PENGUIN CLAS

LYSISTRATA AND OTHER PLAYS

ADVISORY EDITOR: BETTY RADICE

ARISTOPHANES was born, probably in Athens, *c.* 447–445 B.C. and died between 386 and 380 B.C. Little is known about his life, but there is a portrait of him in Plato's *Symposium* and in private life he seems to have been a personal friend of Socrates and Plato. He was twice prosecuted for his outspoken attacks on the prominent politician Cleon. Aristophanes produced his first comedy at the age of nineteen, and in all wrote forty plays of which eleven have survived. *The Wasps*, *The Poet and the Woman* and *The Frogs* are published as a Penguin Classic (one volume).

ALAN SOMMERSTEIN has been teaching Classics at Nottingham University since 1974, and is now the Professor of Greek. He has edited several books on Greek drama and is currently engaged on a complete edition of the comedies of Aristophanes with translation and commentary. He has also translated, for Penguin Classics, Aristophanes' *The Knights*, *Peace* and *Wealth*, published in one volume with *The Birds* and *The Assemblywomen* translated by David Barrett. He is the editor of *The Journal of Hellenic Studies* and joint editor of the new journal, *Drama*.

ARISTOPHANES

THE ACHARNIANS
THE CLOUDS
LYSISTRATA

TRANSLATED WITH
AN INTRODUCTION BY
ALAN H. SOMMERSTEIN

PENGUIN BOOKS

PENGUIN BOOKS

Published by the Penguin Group
Penguin Books Ltd, 27 Wrights Lane, London W8 5TZ, England
Penguin Books USA Inc., 375 Hudson Street, New York, New York 10014, USA
Penguin Books Australia Ltd, Ringwood, Victoria, Australia
Penguin Books Canada Ltd, 10 Alcorn Avenue, Toronto, Ontario, Canada M4V 3B2
Penguin Books (NZ) Ltd, 182–190 Wairau Road, Auckland 10, New Zealand

Penguin Books Ltd, Registered Offices: Harmondsworth, Middlesex, England

This translation first published 1973
23 25 27 29 30 28 26 24

Printed in England by Clays Ltd, St Ives plc
Set in Monotype Bembo

To the memory of

FRANK EZRA ADCOCK

ποθεινοῦ τοῖς φίλοις

I've wisdom from the East and from the West,
   That's subject to no academic rule;
You may find it in the jeering of a jest,
   Or distil it from the folly of a fool.
I can teach you with a quip, if I've a mind;
   I can trick you into learning with a laugh;
Oh, winnow all my folly, folly, folly, and you'll find
   A grain or two of truth among the chaff!

I can set a braggart quailing with a quip,
   The upstart I can wither with a whim;
He may wear a merry laugh upon his lip,
   But his laughter has an echo that is grim!
When they're offered to the world in merry guise,
   Unpleasant truths are swallowed with a will –
For he who'd make his fellow, fellow, fellow creatures wise
   Should always gild the philosophic pill!

W. S. GILBERT – *The Yeomen of the Guard*

CONTENTS

INTRODUCTION

The eleven surviving plays of Aristophanes are all that we have, apart from fragmentary quotations, of one of the most remarkable branches of ancient literature, the Old Comedy of Athens. Of Old Comedy I will say more presently: first something on Aristophanes himself, his life, times, work and thought.

Aristophanes, son of Philippus, of the 'deme' or ward of Cydathenaeus in the city of Athens, was born in about 447 B.C. The actual date of his birth was not known, it would seem, to scholars of later antiquity; the approximate date I have given is inferred from the fact that when he wrote his first comedy, *The Banqueters* (which was produced in the spring of 427, but must have been written several months earlier), he must have been old enough to be fully conversant with the matter and manner of the comic craft* – hence probably at least eighteen – and at the same time young enough to compare himself to an unmarried mother (see *The Clouds*, lines 530–2, p. 135) in a society where all girls for whom a husband could be found were married in their teens. *The Banqueters* was not only accepted for performance at the showpiece festival of the City Dionysia, but placed second out of the three competing comedies. The following year Aristophanes won first prize with *The Babylonians*, and earned a prosecution by Cleon for anti-Athenian propaganda (see

---

*It was literally a craft, and like other crafts was frequently handed down from father to son. Aristophanes' own son Araros became a successful comic poet; the great tragic poets, Aeschylus, Sophocles and Euripides, all had sons who wrote tragedies, as did such lesser lights as Carcinus (*The Clouds*, line 1261, p. 164).

Introduction to *The Acharnians*). From then on his reputation was established. In a career of some forty years he had forty plays produced: those that survive today are *The Acharnians* (produced in 425), *The Knights* (424), *The Clouds* (423, but revised later), *The Wasps* (422), *Peace* (421), *The Birds* (414), *Lysistrata* and *The Poet and the Woman*★ (411), *The Frogs* (405), *The Women's Assembly*★ (*c.*392), and *Plutus* (388). Of these, *The Acharnians*, *The Knights* and *The Frogs* won first prize, and *The Wasps* was only defeated because Aristophanes had also entered another play, *The Preview*, at the same festival.† *Peace* and *The Birds* also came second; the original version of *The Clouds* was placed third and last. For the other four extant plays the results are not known.

After the production of *Plutus* Aristophanes wrote two more comedies, which were produced by his son Araros; Araros is known from an inscription to have won first prize for comedy in 387, and this may well have been with one of his father's plays. Aristophanes probably died not long after this, although the date of his death is not known with certainty.

It was most likely soon after Aristophanes' death that Plato wrote his *Symposium*, which purports to be an account of a dinner party given by the tragic poet Agathon in 416 at which both Socrates and Aristophanes were present. This work, fictional though it no doubt is, is nevertheless the only source we have for knowing what Aristophanes was like, so to speak, outside working hours; and it is an authoritative source, for Plato was almost certainly a personal friend of Aristophanes.‡

★These plays are often referred to by their Greek titles *Thesmophoriazusae* and *Ecclesiazusae* respectively.

† *The Preview* was given to Philonides to produce. Our information about this particular contest depends on a corrupt passage of an ancient synopsis of *The Wasps*, and the statement in the text is not quite certain. See D. M. MacDowell's edition of *The Wasps* (Oxford, 1971), pp. 20 and 124.

‡ It is not certain whether the epitaph on Aristophanes, describing his soul as a temple of the Graces, is really by Plato; but it is certain that in

The first we hear of Aristophanes in the *Symposium* is that, like all the other guests (except Socrates), he has a hangover from the previous night's party, or, as he puts it, 'I had a bit of a dip yesterday too.' When his neighbour Eryximachus, a medical man, proposes that all the guests should make speeches in praise of love, Socrates comments that Aristophanes can hardly refuse, 'seeing that he devotes his whole life to Dionysus and Aphrodite'. Aristophanes' turn to speak eventually comes, but he is in the middle of an attack of hiccups (Dionysus jealous of Aphrodite?) and Eryximachus has to speak before him, as well as prescribing treatment for his complaint. By the end of the doctor's speech Aristophanes has recovered, and is ready to begin; but he is almost immediately accused of trying to be funny. 'Oh,' he rejoins, 'it's not that I'm afraid of – if I'm funny, so much the better – but I'm worried I may make a fool of myself.' He then makes his speech. Originally, he says, human beings had four legs and double the present number of all other organs, and there were three sexes, male, female and hermaphrodite; but when they tried to fight against the gods Zeus punished them. He was unwilling to destroy them, because that would mean no more sacrifices for him and the other gods, so he hit upon an ingenious plan: he sliced them all in half, thus simultaneously reducing their strength and increasing the number of people available to offer sacrifices. This, says Aristophanes, is the reason why even now there are three kinds of person – heterosexuals, and female and male homosexuals – because 'each of us is always looking for his other half'; and it is this desire and pursuit that we call love, and in its fulfilment that the hope of happiness lies.

There is plenty that is ludicrous here, and a good deal that is

---

The Women's Assembly Aristophanes makes fun of proposals for a communistic society which correspond in some detail with those published long afterwards by Plato in his *Republic* (Book V), and it is hard to see how he can have heard about them except from Plato himself – perhaps at another dinner party.

serious (as the Chorus of *The Frogs* remark). And the speech appears to be taken seriously by the others present; so seriously, in fact, that Socrates makes a point later on of saying that Aristophanes' thesis needs to be qualified: 'We can love neither a half nor a whole, unless it is something good.' At the end of Socrates' speech, Aristophanes is just about to say more about this, when the proceedings are interrupted by the arrival of Alcibiades.

Rather surprisingly, Socrates is not made to show any resentment, nor Aristophanes any embarrassment, on the subject of *The Clouds*; this although Plato believed, as we know from his *Apology*, that *The Clouds* was a factor in creating the prejudice that contributed to Socrates' condemnation in 399. I think we must here regard Plato as being faithful to the relations between the two men at the assumed date of the party. Neither Socrates nor Aristophanes could have any idea in 416 what would happen in 399, a lost war and two revolutions later.

For Aristophanes' lifetime was a time of extreme political turbulence. At the beginning of his career Athens was at the height of her power and fame. For a generation the city had been governed by a radical form of democracy, under which all citizens had both an equal share in policy decisions (which were taken by an Assembly of the whole citizen body) and an equal chance of appointment to executive office or to the Council which dealt with routine public business and prepared the agenda for the Assembly (since appointment was by lot – military and diplomatic posts necessarily excepted). Such a system might not appear conducive to either rational or consistent policy-making, and the triumphs of Athens between 462 and 431 would scarcely have been possible if one man, Pericles, had not been able to control the Assembly by his personality, his popular policies, and the power that comes from success. Under his leadership Athens transformed what had been a military alliance directed against the Persian empire into a league of subject states paying tribute to herself. Athens was greatly enriched, and spent much of the money on a programme of public building then unparalleled anywhere in Greece;* but the subject states, and others who feared they might become so, were naturally resentful. Eventually Sparta, the greatest military power in mainland Greece (for Athens' empire was an essentially maritime one), was persuaded that Athenian power was a menace to the independence of other states,.and forced Athens into war. This was in 431.

Two years later Pericles died. His successors, Cleon and his like, self-made men for the most part, tended to follow rather than lead public opinion, a failing memorably depicted in *The Knights* where Cleon is presented as a grasping and toadying slave of the personified People of Athens. (These new politicians were also more sensitive to satire: Pericles never prosecuted a comic poet.) The war dragged on indecisively until 421, when, it having become clear that neither side could defeat the other, peace was concluded. Before long, however, Athens was back on her imperial trail, attempting to subdue Sicily, and Sparta again felt compelled to stop her. The Sicilians defeated and destroyed the Athenian expedition; Sparta, on the advice of the brilliant former Athenian general Alcibiades, seized and fortified a base in Athenian home territory; and the crisis resulted which forms the background to *Lysistrata*. For a few months in 411–410 Athens even abandoned her democratic system, but soon restored it, and continued the war. Most of her subject states, however, had by now revolted, and the Spartan alliance, with backing from Persia, was far the stronger side. In 405 Athens suffered a final and catastrophic naval defeat, and the following spring she surrendered unconditionally.

The victors deprived Athens of all her overseas possessions,

---

*This may well have included the reconstruction in stone of the originally wooden buildings of the Theatre of Dionysus where comedy and tragedy were performed.

and even for a time of part of her own territory. A small group of oligarchs seized power and inaugurated a reign of terror, but within a year the democratic system was again re-established, never again to be challenged until Athens fell under Macedonian domination. From now on, however, Athens could never be quite what she had been. She no longer had the resources of the whole Aegean behind her, and while she did again very soon become one of the leading powers of Greece, she never again became *the* leading power. The transformation of Athens from the political to the intellectual centre of Greece was under way.

Aristophanes' work reflects, towards the end of his career, the early stages of this transformation. His last two surviving plays are concerned, not (like *The Acharnians* or *Lysistrata*) with immediate political issues, nor (like *The Clouds* or *The Frogs*) with the moral dangers inherent in contemporary thought and literature, but with the theoretical Utopias that philosophy had begun to construct, and their ludicrous possibilities if put into practice. In these plays he becomes a keen-eyed but detached observer of society. During the war, on the other hand, he is very much part of society; he has his diagnoses for its ills, and his prescriptions as well, and he means them to be taken seriously.

- Of this last point I am sure. It has often been said, especially in recent years, that in Aristophanes political and social thought is purely incidental and always subordinated to the desire to amuse his audience and win the prize. I do not see how this view can be reconciled with the fact that when *The Clouds*, which is in fact, if not in name, a tragedy, failed at its first performance, Aristophanes' reaction was to include in his revision of the play an address to the audience in which, in effect, he rebukes them for not appreciating a comedy whose merits lay 'in her words and in her action'. The Aristophanes of the *Symposium* also seems to expect to be taken seriously, though very much afraid that he may not be. If, then, we ask what were Aristophanes' social, political and intellectual attitudes, we are not talking about something that does not exist.

We certainly cannot detect in Aristophanes any burning attachment to the established democratic system. Again and again he emphasizes the fickleness and gullibility of the sovereign people; and it is noticeable that the politicians about whom he is most venonous are all strongly democratic – Cleon, Hyperbolus, Cleophon, and others. There is no such campaign against more 'right-wing' leaders such as Nicias, and even Alcibiades is attacked on the score of his sexual rather than his political activity. In *The Frogs* Aristophanes explicitly recommends that civic rights should be restored to those who had taken part in the oligarchic coup of 411, and that the direction of affairs should be entrusted to 'men of good birth and breeding' – two classes which would certainly overlap at a number of points. He never goes so far as to express himself in favour of oligarchy, and it would be an exaggeration to describe him as anti-democratic; but he was certainly distrustful of the way the system was currently working.

One of the reasons for this distrust was undoubtedly the eagerness of the Assembly to plunge into war and their reluctance to make peace even when, as in 425 (see Introduction to *The Acharnians*), the opportunity stared them in the face. Aristophanes detests war, at any rate the current war against Sparta, for many reasons, of which the most prominent, in *The Acharnians* and in *Peace*, is the forcible separation of the country people from their land, a separation especially bitter in the 420s when that land was constantly being ravaged by the enemy.* (The return to the land is also mentioned in *Lysistrata*, line 1173, p. 229, as the blessing of peace *par excellence*.)

*Although after 425 there were no further Spartan invasions of Attica, it appears that few of the country people ventured to return to their homes until 421; in *Peace*, produced in that year, the Chorus consists of Attic farmers, who need peace in order to be able to return to their vines and fig trees.

As *Lysistrata* makes quite clear, though, Aristophanes was no simple-minded pacifist, and he had a deep love for his own city.

In the literary and intellectual sphere, as we see from *The Clouds* and *The Frogs*, Aristophanes saw a marked contrast between old and new, Aeschylus and Euripides, traditional and sophistic education. He did not regard the old as perfect; Right in *The Clouds*, for all his high moral tone, is a dirty old man, and Aeschylus is treated as in many ways antiquated and crude. Nor are old men in Aristophanes as a rule morally superior to young men. But he was very suspicious of the new styles. In poetry his treatment of Euripides is on the whole good-natured; serious criticism is reserved for *The Frogs*, when Euripides is dead and his work can be reviewed as a whole. There can be no question, though, what Aristophanes thought of the new kinds of education that were coming into fashion. Not that the attitude he expresses in *The Clouds* was unique to him. One of the plays that defeated *The Clouds* in 423 – *Connus*, by Ameipsias – also included a portrayal of Socrates which, to say the least, did not contradict that in *The Clouds*; and the same is true of all other references in comedy to Socrates, and indeed to philosophers in general, well into the fourth century. The inference can hardly be resisted that this was also the attitude of the ordinary Athenian to such people. It is understandable. The 'enlightenment' of the last third of the fifth century, as is the way of enlightenments, together with a great deal of truth introduced a great deal of nonsense, and dangerous nonsense at that. The ordinary Athenian saw the nonsense, lumped the truth together with it, and rejected the whole package. The intellectual, like Thucydides, distinguished between the two. Aristophanes did not make the distinction.*

* It has been pointed out that Aristophanes' heroes are quite willing to use sophistic methods of argument when it suits them. But this is in the world of comic fantasy; it does not show that Aristophanes approved of sophistic methods, any more than the violence used against the two

The old-versus-new attitude extends even to religion. Although in fifth-century Athens 'impiety' was a serious crime, impiety did not include laughing at the many absurdities in the traditional ideas of the gods and their activities. Aristophanes can happily, in *The Birds*, entertain the idea of the gods being deprived of food and sex by an aerial blockade and then deposed from the sovereignty of the universe; and the theme of Zeus starving from a shortage of sacrifices turns up again in *Plutus* and in Aristophanes' speech in the *Symposium*. Denying the existence of the gods was another thing: this was part of the indictment later preferred against Socrates. That indictment also referred to Socrates allegedly believing in 'other new deities'; and it is new deities and new cults that Aristophanes is particularly scathing about – witness the remarks of the Magistrate in *Lysistrata* (lines 387-9, p. 196) about the worship of Asiatic gods such as Sabazius and Adonis. Otherwise, though he may parody religious observances,* Aristophanes never jeers at them; which is not surprising, for the very performance of one of his comedies was itself part of a religious observance.

Comedy at Athens, like tragedy, was always produced in connection with one of the festivals of the god Dionysus – the Lenaea in the lunar month of Gamelion (corresponding roughly to January) and the City Dionysia in Elaphebolion (corresponding roughly to March). The Lenaea, at which *The*

---

informers in *The Acharnians* shows that he approved of assault and battery. (What the violence *does* show is that Aristophanes disapproved of informers.)

*Even on such parody there were limits. Frequently in comedy preparations are made for a sacrifice, but no animal is ever actually slaughtered; in *Lysistrata*, for example (p. 187), the proposed sacrifice of a sheep is replaced by 'Thasian vine's blood'. This avoidance of actual mock sacrifice can hardly be due to economy (after all, dummy animals could have been used) and must have had a religious motive, at least in origin.

Acharnians and probably *Lysistrata* were produced, was essentially a local Athenian affair, since foreigners were unable to attend in any numbers owing to the extreme difficulty of sea travel in winter. (Aristophanes in *The Acharnians*, p. 71, draws attention to this fact to protect himself from being again accused of 'slandering the City in the presence of foreigners'.) The City Dionysia was the occasion when the wealth of Athens, political, literary and musical, was displayed to the world. Victory at the City Dionysia was thus more highly coveted than at the Lenaea, and defeat more keenly felt.

The City Dionysia lasted for five days in normal times, but during the war with Sparta it was reduced to four. (Comedy was the main sufferer from the curtailment of the programme, the number of competitors being cut from five to three.) Before the festival began, the statue of its patron god, Dionysus Eleuthereus, was brought in procession from a temple just outside the city, near 'Academe's Park' (see *The Clouds*, p. 153), to the theatre, where the god remained throughout the festival,* watching the performances and sometimes (as in *The Frogs*) seeing himself take part in them. On the day after this procession there was another, when numerous sacrifices were offered; the sponsors (*choregi*: see below) of the various performances took a leading part in the procession and dressed themselves magnificently. The rest of this day appears to have been devoted to contests of boys' and men's choruses singing and dancing the lyric performances in honour of Dionysus known as dithyrambs.

On the next day (the second of the festival proper) the dramatic performances began. First, however, various important public ceremonies were performed: announcements were made of the award of golden crowns to citizens who had rendered important services to the state; the gold and silver

---

*At least while performances were in progress; it is possible that at other times the statue was returned to its normal home, in a temple close to the theatre.

brought by the subject states as tribute (see *The Acharnians*, pp. 71 and 78) was displayed to the audience in the theatre; and those young men, just reaching their majority, whose fathers had been killed in battle, paraded in the theatre and were presented with a set of armour at the public expense. Thus the audience which then settled down to watch three tragedies and a satyr play by one poet, and a comedy by another, had been forcibly reminded that it was also the People of Athens, that courage and public spirit had made their city great, and that it was up to them to keep it so.

This audience was enormous by modern theatrical standards. The capacity of the Theatre of Dionysus was about 14,000, and there can be little doubt that it was always full during the Dionysia. There seem to have been no restrictions of age, sex or citizen status governing attendance: Plato in his *Gorgias* (502d) makes Socrates say that 'poets in the theatres' direct their eloquence at a public 'consisting of children, women and men, slave and free, all at once'. This is not contradicted by the fact that Stratyllis in *Lysistrata* (p. 207) can address the audience as though it consisted entirely of adult male citizens; for she is speaking to the audience in its political capacity as 'the People', and only adult male citizens had political rights. In any case, the men will have been in a majority and will have had the exclusive right to the best seats. (A passage in *Peace* implies that the women sat apart from the men, in the back rows.) Many foreigners were present, most notably the official delegates from the three hundred or so Greek states subject to Athens, who had come bringing their tribute; these delegates, as well as Athenian officials and priests, had reserved seats in the best parts of the theatre. The most privileged seat of all, the centre place in the front row, was that of the priest of Dionysus.

Preparations for the festival had begun several months before. Soon after taking office in the summer, the Chief Archon took in hand the arrangements for the City Dionysia, and his colleague the King-Archon (who involuntarily became a performer in *The Acharnians*) those for the Lenaea. These magistrates had two main duties in connection with tragedy and comedy. On the one hand, they had to select the poets who were to be allowed to compete. It is not known how they did this or what advice, if any, they took; for, being chosen by lot, they did not normally have any literary qualifications themselves. There are hints that it was the practice for poets to read their work to the magistrate. This task of his, at any rate, was very delicate and often gave poets occasion for complaint, justified or not.

The other main responsibility of the archon in charge of the festival was to nominate sponsors (*choregi*) to equip the choruses and organize the performances generally. He chose men of considerable means, who were then required to undertake the task as a compulsory civic duty.* Sometimes he received applications from people volunteering to be *choregi*, for despite the expense involved a *choregia* was regarded by many as an honour: defendants in lawsuits often pointed to the number and magnificence of their *choregiae* as proof of their public spirit.

Each comic *choregus* was responsible for one play. Acting on the advice of the poet, he had to train and costume the Chorus, hire any additional singers, dancers or musicians needed (such as appear, for example, at the end of *Lysistrata*), and provide a dinner afterwards for all concerned in the production. He also probably had to pay and costume any actors over and above the three provided by the state (which may explain why, although in some plays Aristophanes certainly needs four

---

*Unlike the poet who thought he ought to have been chosen, the *choregus* who thought his selection was unfair had a remedy available. He could name any man he considered richer than himself and challenge him to take over the *choregia* or, if he refused, to exchange property. The inefficiency of this system appears not to have been a nuisance, for such exchanges of property were still being made in the second half of the following century.

actors, in others such as *The Birds* he goes out of his way to ensure that no more than three are required).

It is not altogether clear how actors were selected. It is known that poets sometimes acted in their own plays, or employed professional actors of their own choice; and it is very tempting to believe that Aristophanes himself took the part of Dikaiopolis in *The Acharnians*. On the other hand, we know that in the early fourth century five principal actors ('protagonists') were chosen by the state and allocated by lot, one to each poet; what we do not know is when this system was introduced. At the Lenaea a prize was awarded to the best comic actor; surprisingly, it was not till a century after Aristophanes' time that a similar prize was introduced at the City Dionysia.

It was normal for poets to produce their own plays, and it was as producers (*didaskaloi*) that their names appeared in the official records of the festivals. Thus Aristophanes himself produced *The Clouds*. For his first play, *The Banqueters*, however, he had asked a friend, Callistratus, to act as producer (probably because he had not attained the age of majority*), and this arrangement was so successful that he frequently repeated it. *The Acharnians* and *Lysistrata* were both produced by Callistratus. There can be little doubt that the audience were well aware of the real identity of the author; indeed in *The Knights*, the first play he produced himself, Aristophanes, through the mouth of the chorus-leader, says to the audience that many of them had been asking him 'why he had not long ago asked for a Chorus in his own name'. (He says that the

---

*This has been doubted, but the evidence seems compelling. On the one hand, there is Aristophanes' own comparison of himself in *The Clouds* (lines 530-2, p. 135) to an unmarried mother (his words mean literally 'I was unmarried and it was not *yet* lawful for me to give birth'); on the other, there is an ancient statement that Menander, in about 324, was the first poet to produce a comedy while an *ephebus* (i.e. between his eighteenth and twentieth birthdays), which suggests that the rule had then been relaxed.

reason is that he considers comic production to be the most difficult job that exists, and goes on to exemplify this statement in considerable detail; he does not deign to mention that had he asked for a Chorus in his own name for the Dionysia of 427, he would not have got one.)

When *choregus*, poet and producer (if any) had completed their preparations, two days before the festival, a preview (*proagon*) was held in the Odeon, not far from the theatre. The poet (or the producer – it is not clear which) presented his actors and chorus, without their masks and costumes, and announced the title of the play. In some cases this will have given the public a fairly good idea what the play was about: after the hints given in *The Acharnians* (pp. 49, 62), they will not have been very surprised when a play announced as *The Knights* turned out to be an attack on Cleon. In other cases the audience would have been put in a mood of mystified expectation: a play called *The Clouds* might have been about anything (since it does not seem that it was announced what roles the actors would play), and certainly no one would expect the Chorus of *The Wasps* to consist, as it did, of elderly jurymen.

Productions at the dramatic festivals were always competitive.* The prizes were allotted by a panel of judges selected by a complicated procedure designed to ensure that the judging should be both competent and fair. Competence was secured by the initial selection, which was made by the Council; the *choregi* were entitled to make nominations at this stage. Corruption was as far as possible eliminated by leaving the final appointment of the judges until just before the contest, and then choosing ten by lot. At the end of the contest the ten voted, but only five of the votes, drawn out of an urn by the presiding archon, were counted. The judges appear to have

---

* *The Frogs*, having won first prize at the Lenaea in 405, was reproduced at the City Dionysia a few weeks later, apparently as a special item not entered for the competition; this is unique in the fifth century. Later, revivals became normal practice.

written their names on their voting tablets, so that, at least in the case of those whose votes were counted, it was known how each judge had voted. Thus there was some possibility of influence being brought to bear on them, either by the general feeling of the audience or by powerful individuals. Nevertheless, the judges' decisions usually seem to have been reasonable from the critic's point of view; and the limits of influence are shown by the fact that Cleon was unable to prevent the victory either of *The Babylonians* or of *The Knights*.

Technically the competition was not between plays or between poets but between choruses; thus when all was ready for a play to begin, the crier proclaimed *Eisage ton choron* ('Bring on your chorus'; this is the proclamation translated in *The Acharnians*, p. 49, as 'Let your play commence'). This practice continued even though it had long been regular for a play to begin with dialogue and for the Chorus only to come on later. The comic chorus consisted of twenty-four; there could also, as in *Lysistrata*, be additional dancers, and any of the actors could be given a song. The Chorus normally has a distinctive character, and some at least of its songs are written to reflect this character; others, however, need not do so. Thus in *The Acharnians* the Chorus consists of old men of Acharnae when it enters, and so it remains for much of the play. But towards the end it becomes (in Dover's phrase) 'the hero's claque'; and at one point (p. 101) it seems to speak as the mouthpiece of the author. Even in *The Clouds*, where the plot requires that the Chorus should retain its character throughout, it can speak (p. 158) as a Chorus taking part in a competition and demand, with menaces, to be given the first prize.

Lysistrata is exceptional in having two choruses, presumably of twelve each. The motive is dramatic, not musical, since all female parts whatever were played by men.*

It was not quite a rule of the competition, but the

*Even the naked girl Reconciliation in *Lysistrata* was played by a suitably costumed man.

overwhelmingly regular practice, that once the Chorus had appeared on the scene it had to remain until the end of the play, and then leave. Some flexibility was allowed: in *The Women's Assembly* the Chorus of women goes off to the Assembly and returns one scene later, and in *Lysistrata*, after the final departure of the Chorus, the actors and additional dancers remain for a concluding song. But in general the Chorus had to be present, and this imposed some restrictions on the plot. In particular, nothing can be done with the knowledge of the Chorus of which it disapproves and which it is willing and able to stop. In tragedy this could be a handicap, and Choruses are sometimes made to take oaths whose implications they do not fully realize, so that when they understand the situation and wish to intervene they cannot do so without perjuring themselves. Aristophanes is able to turn this power in the hands of the Chorus to advantage. In *The Acharnians* the Chorus tries to stop the hero's 'personal peace' by violence. In *Lysistrata* the two Choruses fight each other. Only in *The Clouds*, of our three plays, does the Chorus not intervene in the action; and it turns out in the end that its non-intervention was deliberate, and has far graver consequences than any intervention would have done.

The Chorus normally danced as it sang, and the dance-movements were regarded as an important part of the total effect of a choral ode, but unfortunately we know very little about them.*

In addition to normally having to keep his Chorus on the scene of action, the dramatist was also under a restriction on the number of actors who could have speaking parts. The maximum permitted was four,† and these had between them

---

*The available evidence, mainly derived from vase paintings, is given by T. B. L. Webster in *The Greek Chorus*, London, 1970.

†Excluding (i) the leader(s) of the Chorus(es); (ii) child parts (the Baby in *Lysistrata* was no doubt a doll); (iii) 'barbarians' who said a line or two in broken Greek, such as Pseudartabas in *The Acharnians*.

to play all the characters; indeed, as has already been mentioned (p. 21), some of Aristophanes' plays, such as *The Birds*, seem to have been deliberately constructed so that they could be performed with only three actors. This restriction meant that the author could not, like a modern dramatist, carry a large number of characters through the play, since it would be confusing for the same part to be played by different actors in different scenes;* in comedy, indeed, it is regular for only one or at most two to have parts which bring them on stage in all or most of the scenes, and characters whom one might have expected to be of some importance in the play, like Lampito in *Lysistrata*, can simply disappear. *The Clouds*, with three characters carried through the play, is exceptional in this respect, and presented Aristophanes with a problem for which he found no satisfactory solution. It was impossible for him, with only four actors at his disposal, to have a debate between Right and Wrong with Strepsiades, Pheidippides and Socrates all present; so before the debate begins, Socrates, without giving a reason, has to excuse himself.†

It may be interesting to see how Aristophanes arranged *Lysistrata* in such a way that four actors could play some twenty parts. The first actor takes the part of Lysistrata, who appears in almost every scene. The other three actors seem to have fairly equal loads. The second actor to appear comes on first as Calonice, then in quick succession as First Woman and Fourth Woman, then as Calonice again; after this he would probably not be needed until near the end, when he would again have to make a couple of quick changes, appearing as First Layabout,

*Sophocles, in his last tragedy, *Oedipus at Colonus*, apparently accepts this disadvantage. Tragic poets were limited to only three actors, and the only way that three actors can perform *Oedipus at Colonus* is if the important part of Theseus is shared by at least two of them – possibly all three.

† As the text stands it seems that Socrates has to change mask and costume in no time; but had the revised version of *The Clouds* ever been produced, this change would have been covered by a choral song.

then First Diner, then First Layabout again. The third actor begins as Myrrhine, then takes Second Woman and Fifth Woman, then becomes Myrrhine again for the famous scene in which Cinesias is tantalized; after this he probably takes the parts of the Magistrate,* the Negotiator, the Doorkeeper (who probably remained unseen behind the door) and, in the final scene, the Athenian.

The fourth actor in *Lysistrata* appears to have been a specialist in dialect roles. He appears first as Lampito, then as the Magistrate, then as Third Woman, then as Cinesias (who probably staggered off after singing his last line – p. 220), then in successive scenes as the Spartan Herald and the Spartan Ambassador, and in the final scene as Second Layabout, Second Diner and the Spartan.

The rule about number of actors was rigid, the rule about the continuous presence of the Chorus nearly so. More elastic were certain conventions about the structure of the play. The basic form was something like this:

(1) A prologue (so-called), in which the opening situation was expounded and the movement of the plot begun.

(2) The *parodos* or entry of the Chorus, often marked by a long and varied song-and-dance movement.

(3) A series of scenes interspersed with songs by the Chorus; the central scene was usually a formal debate (*agon*) on the crucial issue of the play, with speech balanced against speech and song against song.

(4) The *parabasis*, in which the Chorus partially or completely abandoned its dramatic role and addressed the audience directly in the absence of the actors. It normally consists of

*I have split the Magistrate's part between two actors in order to give all four Spartan roles to the same actor. The Magistrate of the 'peace negotiation' scene says nothing to show that he either is or is not the same member of the Committee of Ten who appeared earlier in the play. That he is one of the Committee, whether the same one or not, is shown by the fact that he has power to give orders to the Council (p. 222).

three songs (S) and three speeches (s), in the order S_1-s_1, S_2-s_2, S_3-s_3; S_2 corresponds metrically to S_3 and s_2 to s_3, and the first speech (s_1) often ends with a passage to be rattled off very rapidly (theoretically in one breath), called a *pnigos*.

(5) Another series of scenes interspersed with choral songs. The songs in this section generally contained jibes directed at prominent individuals (the Chorus of *Lysistrata*, p. 224, explains why it is departing from this custom); one of them was often expanded into a brief second *parabasis* (as in *The Acharnians*, p. 101).

(6) A concluding scene of general rejoicing, often associated with a banquet or a wedding.

None of the plays in this volume conforms exactly to this pattern, and it is clear that there was no obligation on the poet to follow the conventions at all closely if they did not suit him. The *parodos* of *The Clouds*, for example, consists of only a single song, though a very beautiful one. *The Acharnians* has no *agon*; this is certainly because, if it had had one, somebody would have had to argue in favour of war, and Aristophanes is careful, in all his plays on the theme of peace, not to allow the case for war to be presented. For the same reason, although *Lysistrata* contains a scene in the form of an *agon*, it is completely one-sided: the Magistrate is never given a chance to argue. Again, *Lysistrata*, with its divided Chorus, can have no *parabasis*; in place of this we find a scene between the two Choruses, with alternating song, dance, speeches and violence. The speeches are directed partly at the opposing Choruses, but mainly at the audience; there is even (lines 698–9, p. 209) a direct address to an individual member of the audience. Even the final scene of rejoicing is dispensable; we might have thought that when in *The Clouds* the triumphant Strepsiades took his son home and put his creditors to flight, an ending of that kind was coming, but the Chorus has already (p. 157) given us a hint that it is not to be so, and instead of rejoicing the play ends in destruction. The leader of the Chorus says that it is time to go, and they go – in total silence. The judges evidently did not approve of the original ending of *The Clouds*, and there is evidence that the ending was one of the parts altered when Aristophanes revised the play; the new ending, had the revised version been performed, would have been scarcely more to the judges' liking.

At both the City Dionysia and the Lenaea, comedy and tragedy were performed in the Theatre of Dionysus, which can still be seen just to the south-east of the Acropolis. The plan of the theatre was circular. Over half the circumference was occupied by the spectators' seating, around the circular *orchestra* or dance-floor where the Chorus usually performed. Behind the *orchestra* stood a building called the *skene*, originally no more than a dressing-room, but in Aristophanes' time decorated with an architectural façade and (probably) three doors. Part of the *skene* was on two floors; the upper floor was used a good deal in comedy, as in *The Acharnians*, where Euripides is upstairs writing a play. The rest of the *skene* was lower and had a flat roof: it is on this that Dikaiopolis' wife stands in *The Acharnians* to watch the Dionysiac procession, and in *Lysistrata* the roof does duty as the battlements of the Acropolis. It is likely that the same background was used for every play; when, as in *The Acharnians* and *The Clouds*, the single *skene* building had to represent two or more houses, curtains were hung between the doors.

Whether there was a raised platform in front of the *skene* has long been a matter of controversy, but a painted vase found in Attica, and dating from about 420 B.C., appears to settle the question. The painting shows a comic actor posturing as the hero Perseus, while two spectators look on. The actor stands on a wooden platform approached by four steps. It is thus now generally agreed that there was such a platform in the Theatre of Dionysus; the steps may well have extended the full length of the platform, since in some tragedies a full Chorus of fifteen apparently sits on these steps. There were also probably steps at the ends of the raised platform, which would be used by actors coming in from the wings. Near the top of the central steps stood a small altar, much used in tragedy for prayer and the burning of incense.

The platform was a convenient device for marking off the actors visually from the Chorus, but there was no objection to the actors coming down to the *orchestra* or even to the Chorus mounting the platform, as the Men's Chorus must do ('I doubt if I have any hope / Of hauling these logs up the slope') when attempting to burn the women out of the Acropolis in *Lysistrata*.

Between the ends of the *skene* and the auditorium there were broad side passages (*eisodoi* or *parodoi*) for the entrance and exit of the Chorus and of those actors who did not emerge from the 'house' or 'houses' in the *skene*.

Two pieces of machinery were available for use in tragedy and comedy. One, known as the *eccyclema*, was a device of some kind for bringing tableaux and immobile characters (such as dead bodies in tragedy) out of the *skene* into view; its exact nature is disputed, but it seems most likely, from the language used to describe it in *The Acharnians* (p. 67), that it was a pivoting arrangement rather like the modern revolving stage, such that the whole front of the 'house' opened up. (This is why, later on in *The Acharnians*, Dikaiopolis tells his slave to 'lock up the house' – p. 99.) The other device was a crane from which a car could be suspended, so that gods and heroes in tragedy could be shown flying through the air. It is on this crane that Socrates first appears in *The Clouds*.

The comic actor's costume was traditionally characterized by grotesque padding, and it seems that this was still normal for most characters in Aristophanes' time. Over this actors wore tights and (if playing a male part) a very short tunic which left uncovered a large leather phallus. (Female characters wore long gowns, often dyed yellow.) Much play, of course, is made with the phallus in *Lysistrata*; and in *The*

Clouds, when Aristophanes says that he does not bring on 'a great thick floppy red-tipped leather tool', it is likely that the operative word is 'red-tipped', i.e. circumcised; for at least two jokes in the play (pp. 140, 143) are more easily managed by an actor wearing a phallus than by an actor without one.*

Certain characters would wear special costumes, or carry marks of their identity or profession. Lamachus in *The Acharnians* probably wore a military cloak (*phoinikis*: the 'scarlet uniform' referred to elsewhere by Lysistrata, p. 227). In *Lysistrata*, Lampito and her Peloponnesian companions no doubt wore the sheepskin gowns referred to in the song which closes the play; the Scythian policemen (and policewoman) would be recognized by their bows and quivers, the Spartan herald by his wand of office.

The costumes of the Chorus, if they represented human beings, were similar to those of the actors; it is not certain whether Choruses of men would wear phalluses, but it is most likely that they did (the supernumeraries who represent the Odomantian soldiers in *The Acharnians* would certainly have to). Choruses of animals or birds, on the other hand, gave the costume designer plenty of opportunity to exercise his imagination; it seems he did not give his imagination much rein in the case of *The Clouds*, where the Chorus appears simply as women, and this may have been partly responsible for the play's failure.

Actors and chorus all wore masks, which were typically made with grotesque exaggeration of features. The use of masks may have been religious in origin, or it may have been merely a device employed by early actors to emphasize the

*In any case, many of the claims made by Aristophanes in the *parabasis* of *The Clouds* are blatantly untrue. He explicitly says the play contains 'no torches, shouts, or violence', although the last scene has all three of these; and while it may be literally true that 'no old man with walking-stick applies a well-aimed poke', Strepsiades certainly pokes the Second Creditor with a goad. Thus the *parabasis* cannot be regarded as evidence against the wearing of the phallus in *The Clouds*.

fact that the actor was, for the purposes of the performance, not himself but someone else; masks were retained mainly for two quite practical reasons – firstly, they made it easier for one actor to play many different roles; secondly, in such a large theatre and with only natural lighting, a bold and exaggerated mask would be far more easily visible to the audience than the features and expressions of the actor's own face.

There appears to have been a repertoire of stock masks available for any play; several of them are represented in contemporary art. Some masks, however, must have been unique or nearly so; that of Pseudartabas in *The Acharnians*, for example, must have raised an instant laugh with its single gigantic eye. When a living individual was caricatured on the stage, it was normal to commission a mask recognizably like him. We know that this was so because in *The Knights* Aristophanes apologizes for not using such a portrait-mask for the character who represents Cleon; the mask-makers, he says, were too frightened to take the responsibility of producing one. One reason for the choice of Socrates as the 'professor' in *The Clouds* may well have been that, as we know from other sources, Socrates had an unusually ugly face which lent itself easily to caricature in a mask.

The comic mask normally included a beard, apparently of real hair. The chief character of *The Poet and the Women* is given a shave on stage. Beardlessness at this time was a sign of effeminacy, and so the notoriously effeminate Cleisthenes and Strato (Pseudartabas' 'eunuchs' in *The Acharnians*) are given beardless masks, and Dikaiopolis twits Cleisthenes as 'he of the long black beard'.

The masks and the unchanging back-scene are not the only features of Athenian theatre production that would have been offensive to an audience brought up on early-twentieth-century naturalism. Since the performances took place in the daytime and in the open air, it was not possible to indicate visually whether the action was supposed to be taking place in

daylight or darkness. *The Clouds* begins at night; but the
Athenian audience will only have known this because the
characters are asleep and one of them, on waking, complains
how long the nights are.

Again, it was impossible, except by the use of the *eccyclema*,
to show action taking place indoors. In general this would not
be too disturbing, because much more of the business of Greek
life than of ours was in any case done in the open air; but
sometimes it created difficulties. The first scene of *The Clouds*
may again serve as an example. Strepsiades and his son must
have been lying *in front of* the *skene*. In real life they would of
course have been indoors, since the weather is supposed to be
quite cold, cold enough for Pheidippides to want five blankets; in the play they must needs be outdoors. It would probably be nearer the truth to say that it does not occur to the
audience to ask whether they are inside or outside; they are
too interested in Strepsiades' problems and what he is going to
do about them. When Strepsiades points out to his son the
door of the Thinkery (pp. 115–16), then, indeed, they must be
outside their house;* until that point the question of their
exact location just does not arise.

This indeterminacy of place makes it easy to have changes of
imaginary setting without change of scenery, or gaps in
imaginary time without intervals. (The 'dramatic unities' are
not only not classical, they are not even Aristotelian: they are
Renaissance misinterpretations of Aristotle.) *The Acharnians*
begins on the Pnyx, but when Dikaiopolis walks 'home' (i.e.,
probably, up the steps towards the *skene*) we find we are in
front of his house. In *Lysistrata*, the action is continuous up to
the ignominious retreat of the Magistrate; when the women
next appear, we find five days have elapsed. So long as the

---

*In the original text he does actually point it out. In the present
translation, in which to meet the exigencies of modern staging I have set
the whole opening scene indoors, I make him merely refer to it as 'the
house next door'.

audience knows those facts about the imaginary situation which matter for the purpose of the play, there is no incongruity felt.

Aristophanes' merits as a comedian can for the most part be left to speak for themselves; but I should like to say a few words on two aspects of his technique.

On the one hand, Aristophanes is a master of dramatic structure. It may be of interest to illustrate this from a part of his work that has sometimes been thought rather naive in this respect, the second half of *The Acharnians*.

It has many times been said that in early comedy we tend to find after the *parabasis* a succession of disconnected scenes, and *The Acharnians* and *The Birds* are treated as typical examples. I will not speak here of *The Birds*; but in *The Acharnians*, though we certainly have a succession of scenes, they are not disconnected. Their unifying theme is stated by the Chorus in the centre of this section of the play, at the very beginning of the exquisite ode that sums up the message of the whole play:

> 'Look you, citizens of Athens,
>   See the gain that wisdom brings!'

– 'wisdom' being here synonymous with willingness to make peace. Before and after this ode, the scenes rise to a climax. First, Dikaiopolis sets up his market, and makes an exchange with the Megarian, giving him goods of little value and getting in return goods of perhaps slightly greater value in the two girls; an Informer is driven out with contumely. Then he buys a vast load of good things from the Boeotian, including the much-coveted eels of which Boeotia had a monopoly and which (as Aristophanes again complains in *Lysistrata*) were totally unobtainable in wartime; and for these he pays less than nothing – for that is certainly the price at which we are meant to rate Nicarchus. After this Dikaiopolis chooses his own customers, turning away Lamachus' servant and the Farmer, but condescending, like an amused god, to show favour to an anxious bride. Next he is invited to the usual concluding dinner-party (while the 'unwise' Lamachus is forced to go off and get chilblains) and returns with two ravishing conquests;* but even now he is not finished: the climax is still to come. Dikaiopolis has won the Pitcher Day drinking contest, and he has come to claim a prize from the King-Archon – the very magistrate who is shortly (so the author hopes, and his hopes were justified) going to award another prize to the play itself. And so *The Acharnians* ends.

Another aspect of Aristophanes' genius, which has to be mentioned here because in a translation it cannot be reproduced but only imitated, is his dexterity at all forms of juggling with words. I shall give some examples of this from the beginning of *The Acharnians*. This passage provides a favourable field for word play, because nothing whatever is happening. Dikaiopolis is merely whiling his time away, waiting to see if the Assembly will begin less than five hours late. While he is waiting, he fires off a few jokes.

One of the first of these occurs almost at once. 'The number of things that have pained me,' says Dikaiopolis, 'is *psammakosiogargara*,' literally 'sand-hundred-heaps'. Aristophanes invents these improbable compounds with zest; in *Lysistrata* (p. 198), 'lettuce-seed-pancake-vendors of the Market Square' and 'innkeepers, bakers and garlic-makers' are just one word each (each word filling a whole line of verse). The idea is carried to its logical conclusion at the end of *The Women's Assembly*, where the main item on the menu for the concluding feast is described in one 170-letter word.

Another trick is the so-called *para prosdokian*, 'contrary-to-expectation': the speaker makes us quite sure what we are

*Like the feast, the mute performer(s) representing one or more naked girls appear to have been a regular feature of comedy. Such figures appear towards the end of every extant play of Aristophanes from *The Acharnians* to *The Frogs* inclusive, with the exception of *The Clouds* (where their omission was doubtless unpopular).

going to hear next – and then says something quite different. After completing his list of theatrical joys and sorrows, Dikaiopolis goes on, 'Seriously, though – in all the years I've –' and we expect to hear something like, 'In all the years I've lived, I have never been so distressed as I am now.' What Dikaiopolis actually says is, 'In all the years I've washed, I've never had so much soap in my eyes as – yow! – as I have now.'

Then there is the pun, as dear to Aristophanes as to Shakespeare, or more so. In this speech we have the pun (p. 50) which I have translated into one on 'sale' and 'sail'. In the original it is neater: 'My deme, which never said "Buy charcoal" (*anthrakas priō*), nor vinegar or oil; it knew not "buy" (*priō*), but provided everything for itself without needing a saw (*priōn*).'

On another pun, of rather a different kind, the whole plot of *The Acharnians* depends. Two lines early in the play – one spoken by the demigod Amphitheus to the Assembly, the other later on by Dikaiopolis to Amphitheus – are identical: *spondas poiēsai pros Lakedaimonious monōi*, 'alone to make peace with the Spartans'. But from one use of the line to the other the construction of *monōi*, 'alone', has changed. When Amphitheus uses it, *monōi* agrees with the subject, and the meaning is that Amphitheus is the only person authorized to make peace. In Dikaiopolis' mouth *monōi* is a 'dative of advantage', 'to make peace *for* me alone'. This is the 'personal peace' of which Dikaiopolis afterwards reaps the benefits. It need only be added that when the peace-treaty (*spondai*) is finally brought by Amphitheus, it takes the very agreeable form of three wine-skins suitable for pouring libations (also called *spondai*).*

---

*In *The Knights* Aristophanes introduced *spondai* in the even more agreeable guise of two or three girls, about whom Demos (the personified Athenian People) asks, 'Do you think I could give them a bit of the old thirty years?' – thirty years being, as in *The Acharnians*, the favoured duration for a peace treaty.

My translation is inspired by, and modelled on, David Barrett's magnificent translation in the *Penguin Classics* of *The Wasps*, *The Poet and the Women* and *The Frogs*, and like Barrett's it makes an effort to be a faithful rendering and at the same time 'both readable and actable'. In general, spoken passages are translated as prose, and sung passages as verse; but one or two passages in which the diction or metre of tragedy is imitated are rendered in blank verse, and the speeches in the *parabases* (probably spoken by the Leader of the Chorus through music, while the Chorus danced behind him) in rhymed verse.

To give an idea of the verbal humour which, as I have said, was an essential part of Aristophanes' comic technique, I have often found it necessary to adapt his jokes, or, where even this is impossible, to compensate for their loss by adding something elsewhere. I have generally at such points given an idea in the notes of what the author wrote.

In both *The Acharnians* and *Lysistrata* characters appear who come from parts of Greece other than Athens, and Aristophanes makes use of their dialectal peculiarities for comic purposes. As has become traditional with English translators, I represent his Dorians (a Megarian and several Spartans) as speaking Scots, and his Boeotian (coming from a country justly or unjustly famed for its stupidity) as a generalized 'bumpkin'. My representation of the way they talk is meant to be merely suggestive; Aristophanes himself does not seem to have intended them to speak exactly as real Spartans, Boeotians, etc., would have done.

My stage directions (which correspond to nothing in Aristophanes' Greek text*) assume a modern stage and an audience unused to ancient stage conventions such as those discussed on pp. 28–33 above. Producers are welcome to see in

---

*The only surviving ancient stage directions in these three plays are those for Pseudartabas to shake his head and to nod (*The Acharnians*, p. 54).

the text possibilities of farcical 'business' which I have not noticed. Following Barrett, I have marked act and scene divisions, but, except where there is a change of scene, the divisions are merely intended as points where there might, if desired, be a break in performance. The original production did not have any intervals.

Some of the songs I have written with existing music in mind; where this is the case, it is indicated in the notes. It will be seen that I take this music from two sources. One is well-known traditional tunes; the other is the operas of Gilbert and Sullivan. For there is a great deal in Gilbert that reminds one of Aristophanes, notably in *Princess Ida*, which several times departs from its main source (Tennyson's *The Princess*) in favour of *Lysistrata* (indeed, this is the nearest Gilbert ever gets to actually mentioning sex). If the music I have suggested is used, I would make a plea that music for other songs should be consistent with it in style.

The Gilbertian influence is also responsible for the subtitles which I have added to each of the plays. Aristophanes did not give them subtitles (though one of his lost plays was called *The Dramas, or The Centaur*).

The texts on which this translation is primarily based are, for *The Clouds*, that of K. J. Dover, and, for *The Acharnians* and *Lysistrata*, that of B. B. Rogers. I owe much to both these editors, but I wish to mention particularly Dover's inspired suggestion of 'Right' and 'Wrong' as names for the two Arguments in *The Clouds*, and Rogers' of 'boastard' as a rendering of the Aristophanic compound *kompolakythos* in *The Acharnians* (p. 75). I have occasionally preferred readings or conjectures not adopted by Dover or Rogers, and in one or two places I have disagreed with them on the assignment of lines to characters (always a very tricky matter in ancient comedy).

I should particularly like to thank Mrs Betty Radice for being an even kinder foster-mother to this translation than the

Athenian public was to Aristophanes' *The Banqueters*, and for helping to remove numerous warts that disfigured the infant. I am also grateful to David Watkinson, who read the draft of my translation over a year ago and was the first to encourage me to think it worth publishing, and above all to David Barrett, without whose example it would never have been written, and without whose cooperation once it had been written it might never have seen the light of day. To all, many thanks.

A.H.S.

Cambridge,
April 1972

The Acharnians

or

The Personal Peace

Introductory Note to *The Acharnians*

The Acharnians was produced in January 425 B.C. Almost annually, for six years, the Spartans and their allies had mustered at the Isthmus of Corinth in May, marched into Attica and laid the country waste, destroying not only any corn there might be but also vines and olive trees (contrary to the established rules of warfare among Greek states). And twice a year the Athenian army revenged itself upon the enemy nearest to hand, the Megarians, never rich, now condemned to 'sit by the fire and shrink', everything they grew being methodically destroyed. Everybody was suffering by the war, and nobody had anything much to show for it; the only exception was Boeotia, which had up to now been virtually unaffected, and had indeed got rid of an old enemy by the destruction of Athens' Boeotian ally, Plataea. The Athenian empire was intact, and nothing had happened to induce Sparta to give up her struggle for the 'liberation of Greece'. Meanwhile, the entire population of Attica remained imprisoned in the city and the Piraeus, watching the periodical pillage of their homes, unable to do anything about it; and Sparta, knowing well how they felt, took care to be especially thorough with the property of the inhabitants of the large and important town of Acharnae, seven miles from the city, close to Mount Parnes, in the hope that they would persuade the Generals to march out and give battle to the invaders – a battle that the leaders on both sides knew the Athenians could not win. It was in this situation of interminable, destructive, unprofitable war that Aristophanes composed his third comedy, the earliest which has survived: 'It appeals for peace in every possible way,' as the author of the Greek synopsis rightly says.

But Aristophanes also had a private war of his own. The previous year had seen the production of *The Babylonians*, with its scathing indictments of Athenian politicians and policies, internal and external; and Cleon had prosecuted the author on a charge of 'slandering the City in the presence of foreigners' and, apparently, secured a conviction. This is why Aristophanes is at such pains in *The Acharnians* to point out that no such charge can be made to stick this time, since no foreigners were present at the Lenaea; and, even so, emphatically ascribes the initiation of the events that caused the war to 'a bunch of good-for-nothing individuals', 'not Athens, remember that, not the City'. There is also a hint or two that he will have his revenge on Cleon shortly – as he did, in *The Knights*, the following year.

The Acharnians, however, is essentially an appeal for the ruinous and unnecessary war to be brought to an end. That it has this serious aim does not mean, of course, that the poet is not going to be extremely funny as well; indeed, he is just that. But there is always the serious undertone. The debate in the Assembly, where only one citizen can see through the transparent cock-and-bull stories of the ambassadors; Dikaiopolis' speech on the chopping-block, one of the finest Aristophanes ever wrote, and containing not a single joke; the pathetic sight of the Megarian, selling his own daughters to save them from starvation, and receiving in exchange derisory quantities of the very commodities for the production of which Megara had once been famous; the beautiful ode contrasting the ways of War and 'Reconciliation'; these are of the essence of the play, and Aristophanes' whole heart was in them. It is not at all impossible that he himself took the part of Dikaiopolis, the honest farmer who makes a 'personal peace' and nearly loses his head for it; if not, he surely made certain that the actor who did take the part was equipped with a mask looking very, very much like him.

Of the real people who appear in the play two need special

mention: Euripides and Lamachus. It is very hard to see how the treatment of Euripides in this play could ever have been construed as an 'attack' on him, except by those who, knowing from *The Frogs* that Aristophanes considered Euripides a bad influence on the young, assumed that every time he brought Euripides into a play it must be in order to denounce him. In fact, his primary object here was to give a build-up to the great block-speech, which is an imitation ('parody' would not do sufficient justice to Aristophanes' seriousness) of a speech by the ragged hero in Euripides' *Telephus*. Having got the idea of this speech, what more natural than to send Dikaiopolis to get the necessary rags from Euripides himself; to have some good-natured fun at the tragedian's expense; and (most ludicrous of all) to make him speak throughout in the sort of language he gives to his characters? There is nothing in the scene that Euripides himself could not have laughed at – which could hardly be said of the references in the play to, say, Cleon!

About Lamachus, at this stage of his career, we do not know very much; and we must no doubt believe what Aristophanes says, that he was for war to the death. We need not, however, believe that he was dishonest and a coward; Aristophanes wanted to represent the pro-war party by a single character, and Lamachus, with his crests and Gorgon shield and fiery talk, was an obvious choice. Two years later Aristophanes was faced with a similar problem in choosing a representative 'professor' for the school in *The Clouds*, and the monstrous unfairness of the resulting portrait of Socrates may warn us against believing too much ill of Lamachus. What is certain is that in 415 Lamachus, as one of the commanders of the Athenian expeditionary force in Sicily, urged on his colleagues a bold and aggressive strategy which would probably have resulted in immediate victory; that he was overruled; and that the following year, leading reinforcements in person to help a hard-pressed Athenian detachment before Syracuse, he found himself and a few of his men isolated on the wrong side of a ditch, and died fighting.

A word should be said about the two festivals of Dionysus that are celebrated in the play. The 'Country Dionysia' ought to have been held in the villages of Attica, not in the city, and in December; Dikaiopolis is thus celebrating them in the wrong place at the wrong time (since there is no suggestion that he is able to get back to his home in the country). The 'Festival of Pitchers' was part of the Anthesteria, a three-day festival held in February; its chief feature was the drinking contest, which is described in the play, though it does not take place on stage.

The play won first prize; but its epilogue is a sad one. A few months after it was performed, the audience which had applauded it found a real-life Spartan delegation in Athens with proposals for peace. By the opportunism of their general Demosthenes and his men, the Athenians had fortified the promontory of Pylos and beaten off a naval attack, and now over 400 Spartans were blockaded on the neighbouring island of Sphacteria, many of them full Spartan citizens – and the Spartan citizen body was not large. We do not know what terms were offered, but they must have included an end to Athens' economic war against Megara, and, since this would be regarded by Athens as a very big concession indeed, there must also have been a Spartan *quid pro quo*. It is quite likely that the Athenian Assembly never heard just what the terms were, for Cleon demanded the surrender not only of the 400 but also of various ports and territories which Athens had not held for twenty years, as a preliminary to negotiations. The Spartans naturally refused, and Cleon was thus able to persuade the people that they were insincere, so that the mission came to nothing, and no peace was made. Sphacteria was captured by Demosthenes and Cleon, and most of the Spartans there were taken prisoner and brought to Athens, where they were held as hostages against any further invasion of

Attica, it being announced that as soon as the enemy crossed the border the prisoners would be executed. From then on Spartans entered Attica only on peace missions, and always went home empty-handed. Peace came four years later, after much more suffering, and on much less favourable terms for Athens than she could have got in 425. Much as Aristophanes liked being laughed at, and winning prizes for it, he would probably have liked even more to be listened to.

CHARACTERS

DIKAIOPOLIS *an old farmer*
CRIER
AMPHITHEUS *an immortal*
AMBASSADOR *lately returned from the Persian Court*
PSEUDARTABAS *the Great King's Eye*
THEORUS *ambassador to the King of Thrace*
CHORUS *of old men of Acharnae*
DAUGHTER *to Dikaiopolis*
CEPHISOPHON *Euripides' leading man*
EURIPIDES *the tragic poet*
LAMACHUS *the general*
MEGARIAN
FIRST GIRL
SECOND GIRL } *the Megarian's daughters – disguised as pigs*
INFORMER
BOEOTIAN
NICARCHUS *another informer*
SERVANT *of Lamachus*
FARMER
BEST MAN
FIRST MESSENGER
SECOND MESSENGER

Silent Characters

THE EXECUTIVE COMMITTEE
SCYTHIAN POLICEMEN
SECOND AMBASSADOR
TWO 'EUNUCHS' *attendant on Pseudartabas*
ODOMANTIAN SOLDIERS
WIFE *to Dikaiopolis*

The Acharnians

PIPE BAND *attendant on the Boeotian*

ISMENIAS *the Boeotian's servant*

EEL

BRIDESMAID

TWO DANCING-GIRLS

THE KING-ARCHON

CITIZENS, SLAVES, REVELLERS, LAMACHUS' FRIENDS, *etc.*

ACT ONE

The Pnyx, Athens. Rows of benches are laid out for a meeting of the Assembly; facing them are chairs for the members of the Executive Committee.

[DIKAIOPOLIS *is sitting alone in the front row; no one else has arrived. He yawns, looks around him, sighs, yawns again, and turns to the audience.*]

DIKAIOPOLIS: My heart has drunk deep of the cup of woe, and scant the joys I've known – yes, scant's the word all right; let me see – [*counts on his fingers*] yes, four, that's right. Four things that pleased me, and umpteen trillion of the other sort. Now what was that thing that I enjoyed, that was really pleasurific? Ah yes, I remember – it really warmed the cockles of my heart – when Cleon coughed up his thirty thousand drachs.[1] That sent me. Knights, I love you for that; you deserved well of your country. But then there was something really traumatic, not to say tragic. There was I sitting there, mouth open, ready for a great dollop of Aeschylus, and then in comes the crier, and what do you think he says? 'Let your play commence – Theognis!!'[2] Well, you can imagine, I nearly had heart failure. Which reminds me – another thing that made me really happy – when that lyre-player Moschus got off the stage and Dexitheus came on to play a few Boeotian numbers. To come to this year, though – I nearly broke my neck the other day, trying to see Chaeris,[3] when he was playing the Soldiers' Song;[4] he hardly poked his nose out of the door. Seriously, though – in all the years I've washed, I have never had so much soap in my eyes as – yow! [*hastily wipes it away*] – as

I have now. And do you know why? I'm angry, that's why, angry. Look at this! Plenary session of the Assembly, due to start at sunrise, and not a soul here on the Pnyx! Everybody's down in the Market Square gossiping, that is when they're not dodging the red rope.[5] Even the Executive Committee[6] isn't here. They'll come in the end – hours late – all streaming in together, and push and shove and heaven knows what to get the best seats. That's all they care about. For peace, ha! they don't give a damn. Oh, Athens, Athens, what are you coming to? Now me, I'm always the first to get here. So I sit down, and after a bit, when I find nobody else is coming, I start sighing and yawning and stretching and farting and so on, then I can't think what to do next, so perhaps I do some doodling or pick my nose or tot up my debts – but all the time my heart's in the fields out there, and I'm pining for peace. I'm fed up with the city and just craving to get back to my village. Ah! my village. We had none of this 'Coal for sale', nor oil or vinegar either; we'd never even heard the word 'for sale'. Everything we needed we produced ourselves, and sails we didn't need, 'cause we hadn't any boats.[7] Well anyway – this time I've come prepared: if anybody dares say a word about anything except peace, I'll heckle him like fury until he shuts his cakehole tight.

[*Enter the* CRIER; *then the members of the Executive Committee; then a large and disorderly crowd of citizens.*]

Ah, here they are at last! Twelve o'clock. Well, better late than never. Look at them! Just like I said – all fighting for the best places.

CRIER [*taking his place in front of the Committee*]: Come forward! Come forward! Everyone inside the consecrated enclosure![8]

AMPHITHEUS [*arriving late and breathless, to* DIKAIOPOLIS]: Have they started yet?

CRIER: The Assembly is hereby declared open. Who wishes to speak?

AMPHITHEUS [*rising in his place*]: I do.

CRIER: Your name?

AMPHITHEUS: Amphitheus the Demigod.

CRIER: Are you human?

AMPHITHEUS: No, I am an Immortal. I am a direct descendant of Amphitheus the First, the son of Demeter and Triptolemus, who begat Celeus, who married Phaenarete, that's my grandmother, and begat Lycinus, who begat me; and that makes me immortal. And the gods have commissioned me personally to make peace with Sparta. [*Loud booing.* AMPHITHEUS *raises his voice.*] But, Gentlemen, I am being treated shamefully. I have not been given my expenses. The Executive Committee have vetoed it!

[*The* CHAIRMAN *of the Executive Committee makes a sign to the* CRIER.]

CRIER: Let that man be removed!

[*Two* POLICEMEN, *Scythian archers equipped with bows and quivers, grab* AMPHITHEUS *by the arms and drag him off.*]

AMPHITHEUS [*as his captors take him away*]: My divine ancestors, why do you not help me?

DIKAIOPOLIS [*rising, to the Executive Committee*]: Gentlemen, the arrest of that man was an insult to the Assembly! He only wanted to give us back peace so we could hang up our shields on the wall again where they belong.

[*More booing.*]

CRIER: Silence! Sit down!

DIKAIOPOLIS: I will not, not until the Executive Committee start executing something about ending the war.

CRIER [*ignoring him*]: The ambassadors from the Persian Court!

DIKAIOPOLIS: The Persian Court! I'm sick of all these peacock ambassadors and their tall tales.

CRIER: Silence!

[DIKAIOPOLIS *subsides. Enter the* AMBASSADOR *and his two colleagues, dressed in oriental magnificence.*]

DIKAIOPOLIS [*aside*]: Whew! Holy Ecbatana, what a get-up!

AMBASSADOR: Gentlemen, you will remember that you sent us to the Great King, fixing our expenses at two drachmas per person per day, in the year when Euthymenes was archon.⁹

DIKAIOPOLIS [*aside*]: Six a day for eleven years – oh, God!

AMBASSADOR: And, I may add, we had a very hard time of it. We processed very slowly up the Cayster valley in covered coaches, and we actually had to lie down in them. We endured tremendous privations.

DIKAIOPOLIS: And all the time here was I in the lap of luxury, sleeping among the rubbish on the city walls! Unfair world, isn't it?

AMBASSADOR: And wherever we stopped, our hosts compelled us, willy-nilly, to drink out of gold or crystal cups, insisted that we should have only sweet wine, and even refused to put any water in it.

DIKAIOPOLIS [*aside*]: City of Cecrops, are you blind? Can't you see how your representatives are making fools of you?

AMBASSADOR: Because in Asia, you know, the test of your manhood is how much you can eat and drink.

DIKAIOPOLIS [*aside*]: With us it's how many you can lay – or get laid by.

AMBASSADOR: At the end of three years we reached the Persian capital; but we found the King away – he had gone with his army on an expedition to the jakes, and he stayed there, shitting on top of the Brown Hills, for all of eight months.

DIKAIOPOLIS [*still aside, but loud enough for the* AMBASSADOR *to hear*]: And how long did he take to button up his arse?

AMBASSADOR [*deadpan*]: He waited till the moon was full, and then returned home. Then he gave a dinner for us: we had oxen baked whole in the oven.

DIKAIOPOLIS [*aside*]: Have you ever heard such a liar? You don't bake oxen, you bake bread, you idiot!¹⁰

AMBASSADOR: And to follow – this is the absolute truth – they served us up an enormous fowl, several times the size of – of – of Cleonymus.¹¹ They called it a bezzle.¹²

DIKAIOPOLIS [*aside*]: So that's what taught you to embezzle all those drachs you've been drawing for the past eleven years!

AMBASSADOR: And now we have returned to Athens, and we have brought with us Pseudartabas, the Great King's Eye.¹³

DIKAIOPOLIS [*aside*]: I hope a crow knocks it out – and Your Ambassadorial Excellency's eye with it.

CRIER: The Great King's Eye!

[*Enter* PSEUDARTABAS. *He has one gigantic eye in the middle of his forehead, and he advances gingerly, looking to left and right to see where he is going. He is attended by two 'eunuchs' who try to keep him on a straight course.*]

DIKAIOPOLIS: Heracles and all the gods, man, you look like a bloody battleship rounding a headland. This way for the docks! Why, you've even got an oar-pad – or what is that meant to be?¹⁴

AMBASSADOR: Pseudartabas, will you please deliver the message that the King gave you for the people of Athens?

PSEUDARTABAS: Yartaman esharsha sapitchona satro.

AMBASSADOR: Do you hear what he says?

DIKAIOPOLIS: Yes, but what does it mean?

AMBASSADOR: He says the King is going to send you gold. [*To* PSEUDARTABAS] Gold, tell them more about the gold, and let's understand it this time.

PSEUDARTABAS: You not will get goldu, you Yawonian¹⁵ sack-arsa.

DIKAIOPOLIS: Oh, God, we could understand that all right!

AMBASSADOR: Why, what does he say?

DIKAIOPOLIS: What does he say? He says that us Ionians are sack-arsed idiots, that's what, if we expect to get gold from Persia.

AMBASSADOR: Nonsense. He said we were going to get gold in sackfuls.

DIKAIOPOLIS: Sackfuls indeed! – you're nothing but a bloody liar. Get off with you! I'll do the interrogating myself.

[*The* AMBASSADOR *and his colleagues docilely leave.* DIKAIOPOLIS *confronts* PSEUDARTABAS, *producing a thick leather strap.*]

Look at this and tell me the truth, or I'll paint your face Lydian purple. Is the Great King going to send us gold?

[PSEUDARTABAS *shakes his head.*]

Is everything those ambassadors were saying a load of old codswallop?

[PSEUDARTABAS *gravely nods; so do the 'eunuchs'.*]

Funny, I never knew the Persians nodded like we do. Come to think of it, they don't. I verily believe that our friends here come from somewhere not a thousand miles from Athens! In fact – [*examining one of the 'eunuchs' closely*] I seem to know this one very well indeed. Cleisthenes,[16] isn't it, the son of Athletes?[17] 'O thou that shavest close thy passionate arse!'[18] You, the Great Gorilla himself, he of the long black beard – you, to come here got up as a eunuch! And who's the other? Not Strato,[19] by any chance?

CRIER: Silence! Sit down! – The Council have great pleasure in inviting the Great King's Eye to dinner in the City Hall.

[*Exit* PSEUDARTABAS, *attended by the 'eunuchs'.*]

DIKAIOPOLIS: Hang them all! I can wait here all day for all they care – but those damn pooves, the door's always open for them, they're always invited. I've had enough. I'm going to act. Amphitheus! are you there?

AMPHITHEUS [*who has slipped back in unnoticed*]: Here.

DIKAIOPOLIS: Look, here's eight drachmas. Go to Sparta and make one of those personal peaces you were talking about – for me and the wife and the kids, right?

[AMPHITHEUS *takes the money and leaves unobtrusively*.]
And then the rest of you can go on playing at diplomats till
you drop, for all I'll need to bother!

CRIER: Come forward, the Ambassador to the Court of King
Sitalces of Thrace.[20] Theorus![21]

THEORUS [*coming to the front*]: Here I am.

DIKAIOPOLIS [*aside*]: Here we are – another bloody liar!

THEORUS: Our stay in Thrace would have been much
shorter –

DIKAIOPOLIS [*aside*]: If you hadn't been drawing so much
pay for it.

THEORUS: – if it had not been for a violent snowstorm which
covered the whole country and froze all the rivers, about
Dionysia-time.

DIKAIOPOLIS: I knew Theognis[22] was pretty frigid, but I
never imagined he could do that!

THEORUS: We were able, however, to turn the delay to our
advantage in our negotiations with Sitalces' – wine mer-
chant. The King is your sincere friend, a true lover of
Athens; so true a lover that he goes round writing poems to
you on walls – 'City of Athens, I love you!' – that kind of
thing. When it came to the Festival of the Clans[23] we made
his son an Athenian citizen, and he fell so completely in love
with our sausages that he was beseeching his father to come
to his country's aid in her sore need. And Sitalces, he poured
a libation and swore to bring an army to help us. 'So great
an army,' he said, 'that the Athenians will take it for a
swarm of locusts.'

DIKAIOPOLIS [*aside*]. That's true all right about the locusts;
but the rest, I'll be damned if I believe a word of it.

THEORUS: And now he has sent you a contingent from the
bravest tribe in Thrace.

DIKAIOPOLIS [*aside*]: Now you'll see what I mean.

CRIER: Come forward, the Thracian forces who have come
with Theorus!

[*Enter a group of* ODOMANTIAN SOLDIERS, *ill-dressed, with old and battered shields.*]

DIKAIOPOLIS: What the hell is this rabble?

THEORUS: The Odomantian Army.

DIKAIOPOLIS: Odomantian balls! And while we're in that area, [*examining one of the* ODOMANTIANS *with curiosity*] what on earth has happened here? Tell me, who cut the leaf off your fig?

THEORUS: These are excellent light infantry, and for two drachmas a day²⁴ they will overrun the whole of Boeotia for you.

DIKAIOPOLIS: Two drachmas for that lot, with not a whole prick between them! The oarsmen who saved Athens from the Medes would have something to say about that.

[*Some of the* SOLDIERS *pounce on his lunch-basket and begin to help themselves to the contents.*]

Mr Chairman, I must protest. These Odomantians are pillaging my salad. [*To one of the* SOLDIERS] Put that garlic down, it's mine!

THEORUS: Keep away from them, you stupid fool! The stuff makes them run wild.

DIKAIOPOLIS: Mr Chairman, will the Executive Committee sit idly by and do nothing while an Athenian is maltreated by barbarians in his own Assembly?

[*No answer.*]

Well, at any rate I'm not going to let you ask us to vote them two drachmas a day. Gentlemen, I declare that Zeus has sent a sign! The Assembly must be dissolved. I distinctly felt a drop of rain!²⁵

CRIER: The Thracians will leave, and attend here again the day after tomorrow. The Executive Committee declare this meeting of the Assembly closed.

[*Exeunt all but* DIKAIOPOLIS. *He sadly gathers up the remains of his lunch and walks off, the stage revolving as he goes.*]

SCENE TWO: *An open place in front of two houses. One of them is the house of* DIKAIOPOLIS. *The other represents at first the house of* EURIPIDES, *later that of* LAMACHUS.

DIKAIOPOLIS [*who has now almost reached his house*]: Ah, what a meal that would have been!

    [*Enter* AMPHITHEUS, *running furiously, and carrying three large wine-skins.*]

    Ah, Amphitheus! – back from Sparta already? All O.K.?

AMPHITHEUS [*breathless*]: Not yet, not till I've got clear away from those Acharnians.

DIKAIOPOLIS: Acharnians? What d'you mean?

AMPHITHEUS: Well, I was coming here as fast as I could, bringing you these three peaces[26] [*indicating the wine-skins*], and these old men from Acharnae, blast them, smelt the wine. They're close-grained oak and maple, just like the charcoal they make, and hard as nails – real men of Marathon. And they all yelled at me, calling me all sorts of names, asking how I dared to make peace with the villains who had destroyed their vineyards – and with Spartan wine too! Then they started picking up stones, and I started making myself scarce, and they ran after me, shouting like fiends.

DIKAIOPOLIS: Well, let them. You've got the peaces?

AMPHITHEUS: Yes, here they are – three of them – taste them. This one is for five years. Have a sip.

DIKAIOPOLIS: Ugh! [*He spits out the wine and thrusts the skin from him.*]

AMPHITHEUS: What's wrong?

DIKAIOPOLIS: It's nauseating! It simply reeks of turpentine and shipyards.

AMPHITHEUS [*offering him the second, larger skin*]: Well, try the ten-year one.

DIKAIOPOLIS [*after tasting it*]: No, this one is too acid. More diplomatic missions, I bet, and trying to get the allies to send troops for when the fighting starts again.

AMPHITHEUS [*offering the third skin*]: Ah, but now *this* one –
this is the real thing. Thirty years, by land and sea.

DIKAIOPOLIS [*drinking deep, and gradually breaking into an
enormous smile*]: Why, by all the feasts of Dionysus! It has
the taste of nectar and ambrosia! D'you know what I seem
to feel it saying to me? 'No need to be always wondering
when you're going to hear the order "Come prepared with
rations for three days". You're a free man – you can go where
you like!' Yes, I'll take this one [*hugging it to his bosom*]; and
I hereby [*pouring some of it out on the ground*] make peace with
Sparta. [*He takes another gigantic draught.*] And the Acharnians
– they know where they can go. My troubles are all over! No
more war! [*Hugging the skin even closer*] Now to celebrate
the Country Dionysia![27] [*He takes the skin into his house.*]

AMPHITHEUS: Now to try and get away from those Acharnians! [*Rushes off.*]

[*Enter, as fast as they can, the* CHORUS OF ACHARNIANS.
They are as described by AMPHITHEUS, *very old and very
ferocious, and hot on the track of the traitor.*]

CHORUS [*allegro agitato*]:
        Chase him, chase him, everybody,
        For the traitor must be found,
        Everyone that you run into,
        Ask him where he's gone to ground.

[*By now they are all over the stage. They search intensely in
unlikely places, and finally give up.*]

        Why, our quarry has escaped us!
        Eyes, release a flood of tears!
        Woe is us that we are burdened
        With the weight of sixty years!

        Once our running was Olympic,
        And this villain would not then
        Have so swiftly got away; but
[*adagio*]   That will never be again.

Now my legs have lost their fleetness,
And my joints are stiff and sore,
And the fox has dodged the hunters,
And the hounds can run no more.

[*allegro*]   Still pursue him, still pursue him!
Let him never be at ease!
With the enemy he's treated,
The destroyers of our trees.

Zeus and all ye gods in heaven,
Never shall we rest from war
Till the pillage of our vineyards
Is revenged in Spartan gore.

LEADER [*recitative*]:
Search on, search on, with rock-like constancy[28]
Through all the world, if need be, till he's found.
For never will our wrath be satisfied
Till the peace-monger has been stoned to death.

DIKAIOPOLIS [*within*]:
Keep silent all! – the holy rite begins.

LEADER:
Hush! – did you hear the call for holy silence?
That is our man, about to sacrifice.
He's coming out; so everybody hide.
[*The* CHORUS *conceal themselves. Enter, from the house,*
DIKAIOPOLIS *with his* DAUGHTER, *who carries on her
head a basket containing the requisites for the sacrifice, and two
slaves, carrying between them a phallic symbol mounted on a
pole.* DIKAIOPOLIS' WIFE *watches from the door.*]

DIKAIOPOLIS: Keep silent all! – the holy rite begins. [*Prodding his* DAUGHTER *in the back*] Go on, basket-bearer. [*To one of the* SLAVES] Hold that thing up straight, Xanthias.

[*The* DAUGHTER *advances to the altar.*]

Put the basket down, dear, so we can make the offering.

DAUGHTER [*putting down the basket next to the altar and taking a cake out of it*]: Mum! – can we have the soup spoon, please? I need it to pour the soup over this with.

[*The* WIFE *runs into the house and quickly returns with the spoon.* DIKAIOPOLIS *takes from the basket a pot full of soup, and hands it to his* DAUGHTER, *who ladles some of it on to the cake, which she then places on the altar. Then she takes up the basket again and stands in front of the two* SLAVES, *ready for the procession.*]

DIKAIOPOLIS: Fine. [*Stretching his hands out towards the altar*] O Lord Dionysus, accept with favour this offering and this procession, which I and my household, released from the misery of war, now hold to celebrate thy Country Dionysia; may it be a blessing to us, and may the thirty years' peace that I have made bring me naught but good. Amen. Now, my little beauty, mind how you carry the basket. No laughing, now. Pretend you've got horseradish in your mouth. That's right. My, he'll be a lucky man that marries you! And what wonderful children you'll have! Just think! – half a dozen little kittens in the house, all taking after their mother. Such a farting chorus in the small hours the world will never have heard! Step off, dear; and mind the crowd. We don't want to have anyone snaffling your jewels, now, do we? Xanthias! – make sure it stays upright there behind the basket-bearer. I'll bring up the rear and sing the hymn. [*To his* WIFE] You watch from the roof, dear.

[*She goes into the house.*]

All right, off we go.

[*The 'crowd', which consists only of the* WIFE, *appears on the roof. The little procession circles the altar seven times – first the* DAUGHTER, *then the two* SLAVES, *and lastly* DIKAIOPOLIS, *who sings the following song.*]

O Phales,[29] as with Dionysus from tavern to bedroom
     you roam,
Six years it has been since I saw you, but now at long last
     I am home.
I've made my own peace with the Spartans, I'm finished
     with trouble and war,
And Lamachus, grandson of Ares, won't bother my mind
     any more.

So now I can turn to the pleasures I'd always have chosen
     if I could,
Like finding my neighbour's young slave-girl in the act of
     purloining some wood,
And grabbing her tight (for I never have known her to
     say 'I will not'),
And lifting her up to amuse her, then having it off on the
     spot.

O Phales, come, come to my party to welcome my
     happy release,
And if you feel sick in the morning, just drink off a potful
     of peace;
For now is the time to be merry, with pleasure for one and
     for all,
For the shield that I bore in my battles I've hung up to
     rest on the wall.

[*The procession stops, and* DIKAIOPOLIS *stoops to pick up the
soup-pot, which had been left beside the altar. As he is standing
up, the* CHORUS *rush out, singing and shouting, and throwing
stones at the procession, which scatters in panic, all except*
DIKAIOPOLIS *rushing into the house and banging the door shut.*]

CHORUS:

            That's the man, that's the man!
            Hit him hard, hit him hard,
            As you can, as you can,
            Now we've got him off his guard!

DIKAIOPOLIS: For Heracles' sake, watch out! You're going
to smash the sacred pot.

CHORUS:

> Smash the pot? – no, we'll not,
> No we'll not, no we'll not,
> But we will smash your head,
> And we'll stone you till you're dead!

DIKAIOPOLIS [*who is still trying to shield himself with the pot*]:
But my dear sirs, what have I done?

CHORUS:

> *You* want *us* to tell you what?
> Did you make a peace or not?
> How can you look us in the eye,
> You traitor of the deepest dye?

DIKAIOPOLIS: But you don't know *why* I made peace.
Listen – won't you listen?

CHORUS:

> Listen? – never while we've breath!
> Villain, now you meet your death!
> Die beneath a hail of stones:
> They will serve to hide your bones.

DIKAIOPOLIS: Just let me say something first! Can't you stop
it for a moment?

CHORUS:

> Stop it? – never! – not a word!
> Traitors' tongues must not be heard!
> When *your* wickedness we scan,
> Cleon seems a virtuous man!

[*Addressing* CLEON]

> Don't you grin, though; never fear,
> It'll be *your* turn next year![30]

LEADER: We didn't come here to listen to long speeches from a man who has made – peace – with Sparta! We came here to give him his just deserts!

DIKAIOPOLIS: Look, let's forget the Spartans for a minute, shall we, and just talk about the peace? Yes, I made peace. Now, was I right to make it?

LEADER [*spluttering*]: Right?! To come to terms with that lot? Don't you know that to a Spartan his pledged word, his oath, his most solemn sacrifice, counts for nothing?

DIKAIOPOLIS: Oh, I know we always say hard things about the Spartans; but are they really responsible for everything?

LEADER: The Spartans not responsible?! You talk flat treason like that, and you expect to escape with your life?

DIKAIOPOLIS: Yes, and I say it again, they're not responsible for everything. In fact I could prove to you quite clearly that they have a good many legitimate grievances against us.

LEADER: This is really beyond all bearing! Pleading the enemy's case!

DIKAIOPOLIS: Truth and justice, that's what matters, and that's what I'm going to plead the case of. The People [*indicating the audience*] will be my judges. And – and – [*a brilliant idea strikes him*] – if you like, I'll make my speech with my head on the block, and if I don't convince you, well then, you can decapitate me on the spot![31]

LEADER [*quite unimpressed*]: What are you waiting for, boys? Let's paint him red!

DIKAIOPOLIS [*who has had another brilliant idea*]: Well, well, the charcoal in your hearts has blazed up all right! Now then, gentlemen of Acharnae, are you going to let me speak or not?

LEADER: Certainly not.

DIKAIOPOLIS [*not particularly worried*]: Looks like I'm for it, then.

LEADER: I'd sooner die than listen to you.

DIKAIOPOLIS: Oh, please don't do that.

LEADER: No, we won't; but you will! [*He is ready to throw the first stone.*]

DIKAIOPOLIS: I don't think so. [*Mysteriously*] If you lift a finger against me, I will kill your nearest and dearest. I am holding them as hostages, and I will execute them at the slightest provocation. [*He goes into the house.*]

LEADER [*to his colleagues*]: You any idea what he means – these threats he's making? He doesn't maybe have one of our children locked up in there? Why's he so damn confident?

DIKAIOPOLIS [*emerging triumphantly, carrying in one hand a sword, and in the other a wickerwork scuttle full of coal*]: Right. I'm ready. Stone me whenever you want to. Only if you do, I'll kill this one.³² We'll soon know if any of you has any respect for common hum – for common coality.

LEADER: No, no! It's one of us! Don't, in the gods' name, don't!

DIKAIOPOLIS: I will. It's no good your shouting. I'm not listening.

LEADER: Don't kill him! We grew up together – it would break all our hearts!

DIKAIOPOLIS: You wouldn't listen to me, and I'm not going to listen to you. [*He draws back his sword to run the scuttle through; but he is interrupted by agitated music and mute appeals from the* CHORUS.]

CHORUS:
All right, you can tell us what makes you so fond
   Of the men who our homes would destroy.
For let come what may, I will never betray
   My dear little coaly-faced boy.

DIKAIOPOLIS: Not till you've dropped those stones.

LEADER [*as the* CHORUS *lets some of them fall*]: There you are. Now put your sword down.

DIKAIOPOLIS: You can't fool me! You've still got some hidden away in those cloaks.

64

CHORUS [*rhythmically shaking the remaining stones out of their cloaks*]:
Look, how can you doubt that we've shaken them out?
   Our missiles all lie at our feet.
Now no more excuses, but put down that sword –
   And do it in time with the beat!
[*On the final shake, slightly off the beat,* DIKAIOPOLIS *drops his sword.*]

DIKAIOPOLIS [*reflectively*]: I *thought* I'd manage to quiet you down in the end. But it very nearly cost the lives of some innocent coals from Mount Parnes. Will they ever forgive their neighbours? [*He hands the scuttle to the* CHORUS, *who greet it rapturously; then inspects his sooty clothes.*] Well, they've got disgusting manners, I must say! Shitting all over me, like a bloody cuttlefish! But seriously – it's not right that people should have tempers like sour wine, to want to yell and throw stones, and refuse somebody a hearing, just because he wants to say something nice – and true – about the Spartans for a change? And don't forget my offer: to say it with my head on the block. And don't think I don't love my own life, either.

CHORUS:
Now don't dilly-dally, but bring out the block,
   And let's see how your argument goes.
We're most curious to find what it is you've in mind
   To say on behalf of our foes.
[*During this chorus* DIKAIOPOLIS *goes into the house and shortly returns with an enormous butcher's block. He has also put on a bald wig, in which he bears a remarkable resemblance to the* AUTHOR.]

LEADER:
You offered of your own accord to stand your trial this
   way;
So set it down, and let us hear just what you've got to
   say.

DIKAIOPOLIS [*putting down the block, front facing the audience*]:
There you are. There's the block, and here's little me ready
to speak. You needn't worry about me putting any fancy
dress on my ideas: I'm just going to say what comes into my
head in defence of Sparta. [*The thought of the word 'head'
somewhat unnerves him.*] But it won't be easy. You know
what country people are like. Any smooth-tongued fellow
will be sure to be a hero with them, whatever he says, right
or wrong, so long as it flatters their country and themselves.
They could be bought and sold, and never know a thing
about it. And the senior citizens, who serve on juries –
they've got sharp teeth, votes they call them, and they're
never happy except when they're biting someone. I know
that better than anyone now, after my little brush with
Cleon over last year's play. He dragged me into the Council
Chamber and made all sorts of trumped-up accusations
against me; his mouth spewed out a torrent of sewage,
nearly enough to drown me with lies – and I very nearly did
drown. So this time [*to the* CHORUS] I'd be very grateful if
you allowed me time to dress up properly for my trial, look
really poor and downtrodden, you know.

CHORUS:
>Why all this delay? – why, why do you stay,
>>And wriggle first this way then that?
>We don't mind if you use Hieronymus' hair[33]
>>For an invisibility hat!

LEADER:
>Prepare yourself with all the tricks from Sisyphus'[34]
>>store,
>If you desire, but once you're ready, temporize no more!
>[*The* CHORUS, *with meaningful looks, retire to the far side of
>the stage.*]

DIKAIOPOLIS: Now's the time I must show myself a man.
I'd better go and see Euripides. [*He goes up to* EURIPIDES'
house and knocks.] Boy! Boy!

CEPHISOPHON[35] [*a man of middle age and great stature, opening the door; in a resonant stage voice*]: Yes, who's that?

DIKAIOPOLIS: Is Euripides at home?

CEPHISOPHON: He is and is not, if you understand.

DIKAIOPOLIS: He is and is not . . . I must be a bit dim today. Could you explain?

CEPHISOPHON: Why, certainly. His *mind* is not at home, it's out looking for stray verses to find a kind home for; but he *himself*, you see, *is* at home, upstairs, writing a play.

DIKAIOPOLIS: How lucky a man must be whose very slaves are such clever – actors! Can you call him down?

CEPHISOPHON: No, it is not possible.

DIKAIOPOLIS: But can't you *make* it possible?

[CEPHISOPHON *begins to shut the door.*]

If you shut me out I won't go away – I'll just keep on knocking.

[CEPHISOPHON *shuts the door firmly.* DIKAIOPOLIS *knocks loudly for some time, to no avail. Then he has an idea.*]

Euripides! Euripikins! If e'er you answered mortal's earnest prayer, answer me now. It is Dikaiopolis from Cholleidae calling you – that's me.

EURIPIDES [*from inside, on the top floor*]: Go away. I'm busy.

DIKAIOPOLIS: You don't need to come down. Why not use that mechanical gubbins?

EURIPIDES: No, it is not possible.

DIKAIOPOLIS: But can't you *make* it possible?

EURIPIDES: Very well. I *am* too busy to come downstairs, but I'm coming round now.

[*The façade of the house revolves, disclosing, on the upper level,* EURIPIDES' *study. He is sitting writing, at a table full of books. On the walls hang numerous ragged or patched bits of old clothing; more are seen in open cupboards, some of them labelled with the names of famous characters in* EURIPIDES' *plays. A slave is in attendance.*]

DIKAIOPOLIS: Euripides –

EURIPIDES: What sayest thou?

DIKAIOPOLIS: Now I know why you put so many cripples in your plays.³⁶ They all fell downstairs when they came to see you. And the state of your wardrobe! – it's really tragic! – that will explain the beggars. But what I came for, Euripides – please, I beg of you, could you give me a rag or two out of one of your old plays? I've got to make a long speech to the Chorus in the next scene, and if I make a hash of it – [*He draws his finger across his throat with the appropriate sound.*]

EURIPIDES: Which wouldst thou have? Perchance thou seekest these, wherein ill-fated Oeneus³⁷ once appeared.

DIKAIOPOLIS: No, I don't want Oeneus'. Someone, I don't remember his name, but much more beggarly than that.

EURIPIDES: Then these, blind Phoenix's?³⁸

DIKAIOPOLIS: No, not Phoenix. Someone worse off still.

EURIPIDES [*to himself*]: Whose tattered raiment doth the fellow seek? [*To* DIKAIOPOLIS] Meanest thou then the beggar Philoctetes?³⁹

DIKAIOPOLIS: No, much, much, much more beggarly than that.

EURIPIDES [*pointing to yet a fourth outfit*]: Is this perchance the squalid garb thou seek'st, which once was borne by lame Bellerophon?⁴⁰

DIKAIOPOLIS: No, not Bellerophon either. The man I'm after, though, he was lame too – *and* a beggar – oh, yes, and he was a very clever speaker, very glib.

EURIPIDES: I know the man: 'tis Mysian Telephus.

DIKAIOPOLIS: Yes – that's right – Telephus. Please, just as a favour, could you give me his clothes?

EURIPIDES: Give to him, slave, the rags of Telephus. They lie above Thyestes',⁴¹ and below poor Ino's robe.⁴²

[*The* SLAVE *has now found the tunic, which consists chiefly of holes.*]

Here, catch. [*He throws it down to* DIKAIOPOLIS.]

DIKAIOPOLIS [*inspecting it*]: 'O Zeus who seest through and under all!' – Euripides, since you have been so kind, could you possibly give me the things that go with the outfit? The Mysian cloth cap, for example?

> 'For I this day must seem to be a beggar –
> Be who I am, but not appear myself.'⁴³

Or to be more accurate – the audience have got to know who I am, but the Chorus have got to be fooled, at least until my telling Telephean phrases have knocked them into the middle of next week.

EURIPIDES: I'll give it thee; for subtle are thy schemes, and intricate the courses of thy mind. [*He throws down the cap;* DIKAIOPOLIS, *who has by now struggled into the tunic, puts it on, and is at once delighted.*]

DIKAIOPOLIS:

> 'O be thou blest; and as for Telephus,
> Thou knowest what I wish as touching him.'

Dear me! [*patting the cap*] you're making me quite poetic already. Now – I still need a stick, if I'm to be a proper beggar.

EURIPIDES [*who is getting exasperated*]: Take this, and quit thou straight these marble halls. [*Throws down a crooked walking-stick*]

DIKAIOPOLIS [*to himself*]: Seest thou, my soul, how I am thrust away? – and I haven't got half the things I came for yet. I've got to be a really glutinous and limpet-like wheedler. [*Aloud*] Euripides, could you give me a little wicker basket? – preferably one that's fallen on to a lamp and got a hole burnt in it.

EURIPIDES: Why needest thou the basket-maker's product?

DIKAIOPOLIS: I don't need it at all – I just want it.

EURIPIDES [*throwing down the basket*]: Know that thou vexest me, and go from hence.

DIKAIOPOLIS: Oh, very well. And 'be thou blest' – just like your mother used to be![44]

EURIPIDES: I say, be gone.

DIKAIOPOLIS: Won't you give me just one little drinking cup – chipped if possible?

EURIPIDES[*flinging it down so hard that* DIKAIOPOLIS *only just catches it in time to stop it breaking*]: Take it and go, thou troubler of our house!

DIKAIOPOLIS [*aside*]: Little does he know what trouble he's bringing upon himself! – Euripides, my sweet, lovely Euripides, just this one thing more: could I just have a little pot, with a hole in it, stuffed up with sponge?

EURIPIDES: Thou'lt rob me soon of all my tragic art. Take it and go!

DIKAIOPOLIS [*trying to find a spare pair of fingers to hold the pot*]: All right, I'm going. No, silly me, I can't go yet. I still need one thing more, or else all the rest will be useless. – My very dearest Euripides, do listen! I'll go away and never come back – if you only give me some cast-off cabbage leaves to put in my basket.

EURIPIDES: Thou art my ruin! Here. Alas, my plays, all gone!

DIKAIOPOLIS: Honestly, that's all. I'm going. I've obviously upset you – 'yet thought I not the kings would hate me so.'[45] [*He is going this time, but suddenly stops and puts his hand to his head.*] Ye gods, I'm done for! I forgot the most important thing of all! [*Returning to the house*] Euripikins – I really love you, you know that – and may Zeus strike me dead if I ever ask you for anything again except just one thing – just one thing. Euripides, could yôu give me some of the parsley your mother left you?

EURIPIDES: He is a mocker. Close the palace gates. [*The house closes up, and* EURIPIDES *disappears.*]

DIKAIOPOLIS: Well then, my soul, we'll have to do without the parsley. [*Goes back towards his own house, but stops on seeing the block.*] Do you know what you've let yourself in

for? – making a speech in defence of Sparta? Forward, my
soul! On your marks – set – go! [*He remains petrified.*] Come
on, now. What are you afraid of? You're full of Euripides,
after all. That's better. All right, my soul, let's go. Let's say
what we want to say, and then, if they want our head, they
can have it! Be brave – come on. [*He makes a sudden dash for
the block and lays his head on it.*] Well done, heart.

CHORUS:
> What will he say? What will he do?
> I marvel at his gall,
> Who dares to risk his neck and speak
> Alone against us all.
>
> He does not tremble, does not flinch:
> I think he thinks he'll win!
> All right then; this is what you chose;
> We're ready, so begin.

DIKAIOPOLIS: Don't hold it against me, gentlemen,[46] if,
though a beggar – and a comic poet at that – I make bold to
speak to the great Athenian people about matters of state.
Not even a comedian can be completely unconcerned with
truth and justice; and what I am going to say may be
unpalatable, but it's the truth. At least this time I can speak
freely, with no risk of being charged by Cleon with slandering the City in the presence of foreigners.[47] This time we're
all by ourselves; it's only the Lenaea, and there aren't any
foreigners here yet, either with tribute or with troops. We're
all by ourselves, all grain, no chaff. The foreigners who live
here you can think of, if you like, as bran. Now let's be
clear about this: I hate the Spartans as much as any man
here. I hope Poseidon sends an earthquake from his home on
Mount Taenarum[48] and brings all their houses to the
ground. I've had vines of mine chopped down as well. But
after all – we're all friends together here, and we can speak

71

our minds – why should we blame it all on the Spartans? It was Athenians – Athenians, mind you, not Athens, remember that, not the City – but a bunch of good-for-nothing individuals, not even real citizens but aliens who had wormed their way in, bad stuff through and through – it was them that started the whole thing. They started bringing charges against the Megarians. First it was their woollies, and before long, whenever they saw anyone with a watermelon, or a young hare or a piglet, or some garlic and rock-salt, 'Ah!' they said, 'Megarian contraband,' and had them confiscated and put under the hammer that very day. Well, that was minor – just our national sport, as you might say; but then some young chaps got drunk and, for a lark, went to Megara and kidnapped their tart Simaetha. Well, this raised the Megarians' hackles, and they stole two of Aspasia's[49] girls in retaliation. And that, gentlemen, was the cause of the war that has been raging throughout Greece these six years: it was all on account of three prostitutes. Because Pericles, Olympian Pericles, sent out thunder and lightning and threw all Greece into confusion. He began making laws written like drinking songs,

'No Megarian shall stand
On sea or on land,
And from all of our markets they're utterly banned.'[50]

Well, pretty soon the Megarians were starving by slow degrees, and not unnaturally they asked their allies the Spartans to try and get the decree reversed, since after all it had only been made, as I said, because of three prostitutes. They asked us, more than once, but we refused, and so the shields began to clash. I hear someone say that they ought not to have declared war. Well, what ought they to have done? Tell me that. And tell me something else. Suppose a Spartan customs officer had confiscated and sold a puppy from Seriphos[51] or some such spot on the map, alleging that

72

it was being smuggled – would you have sat by and done
nothing? Of course not. You'd have launched a fleet of
three hundred instantly, and the City would have been full
of military preparations – ships' captains shouting for
sailors, pay being distributed, figureheads of Athena being
gilded, the Piraeus corn market all a-bustle with rations
being doled out everywhere; people buying water-bottles
and jars and rowlock thongs at one stall, garlic, onions and
olives at another; farewell parties being held, with the best
anchovies and flute-girls, and maybe later a bloody nose or
two; and down at the docks they'd have been planing spars
into oars, driving in rivets, putting on thongs, and the
masters of the oarsmen meanwhile practising trills and runs
on their flutes.[52] You know as well as I do that's what you'd
have done; 'and do we think that Telephus would not?'[53]
If we do, we're even stupider than I thought.

[*Half the* CHORUS *go over to where* DIKAIOPOLIS *is lying and
stand around him with every show of enthusiastic approval. The
other half advance menacingly and angrily upon them and him.*]

FIRST SEMICHORUS:
How dare you, monster, say such things, and say them, too,
    of us!
Suppose we *had* the odd informer, why make all this fuss?

SECOND SEMICHORUS:
So may the great Poseidon help me, I declare that I
Thought all he said was true and just, without a single lie.

FIRST SEMICHORUS [*trying to break through the cordon around*
DIKAIOPOLIS]:
Well, true or false, he had no right to utter treason here,
And he must learn that talk like that is going to cost him
    dear.

SECOND SEMICHORUS [*overpowering and pinioning them*]:
Whatever violence you use, we're ready to receive it;
And if his head should hit the ground, your feet will
    quickly leave it!

73

FIRST SEMICHORUS [*struggling to free themselves*]:
Lamachus, Hero of Lightning and Lord of the Gorgon
Crest,
Our tribal champion, come quickly, thy servants are sore
distressed!
And every general and captain who ever has stormed a
wall,
Be quick to come to our rescue, and do not neglect our
call!
[*A great war-cry is heard, the greatest probably since Achilles,
and* LAMACHUS *bursts on to the stage. He is dressed in full
armour, his shield bearing a horrific Gorgon's head, and wears a
helmet with an enormous triple crest and two ostrich feathers.
The* SECOND SEMICHORUS, *dumbfounded, let go of their
prisoners.*]

LAMACHUS [*bombastically*]: Whence came the cry of battle
that I heard? Whom must I aid, and where my havoc
wreak? Who has aroused the Gorgon on my targe?

LEADER OF SECOND SEMICHORUS [*whose panic has given place
to uncontrollable hilarity*]: O Lord Feathercrest, what a get-up!

LEADER OF FIRST SEMICHORUS [*indicating* DIKAIOPOLIS]:
It's *him*. He's been doing nothing but slander the City for
years.

LAMACHUS [*grabbing* DIKAIOPOLIS *by the scruff of the neck*]:
How dare you do such a thing? You, a beggar!

DIKAIOPOLIS [*wriggling free*]: Oh, great Lamachus, do pardon
me. Even a beggar has the right to say just a little occasionally.

LAMACHUS: What did you say about us? [*Gives him a shake.*]
Come on, out with it.

DIKAIOPOLIS: I – I don't remember at the moment. It's that
armour of yours, it makes me all giddy. Please take away
that bugaboo!

LAMACHUS [*reversing his shield*]: There you are.

DIKAIOPOLIS: No – on the ground, face down, so.

74

LAMACHUS [*complying*]: There.

DIKAIOPOLIS: Now could you give me that plume off your helmet?

LAMACHUS [*handing him a gigantic feather*]: Here's a bit of down for you.

DIKAIOPOLIS: Right. Now could you hold my head so that I can be sick? It's that crest of yours does it.

LAMACHUS [*trying to grab the feather back*]: What do you think you're doing, using one of my feathers to help you throw up?

DIKAIOPOLIS: *One* feather!! For heaven's sake, what bird does it come from? Not a *boastard*?

LAMACHUS [*trying to throttle him*]: Why, you little so-and-so, I'll –

DIKAIOPOLIS [*wriggling free again*]: No, no, Lamachus, don't. Why should a great big chap like you want to murder a little fellow like me? If you *must* prove your strength, why don't you trim my wick? You're well enough equipped to do it!

LAMACHUS: How dare you talk to a general like this?

DIKAIOPOLIS: Why shouldn't I?

LAMACHUS: Because you're a beggar, that's why.

DIKAIOPOLIS [*throwing off his rags*]: I, a beggar? I'm no beggar. I'm an honest citizen. I've never run for office in my life, and ever since the war started I've been in the front line. And *you*, ever since the war started you've been in the pay queue!

LAMACHUS: I was democratically elected –

DIKAIOPOLIS: By a couple of benighted cuckoos, yes. That's the sort of thing I got fed up with, and that's why I made peace. I just couldn't stand seeing sixty-year-olds called up for active service, while young people like you got as far away from the scene of action as you possibly could[54] – to Thrace, perhaps, on three drachmas a day, I don't know who, Teisamenus, Phaenippus, Hippo-bloody-archides; then there's Chares and his lot, and another gang up in

75

Chaonia – there's Geres, Theodorus, and some line-shooter from Diomeia – what was his name? – anyway, then there's a whole lot more in Sicily, in Camarina, Gela, Catana, Ridicula, and I don't know where else –

LAMACHUS: They were democratically elected too.

DIKAIOPOLIS: Then how come it's always you that get every well-paid post going, and never any of these people [*indicating the* CHORUS]? You, for instance, Marilades – you're getting on in years; have you ever been an ambassador?

[MARILADES *shakes his head.*]

He hasn't, you see; and yet he's a perfectly honest and hard-working man. How about you, Anthracyllus? or you, Euphorides? or you, Prinides? Any of you ever been to Chaonia or to Ecbatana?

[*All shake their heads.*]

None of them, you see. But Coesyra's son,[55] and Lamachus here, they're on every embassy we send; and yet only the other day they got so behind with their club subscriptions that their colleagues were warning them they'd better make themselves scarce – 'Get away!' they said, as if they were emptying their slops into the street.

LAMACHUS: Oh, Democracy! this is intolerable!

DIKAIOPOLIS: Anything's intolerable to you, unless you get paid.

LAMACHUS [*who has now had enough, and observes that the* CHORUS *have all gone over to* DIKAIOPOLIS' *side*]: Very well, gentlemen, if that's what you think, I'm off. I'm going to fight the Peloponnesians, the whole damn lot of them, and send them helter-skelter all over the place, by land and sea, everywhere, to the utmost of my power. [*He departs in a great rage.*]

DIKAIOPOLIS: Well, what I say to the Peloponnesians is – come to my market, all of you, especially the Megarians and Boeotians. [*Looking after the departing 'hero'*] But *not* Lamachus.

[*Exit* DIKAIOPOLIS. *The* CHORUS *come forward and address the audience.*]

CHORUS:

He has won the debate and converted the State
(At least, so we hope) to his view.
Now let's strip for the dance and make use of our chance
To convey our opinions to you.

LEADER:

Since first our poet started writing comedies, he's never
Made use of his Parabasis to say that he is clever.
But since his foes have charged him (and in hasty
    judgement sitting
The jurymen condemned him when they should have
    been acquitting)
With slandering the People and the State, he wants to
    find
If, true to your tradition, you since then have changed
    your mind.

He says that all the good he's done deserves some
    recognition:
For now you do not gawp at every diplomatic mission
That comes from foreign parts and tries to flatter and
    entreat you;
He's taught you all their tricks, and now you *never* let
    them cheat you!
It used to be they only had to call you 'violet-crowned'[56]
And you sat up so, your undersides were almost off the
    ground;
And if they'd called your city 'rich and shining', you'd
    have been
All hooked upon an epithet more fit for a sardine.
And that's not all he's done: last year he tried to
    demonstrate
Exactly what 'democracy' means to a subject state.

That's why, next Dionysia-time, when all your allies bring
Their tribute, every one enthusiastically will sing
The praises of our poet, of that rash and headstrong
    youth
Who actually dared to tell the Athenians the truth.

Indeed his fame has reached so far (or so our spies report)
That when the Spartans sent their envoys to the Persian
    court,
The King, who cross-examined them to learn who'd win
    the war,
Asked just two questions: first about the ships – which
    side had more;
And then he asked: 'That comic poet, what's-his-name,
    the one
Who wrote *The Babylonians* – which side's he hardest on?
That city, my prediction is (although it may surprise
    them),
Will win the war hands down if he continues to advise
    them.'
That's why the peace proposals made by Sparta never
    lack
A clause that stipulates that we must give Aegina back.
It's not the island that they want: they'd willingly forgo
    it,
Only it offers them a chance to take away our poet.[57]

Be sure, though, and hold on to him. He'll carry on
    impeaching
Every abuse he sees, and give much valuable teaching,
Making you wiser, happier men. There won't be any
    diddling
Or flattery or bribes, or any other kind of fiddling,
Nor will you drown in fulsome praises, such as all the rest
Bestow on you: he thinks his job's to teach you what is
    best.

So, though Cleon may itch
    For another big fight,
He will never prevail,
    For both justice and right
Are my allies, and I
    Have no fear of defeat,
For I am, unlike him,
    Neither coward nor cheat.

CHORUS:

Come hither, glowing charcoal Muse,
With fiery power thy friends infuse.
As from the coal the sparks arise
When fanned, as on the embers fries
A dish of sprats, while servants shake
The bright-crowned Thasian sauce, and bake
A cake or two, so send thy gleam
To us the members of thy deme,
That we may sing in concord fair
A proud melodious country air.

LEADER:

We think it is high time that someone spoke
About the way you treat us older folk.
Time after time our valour's saved the City
In naval battles; yet you have no pity
For our old age, but let the younger sort
On trumped-up charges haul us into court,
Young orators who mock us left and right,
Knowing *our* verbal fire's extinguished quite.
We stand there leaning on our staffs and pray
To Lord Poseidon for a storm-free day;
But mist beclouds our eyes, and we can trace
Only the dimmest outline of the case.
The young accuser, scorning others' aid,
Pelts us with small round phrases deftly made,
Then calls us up, puts questions with a catch,

And leaves the accused without a straw to snatch.
He stammers a few words, but soon it ends,
And home he goes convicted to his friends,
And sobbing says: 'The little cash that's mine
Must go, not on a coffin, but a fine!'

CHORUS:

It's a scandal and a shame to dishonour and defame
    And to laugh at and humiliate in court
One who's snowy-headed now, but whose sweat
        bedewed his brow
    When the Persian foe at Marathon he fought.

For at Marathon – ah! then we were proved courageous
        men
    As hotly we pursued the fleeing Mede;
But now it seems the boot's been transferred to the other
        foot,
    And *we're* persecuted, *we* for mercy plead.

And then when we've said our say, all the jurors vote one
        way –
    They don't care if we are guilty or we ain't;
Why, it's got so bad I guess even Marpsias[58] would
        confess
    That we have *some* cause for justified complaint.

LEADER:

Pity brought tears into my eyes to see
How it befell Thucydides[59] to be
Lost in the Scythian wilderness, and stung
By young Cephisodemus' adder-tongue.
How shameful, that a bent old man should face
That taunting scion of the archer race!
When he was young and his reactions fleeter,
He'd not have stood such insults from Demeter!
No, he'd have floored them all with verbal violence,
Shouted three thousand Scythians into silence,

And proved himself a better archer than
Cephisodemus, yes, and all his clan.
But if on trying old folk you insist,
Then put their names upon a separate list.
If the defendant's old, then don't be ruthless,
But choose a prosecutor who is toothless;
And for the young reserve the subtleties
Of smart young queers like Alcibiades.
Then will this just old saw of Athens hold:
'The young should fight the young, the old the old.'

ACT TWO

SCENE: *the same.*

[*Enter* DIKAIOPOLIS, *carrying three leather thongs and a number of boundary stones, which he begins to set out in a large circle. Meanwhile two* SLAVES *set up a trading stall for him.*]

DIKAIOPOLIS: Right then, there's the boundaries for my market. Within these limits all Peloponnesians, Megarians and Boeotians have full trading rights – to trade with me, that is; Lamachus is excluded. I have held an election by lot for the office of Market Commissioners, and I declare these three thongs from Lepri duly elected. No informers will be admitted – it's your job [*to the thongs*] to see to that – or any other bird of that feather.[60] [*He hangs up the thongs at the side of the stall.*] But I'd better go and get my engraved copy of the peace treaty and put it on display here. [*Goes into his house.*]

[*Enter a* MEGARIAN *with his two little* GIRLS. *He carries a sack containing various bits and pieces whose nature and purpose will be clear from what follows. All three are very emaciated.*]

MEGARIAN: Weel, hullo, Athenian market. We Megarians havena seen ye for a lang time, and we lo' ye dearly, aye, by the great god of friendship, as though ye were our ain mither. You twa puir bairns, will ye help your auld father? Go over there and see can ye find a meal-tub anywhere aroond.

[*The* GIRLS *go over to the market-stall; but find nothing edible.*] Listen, then, and dinna let your bellies – I should ha' said, your minds wander. Which wuid ye rather – be sold as slaves, or starve tae death?

GIRLS: Be sold! Be sold!

MEGARIAN: I go along wi' that. But wha's sae far gone in his mind that wuid buy ye? He'd want tae be paid tae tak ye! Havena fear, though; I've a guid Megarian trick up my sleeve. I'll dress ye oot as canties – is it piglets they ca' them here?[61] – and sell ye that way. First of a', [*burrowing in the sack*] pit on these trotters. And for the dear's sake luik like ye had a guid sow for a mither. For Hermes knows, if ye come hame again, ye'll ken for real what starvation is. Pit on these snoots, that's recht. Now get into this sack

[*the* GIRLS *do so*]

and let oot some grunts and oinks. Soond like the wee canties do at the Mysteries doon at Eleusis.[62] I'll call and see if I canna get Dikaiopolis to come oot. Dikaiopolis! Will ye buy a brace o' canties?

DIKAIOPOLIS [*coming out of the house*]: Good heavens, a Megarian!

MEGARIAN: We're come tae do business.

DIKAIOPOLIS [*trying to find something to say*]: How – how are you getting on, where you come from?

MEGARIAN: Och, no badly. We sit by the fire and shrink.

DIKAIOPOLIS [*misunderstanding him*]: Not bad either, especially with a bit of music added. How are you managing otherwise?

MEGARIAN: Och, so-so. When I left tae come here, the government was doing its best tae see we achieved a speedy and complete catastrophe.

DIKAIOPOLIS [*ironically*]: Then you'll be out of the wood before long.

MEGARIAN [*dead serious*]: Exactly.

DIKAIOPOLIS: What else is up at Megara? What sort of price is corn there?

MEGARIAN: It's sae high, the gods in heaven are takkin' it a'!

DIKAIOPOLIS: Well, anyway, what have you got to sell? Salt?

MEGARIAN: Salt! Din ye own the whole of the sea already?

DIKAIOPOLIS: Garlic, then?

MEGARIAN: Dinna mak me laugh! Every time ye raid our country, ye uproot them a', as though ye were fieldmice! Garlic!

DIKAIOPOLIS: Well, then, what do you have?

MEGARIAN: I hae some canties for the Mysteries.

DIKAIOPOLIS [*very excited*]: Where are they? Let's see them.

MEGARIAN: Och, but they're pretty. Feel them if ye like. [*Fishes one of the* GIRLS *out of the sack and hands her to* DIKAIOPOLIS.] Isna she lovely and fat?

DIKAIOPOLIS: What the devil is this?

MEGARIAN: Why, a cantie.

DIKAIOPOLIS: What do you mean? What sort of – what sort of what-you-said is this?

MEGARIAN: A Megarian one, of course. Din ye see it's a cantie?

DIKAIOPOLIS: Well, I can't see it.

MEGARIAN [*handing him the other* GIRL]: No? – luik at this one, then. Will ye no believe your ain eyes? Ye say that one wasna a cantie. Wuid ye mak a bet? I'll lay ye a poond of salt with some thyme in it that this is a proper pure-bred Greek cantie.

DIKAIOPOLIS: Ah yes, I see – and it belongs to a human being too.

MEGARIAN: Weel, holy Diocles,[63] of course it does! It belangs tae me!

[DIKAIOPOLIS *eyes him in astonishment, unsure not so much of the* MEGARIAN's *sex as of his sanity; the* MEGARIAN *is blissfully unaware of his amazement.*] Wha did ye think I'd stolen them from? Wuid ye like tae hear them talk?

DIKAIOPOLIS [*humouring him*]: By all means.

MEGARIAN: A' right. [*To* SECOND GIRL.] Let's have a grunt from ye, my wee cantie, the noo.

[*Silence.*]

What, ye willna? How dare ye, ye little rascal? [*In her ear.*] Gie us a grunt, or as Hermes is my witness I'll tak ye hame!

SECOND GIRL: Oink, oink!

MEGARIAN: A' right, are ye satisfied? Is that a cantie or isna it?

DIKAIOPOLIS [*who at last understands what the* MEGARIAN *is talking about, but is unwilling to lose the magnificent joke he has just previously thought of*]: Well, I suppose you could say it is, but – ha! ha! – it'll be a real cunt in five years' time, won't it? Ha! ha! ha!

MEGARIAN [*on whom this is completely lost*]: Och aye, she'll tak after her mither.

DIKAIOPOLIS [*who has been examining the* SECOND GIRL]: This one's no good. What are you trying to palm off on me? I can't sacrifice this.

MEGARIAN: And why not, pray?

DIKAIOPOLIS: Where's its tail?

MEGARIAN: Och, it's young yet. Wait till it grows up, then it'll have a beautiful fat red one. [*Noticing that* DIKAIO- POLIS *seems inclined to doubt this, but not very clear why.*] Din ye want tae rear them? Luik at this one [*handing over* SECOND GIRL]: isna she pretty?

DIKAIOPOLIS [*examining her*]: She's just the same as the other one!

MEGARIAN: So I shuid think, too; they're full sisters. Ye ken, when they get a wee fatter and grow a bit of hair, cantics is the perrfect sacrifice tae Aphrodite.

DIKAIOPOLIS: But you don't sacrifice these to Aphrodite.

MEGARIAN: Not sacrifice canties tae Aphrodite? – wha *do* ye sacrifice them to, then? But ye ken, if ye stick them on a spit, ye'll find they're delicious.

DIKAIOPOLIS: [*who has decided, out of pity, to buy the 'pigs'*]: Can they eat yet without their mother?

MEGARIAN: Aye, and withoot their father forby.

DIKAIOPOLIS: What do they like having?

MEGARIAN: Whatever ye gie them. Ask them yersel'.

DIKAIOPOLIS [*to* FIRST GIRL]: Piggy-piggy!

FIRST GIRL: Oink! Oink!

DIKAIOPOLIS: Piggy, do you like chick-peas?

FIRST GIRL [*half-heartedly*]: Oink! Oink!

DIKAIOPOLIS: How about Phibalian figs?

FIRST GIRL [*greedily*]: Oink! Oink! Oink!

DIKAIOPOLIS [*turning to* SECOND GIRL]: What about you?
Do you like them too?

SECOND GIRL: Oink! Oink!

DIKAIOPOLIS: Yes, you do all right! Boy!

[*A* SLAVE *runs out of the house.*]

Bring out some of our figs for these piglets, will you? [*The
figs are brought. He scatters them in front of the* GIRLS.] I
wonder if they're going to? Whew! – they are – listen to
them! Mighty Heracles! Where do they come from? Not
Aet-olia,⁶⁴ by any chance? Good God! They haven't
guzzled them all in this time?!

MEGARIAN: Matter of fact, no. I did snitch ane for mesel'.

DIKAIOPOLIS: Well, I must say they're not a bad pair of
beasts. How much are you asking for them?

MEGARIAN: For this one, a bunch of garlic. And for the
ither – let me think – och aye, four poond o' salt.⁶⁵

DIKAIOPOLIS: It's a deal. Just wait a moment, could you,
please? [*He goes into his house.*]

MEGARIAN: Very weel. O Hermes, god o' marketing, if I
cuid anely sell my wife and my mither as easily!

[*Enter an* INFORMER.]

INFORMER: May I ask you, sir, where you are from?

MEGARIAN: I'm come frae Megara tae sell my ca – my pigs.

INFORMER [*taking hold of the sack, into which the two* GIRLS
have again climbed]: In that case I denounce these piglets as
contraband of war, and I shall lay information against you.

MEGARIAN: Here we are again, back where the whole sair tale
began!

INFORMER: I'll teach you to talk Megarian! Let go of that sack!

MEGARIAN [*holding desperately on to it*]: Help! help! Dikaiopolis! I'm being informerized!

DIKAIOPOLIS [*re-emerging*]: Who by? Who's trying to charge you? [*Takes down his three thongs.*] Come on, Market Commissioners, let's get rid of these informers. [*To the* INFORMER] What do you think you are charging people like this, a bloody bull?

INFORMER: I've got a right to report enemy aliens!

DIKAIOPOLIS: Well, run off and do it somewhere else, or you'll get what for.

[*Exit* INFORMER, *helped somewhat by the thongs.*]

MEGARIAN: What a plague ye have here in Athens!

DIKAIOPOLIS: Don't bother about them, my dear chap. Look, here's what you wanted for the pigs: here's the garlic, and the salt. Good-bye, and the best of luck.

MEGARIAN: It isna common at Megara tae have that.

DIKAIOPOLIS: Well, if you don't want it, I can always use it.

MEGARIAN [*to the* GIRLS *in the sack*]: Weel, my wee canties, ye'll be withoot your father noo. Be guid. And if anyone gives ye some cake, dinna forget tae put some salt on.

[*He leaves with the garlic and salt.* DIKAIOPOLIS *takes the sack with the* GIRLS *into his house.*]

CHORUS:[66]

Oh, how happy is our hero and how well his plans succeed!
He is going to reap the harvest of his bold and fearless
    deed;
And Ctesias will find that he is forced to leave with speed
    If he tries to play informer in the market.

Dikaiopolis need never more frequent the Market Square;
He's escaped from all the bugs that you contract if you
    go there

From Cleonymus[67] and Prepis, from the glutton and the
    queer,
And Hyperbolus'[68] indictments in the market.

He will never meet Cratinus[69] of the fancy crew-cut
    head,
Who can write an instant dithyramb, but, after all's been
    said,
Is a lazy yawning drone who saves his energies for bed
And who smells like a goat in the market.

From the mockery of Pauson[70] he has got away at last,
And his meetings with Lysistratus[71] belong now to the
    past,
Whose idea of having fun is just to shiver and to fast
Forty days every month in the market.

[*Enter a* BOEOTIAN *with an enormous and very heavy sack of
wares, attended by a slave,* ISMENIAS, *and followed by a pipe
band.*]

BOEOTIAN: Ar, boi Heracles, this back o' moine be toired.
Here, Ismenias, moind how you put down thaht mint plant.
And you, my Theban poipers, get out your mouthpieces
and let's hear 'The Dog's Arse'.

[*Raucous music.* DIKAIOPOLIS *comes out of the house
brandishing his thongs.*]

DIKAIOPOLIS: Stop that din, damn you! Must I have these
wasps buzzing all round my house? Where did all these
blasted bumble-bees come from? One Chaeris in town is
enough! [*Drives the pipers away.*]

BOEOTIAN: Boi Iolaus,[72] sir, that be a great favour you have
just, as you moight say, performed for me. They have been
blowing moi ears off all the way from Thebes, and not only
my ears; just look at what they've done to those mint
flowers! Would you care to buy any of my wares? Some
chickens, perhaps? Some four-winged locusts?

DIKAIOPOLIS [*shaking his hand enthusiastically*]: A Boeotian! –
from the land of barley buns! How do you do, my dear
chap? What have you got with you?

BOEOTIAN: Whoi, sir, oi've brought all the goodies Boeotia
produces. Let me see, oi've – [*burrowing in the sack*] mar-
joram and mint, door-mats and lamp-wicks, and then ducks
and jackdaws and woodcocks and coots and sandpipers and
divers and –

DIKAIOPOLIS: Better wrap up: I can see you've brought fowl
weather!

BOEOTIAN: Do you moind, oi'm not finished yet. Oi also
have geese and hares and foxes, moles and hedgehogs, cats
and beavers, some otters, and – oh yes, oi nearly forgot –
some eels from Lake Copais.

DIKAIOPOLIS: Man's highest joy! The eels – you've really
brought your eels? Let me give them a formal welcome.

BOEOTIAN: O eldest of the daughters of Copais,[73] come out
here and say hullo to the gentleman, will you? [*A giant* EEL
emerges from the sack.]

DIKAIOPOLIS [*to the* EEL]:

    My long-lost love! how blessed thy return,
    How joyful will the chorus members be,
    How glad the gastronomes, that thou hast come!
    Slaves, bring me out my brazier and my bellows!

[*Enter* SLAVES *with cooking appliances; also two of* DIKAIO-
POLIS' *children.*]

    Behold the greatest eel that ever was,
    After six years of absence hither come,
    Long pined for. Greet her kindly, little ones;
    To honour her I'll give you all some coal.
    Go, take her in: for nor alive nor dead
    Would I be parted from my well-loved eel![74]

[*The* EEL *and cooking appliances are solemnly removed.*]

BOEOTIAN: Ahem – may oi expect to be paid for this, sir?

DIKAIOPOLIS: Not for that, that's got to go to pay your

market dues. Is there anything else you're interested in selling, though?

BOEOTIAN: Interested in selling? The lot, sir, the lot.

DIKAIOPOLIS: How much for? Perhaps you'd like some goods you could take back with you?

BOEOTIAN: Boi all means. Some local product of yourn that's unobtainable in Boeotia.

DIKAIOPOLIS: Well then, how about, say, some Phalerum whitebait? Or some best Attic pottery?

BOEOTIAN [*shaking his head*]: No need, we've got plenty of both. No – something we don't have at all, and that you produce lots of.

DIKAIOPOLIS [*scratching his head*]: Something you don't have ... I've got it! An informer! Why not pack up an informer – with care, of course, like a piece of pottery – and take him home with you?

BOEOTIAN: Ar, by the Two Gods,[75] that be a great idea of yourn. He'd be a good investment – he'd fetch as much as a monkey, and he wouldn't need to be taught any tricks!

DIKAIOPOLIS: What luck! Here comes Nicarchus looking for someone to denounce.

BOEOTIAN [*looking at* NICARCHUS, *who is just coming on*]: Not very big, is he?

DIKAIOPOLIS: No, but what's there is bad, that's all that matters.

NICARCHUS [*pointing at the sack*]: To whom do these goods belong?

BOEOTIAN: They're moine. Oi brought them from Thebes, as Zeus is my witness.

NICARCHUS: In that case I hereby denounce them as contraband of war.

BOEOTIAN: War? You're making war against innocent little birds? Are you sure your head hasn't gone soft?

NICARCHUS: Don't laugh. I am going to lay an information against you personally as well.

BOEOTIAN: Pardon me, sir, but what have I ever done to you?

NICARCHUS: Well – for the benefit of these others [*indicating the* CHORUS *and the audience*] – I had better explain. You are attempting to import enemy-made lamp-wicks.

DIKAIOPOLIS: I wish you'd be a bit clearer about why you're denouncing these lamp-wicks. I'm still quite in the dark.

NICARCHUS [*holding one of them up*]: Do you realize that this could be used to set fire to the Docks?

DIKAIOPOLIS: Set fire to the Docks? A lamp-wick?

NICARCHUS: Certainly it could.

DIKAIOPOLIS: How could you do that?

NICARCHUS: If a Boeotian put one of these wicks into a hollow reed, waited for a northerly gale, lit it, put it down a sewer leading to the Docks – then if once any of the ships caught fire, they'd all be ablaze in no time.

DIKAIOPOLIS: Set ablaze by a wick in a hollow reed? You know what you can do with that story! [*Plies his thong on* NICARCHUS' *back.*]

NICARCHUS: Help! Assault! [*He is seized and overpowered.*]

DIKAIOPOLIS [*to* ISMENIAS]: Bung up his cakehole, will you? [ISMENIAS *puts his hand over* NICARCHUS' *mouth.*] Now let's have some straw and stuff for packing. We don't want him to get broken while this chap's taking him north.

CHORUS [*while* SLAVES *bring out straw and rope*]:
    Be careful how you pack the goods,
      And tie them nice and tight.
    For this fine Theban fellow's sake
    We shouldn't like to see them break,
      And if you don't, they might.

DIKAIOPOLIS [*at work wrapping* NICARCHUS *in straw and tying up the bundle*]:
    I'm being careful; after all,
      This pot is not first-rate;

[*He strikes the 'pot', which squeals loudly.*]
>It doesn't have an honest ring;
>I think it's cracked.

[*Strikes it again.*]

>>>>A poor-class thing –
>An earthen reprobate!

LEADER:

>What is there one can use it for?

DIKAIOPOLIS:

>It serves for many needs:
>A mixing-bowl for witches' brew
>Or lawsuit-juice, a lantern too
>To light up shady deeds.

CHORUS:

>I don't think I would ever use
>A pot like that – would you?
>It keeps on making such a sound,
>I'm sure that it will soon be found
>To break, untouched, in two.

DIKAIOPOLIS [*who has now finished the job,* NICARCHUS *still kicking and squealing*]:

>That's done it strong and firm, my friend;
>No risk the knots will go;
>His weight won't break your porter's back,
>So just you bung him in the sack
>And carry him like so.

[NICARCHUS *is shoved head first into the* BOEOTIAN's *sack.*]

LEADER:

>That's got it fine.

BOEOTIAN:

>>>With all this straw
>Oi feel loike oi've been reaping!

CHORUS:

> Well, may your harvest bring you wealth,
> And let us hope Nicarchus' health
> Does not improve with keeping.

DIKAIOPOLIS: The blighter was a devil to tie up. There's your pot, old chap, all ready to go.

BOEOTIAN: Shoulder to the burden, then. Come on, Ismenias. [ISMENIAS *puts the sack on his shoulder, and both set off.*]

DIKAIOPOLIS [*as they leave*]: Mind how you carry him. I know he's low-grade stuff, but all the same. If you make a profit on these goods, you'll be the first person who ever got anything good out of an informer!

[*Enter, from the other house, the* SERVANT OF LAMACHUS.]

SERVANT: Dikaiopolis!

DIKAIOPOLIS: What do you want?

SERVANT: Lamachus wants to buy some of your stuff for the Festival of Pitchers.[76] Here's a drachma he'll pay for some of your thrushes, and three he'll give you for a Copaic eel.

DIKAIOPOLIS: Lamachus? And who may he be? I don't think I know him.

SERVANT:

> The dreaded warrior with the bull's-hide shield,
> Bearing the Gorgon's head, who brandishes
> Three mighty crests that cast a fearful shade.

DIKAIOPOLIS: *That* Lamachus? I wouldn't sell him anything if he gave me his shield! He's got some salt fish already; let him brandish his crests over them, if he wants any seasoning! And if he complains, I'll set my Market Commissioners on to him.

[*Exit* SERVANT, *hastily.*]

Well, I'd better take my purchases in. [*Sings to himself.*] 'Hear the sound of blackbirds' wings' – and thrushes' ... Here goes. [*Gathers all the* BOEOTIAN's *birds up in his arms, and staggers into the house.*]

CHORUS:
    Look you, citizens of Athens,
      See the gain that wisdom brings!
    See how peace has given our hero
      Lavish store of precious things,
    How there come to him unbidden
      Dainty dishes fit for kings.

    I will never ask the War-god
      At my future feasts to dine.
    When he has some drink inside him
      He'll to violence incline,
    Gatecrash other people's parties,
      Break the jugs and spill the wine.

    I would try to pacify him –
      'Have some wine, your sorrows drown!'
    But he'd spurn the cup of friendship,
      Leave with a portentous frown,
    Go and burn up all my vine-props,
      And my precious vines cut down.

[*Feathers fly out of the door of* DIKAIOPOLIS' *house. A beautiful woman comes out of heaven, like a goddess in tragedy, and remains suspended in mid-air while the* CHORUS *complete their song.*]

    See the tokens of rejoicing
      Lie before our hero's door!
    Welcome, Reconciliation,
      Maid divine whom we adore,
    Full of Cytherean graces,
      Face we never saw before!

    O that, as in Zeuxis' picture,
      Eros could unite us twain,
    Garlanded with springtime flowers!
      I am sure I'd stand the strain,

You and me, two veteran wrestlers,
  Grappling twice and once again.

First I'd plant a few young fig-trees,
  Then some vines across the way,
Then of olive-trees a circle,
  So that with the least delay
You and I could be anointed
  Ready for the holiday.

[*Re-enter* CRIER, *bearing a proclamation.*]

CRIER: Oyez! Oyez! Oyez! According to ancient custom, when the trumpet sounds, all are to begin drinking from their jugs; and whoever is the first to drink his jug off will win a skinful of Ctesiphon![77]

[*The front of the house swings open, and reveals* DIKAIO-POLIS *frenziedly engaged in cooking.*]

DIKAIOPOLIS: Boys! Women! What are you doing? Didn't you hear the proclamation? Get the hares braised – get the spit turning – take them off – quick! Get those garlands ready! Let's have the skewers so I can put the thrushes on them!

[*A* SLAVE *runs and brings him a pair of skewers, on each of which he impales a thrush, and sets them to roast on the fire.*]

LEADER:
  How wise you are and how fine your feast!
    My eyes with envy burn.

DIKAIOPOLIS:
  What will you say when you see the thrush
    Roasted and done to a turn?

LEADER:
  I think on that you're probably right.

DIKAIOPOLIS:
  Someone rake out the grate!

LEADER:
  I've never known such an expert cook
    A citizen of our state.

[*Enter a* FARMER, *weeping bitterly*.]

FARMER: Help me! Help me!

DIKAIOPOLIS: Heracles save us, who's this?

FARMER: A man that fate has ruined.

DIKAIOPOLIS: Well, don't sneeze on me, then.

FARMER: My dear friend, I know that you, and you alone, possess peace. [*Holding out a cup made from a hollow reed*] Please give me a little – even five years would be enough.

DIKAIOPOLIS: Why, what's happened to you?

FARMER: I – I've lost my oxen! I'm ruined!

DIKAIOPOLIS: How did you lose them?

FARMER: I live at Phyle, you see, near the border, and the Boeotians carried them off!

DIKAIOPOLIS: How appalling! I wonder you're not in mourning.

FARMER: They were life itself to me! They were the source of all the good manure I ever got.

DIKAIOPOLIS: Well, what do you want, then?

FARMER: I've cried my eyes out for them. Please, if you care for poor Dercetes of Phyle, rub some peace on my eyes.

DIKAIOPOLIS: I'm very sorry for you, but I don t happen to be the state physician.

FARMER: Please! – If only I can get my oxen back –

DIKAIOPOLIS: No. Go to Pittalus'[78] and do your sobbing there.

FARMER: Couldn't you just put a teeny weeny drop of peace into my reed?

DIKAIOPOLIS: Not a sausage. *Will* you go away and moan somewhere else?

FARMER [*departing*]: My poor oxen! All the ploughing you did for me!

LEADER:
        I think our hero likes his peace:
        To share it he does not wish.

DIKAIOPOLIS [*to a servant*]:
> Now pour some honey into the tripe
> And broil the cuttlefish.

LEADER:
> O did you hear that stirring song?

DIKAIOPOLIS:
> Now turn the eels about!

LEADER:
> Our mouths are watering fit to burst
> With the smell and the things you shout.

DIKAIOPOLIS [*handing some more meat to the servant*]: Roast this, will you, nice and brown?

[*Enter a* BEST MAN *in festive dress, carrying several slices of meat, followed by a* BRIDESMAID.]

BEST MAN: Dikaiopolis!

DIKAIOPOLIS: Who's that?

BEST MAN: I've come from a wedding. The bridegroom asked me to give you these [*showing him the meat*].

DIKAIOPOLIS: Very kind of him, whoever he is.

BEST MAN: And in return he wants you to give him just a thimbleful of peace, in this bottle. You understand he's keener on making love than war just at the moment.

DIKAIOPOLIS [*with a gesture of rejection*]: Take that meat away; I don't want any of it. I wouldn't give you any of my peace for a thousand drachmas. [*Noticing the* BRIDESMAID] Who's she?

BEST MAN: She's the bridesmaid, and she's got a request from the bride to make in your private ear.

DIKAIOPOLIS: All right, let's hear what she has to say. [*He bends down to let the* BRIDESMAID *whisper to him.*] Ha! ha! ha! Gods in heaven! – do you know what the bride's message was? 'Please do me a favour and keep my husband's prick at home for me.' Very well, I will. Boy! – bring the peace here. I'll give her some specially. She is a woman, and

97

it would be wrong for her to suffer by the war. [*The wine-skin is brought.*] Put the bottle to the spout, my dear. Do you know what to do with it? Tell the bride this: any time they're preparing the army lists, just smear a little of this on to his prick at night, and you're safe. [*To the* SLAVE] Take the peace away and bring me the cup, so I can start pouring my wine into the jug.

[*The* BEST MAN *and the* BRIDESMAID *joyfully leave.*]

LEADER: Here comes someone in a hurry – bringing bad news, by the look of his face.

[*Enter* FIRST MESSENGER, *running towards* LAMACHUS' *house.*]

FIRST MESSENGER: O War! O Ares! O Lamachus! [*Knocks furiously.*]

LAMACHUS [*emerging, without his armour*]: Who is it knocks without these brazen halls?

FIRST MESSENGER: Orders from the Generals, sir. You're to go immediately, with all your troops and all your crests, take up a position in the snow and keep a look-out for enemy raiders. There's been a report that the Boeotians may take advantage of the festival to do a bit of rustling.

LAMACHUS: O General Staff, more numerous than kind! What! – even for the feast have I no respite?

DIKAIOPOLIS: Time for the Lamachean Expedition!

LAMACHUS: I've got quite enough without *you* laughing at me.

DIKAIOPOLIS [*putting his fingers on his head to suggest the shape of a locust*]: Like to have a fight with Geryon, Heracles? I can't manage three bodies, but will four wings do?

LAMACHUS: Alack, what news have I received this day!

DIKAIOPOLIS: Alack, what's this fellow coming to tell me?

SECOND MESSENGER [*running up to* DIKAIOPOLIS]: Dikaio-polis!

DIKAIOPOLIS: Yes?

SECOND MESSENGER: Message from the Priest of Dionysus.

You're to come to dinner as quickly as possible. Bring a
boxful of meat and your jug. Hurry up, you're keeping
everybody else waiting. He's got everything ready.
Couches, tables, headrests, blankets, garlands, myrrh, the
lot; the nuts and raisins are out, so are the tarts, and sponge-
cakes and flat-cakes and seed-cakes and honey-cakes and
heaven knows what else – oh yes, and lovely dancing-girls,
'beloved of Harmodius',[79] as you might say. Come on,
hurry! [*He runs off.*]

LAMACHUS: Woe is me!

DIKAIOPOLIS: It was you chose to enlist under the Gorgon.
[*To his* SLAVE] Lock up the house and get the dinner ready
for me to take, will you?

> [*The* SLAVE *swings the front of* DIKAIOPOLIS' *house back
> into place.*]
>
> [*In the ensuing scene slaves of both* LAMACHUS *and*
> DIKAIOPOLIS *are kept busy carrying out their masters'
> instructions.*]

LAMACHUS: Boy! – bring me out my provision basket.

DIKAIOPOLIS [*mimicking him*]: Boy! – bring me out my
dinner box.

LAMACHUS: Bring some salt with thyme in it, and some
onions.

DIKAIOPOLIS: I'm fed up with onions. Bring me some slices
of fish.

LAMACHUS: Now some salt fish in a fig-leaf. Be sure and
make it stale.

DIKAIOPOLIS: Yes, I wouldn't mind a fig-leaf pancake either.
I'll cook it when I get there.

LAMACHUS: Bring me the feathers for my helmet.

DIKAIOPOLIS: Bring me the pigeon and thrush.

LAMACHUS: This ostrich feather is lovely and white.

DIKAIOPOLIS: This pigeon's meat is lovely and brown.

LAMACHUS: Bring me out my three-plumed crest.

DIKAIOPOLIS: And could I have my pot of hare's meat?

LAMACHUS [*inspecting his crest*]: Don't say the moths have eaten them!

DIKAIOPOLIS: Don't say I'm going to eat this hare stew before dinner even begins!

LAMACHUS [*turning haughtily to* DIKAIOPOLIS]: Sir, would you mind not making fun of my equipment?

DIKAIOPOLIS: Sir, would you mind not looking hungrily at my thrush?

LAMACHUS: Sir, would you mind not speaking to me in that manner?

DIKAIOPOLIS: Not at all; but my boy and I have a little argument going. [*To the slave*] Let's make a bet of it, Lamachus here can be the judge: which is nicer to eat, locusts or thrushes?

LAMACHUS: Damn your insolence!

DIKAIOPOLIS: I think he prefers the locusts.

LAMACHUS: Boy! – take my spear off the peg and bring it to me.

DIKAIOPOLIS: Boy! – take my black pudding off the fire and bring it to me.

LAMACHUS: Better take the case off the spear. Hold the other end, boy.

DIKAIOPOLIS [*taking one end of the black pudding*]: And you, boy, hold on to the spit.

LAMACHUS: Bring me the stand for my shield.

DIKAIOPOLIS: Bring me the rolls for my stomach.

LAMACHUS: Now, please, the Gorgon shield itself.

DIKAIOPOLIS [*trying to think of something remotely resembling that unique object*]: I know. Now, please, a round cheese-cake.

LAMACHUS: This mockery is absolutely disgusting!

DIKAIOPOLIS: This cheese-cake is absolutely delicious!

LAMACHUS: Pour out the oil, boy. [*The slave does so, and begins to polish the shield.*] I can see the face of an old man who's going to be prosecuted for draft-dodging.

DIKAIOPOLIS: Pour out the honey. [*Pretending to look at himself in the honey.*] *I* see the face of an old man who is going to tell Lamachus, the son of – of Gorgonus, to jump in the lake!

LAMACHUS: Bring me my sturdy breastplate.

DIKAIOPOLIS: Bring me my sturdy wine-jug.

LAMACHUS: This will defend me stoutly against the enemy.

DIKAIOPOLIS [*displaying the jug*]: *This* will defend me stoutly against the other guests.

LAMACHUS: Tie all my kit to the shield, boy.

DIKAIOPOLIS: Tie up my dinner in the box, boy.

LAMACHUS: – And I'll take the provision basket myself.

DIKAIOPOLIS: – And I'll take my coat and go.

LAMACHUS: All right, boy, take the shield and let's be off. Brr! it's snowing. Wintry weather!

DIKAIOPOLIS: All right, then, take my dinner and let's go. Party weather!

[*Exeunt, on one side,* LAMACHUS *and his slave; on the other,* DIKAIOPOLIS *and his slave, each loaded as described.*]

CHORUS:
> Go to war, and may fortune go with you!
>   How different the paths that you tread!
> One leads to the wine and the garlands,
>   The other to chilblains instead;
> But our hero, we fancy, will finish
>   With the best of the bargain in bed.

LEADER:
> As for Antimachus,[80] the son of Splutter,
> I hope Zeus visits him with ruin utter.
> Not just because his lyrics show no skill;
> Though mean his verse, the author's meaner still.
> Once, having seen his comic chorus win,
> He gave a feast – and wouldn't let me[81] in.
> O Heracles! next time he wants a dish
> Of lovely, well-cooked, sizzling cuttlefish,

Just as it's lying waiting safe and sound,
See that the table tips and goes aground;
Then, as he's just about to pick it up,
Let the dog snatch it, run away and sup!
My malediction has not reached its height:
May other terrors come on him by night!
When coming home from riding, flushed and red,
May hooligans pounce and smash his fevered head!
Then let him find the stone he stoops to take
Is nothing but a turd of recent make!
And lastly let him with his lump of shit
Miss him he aims at, and Cratinus[82] hit.

[*Enter the* SERVANT OF LAMACHUS.]

SERVANT: All of you in Lamachus' house, bring water –
hot water! Heat it up in pots – lots of it! Get some lint and
salve, and some greasy wool, to make a bandage for his
ankle! The master has been wounded by a stake in crossing a
ditch. His ankle is dislocated, and his head's broken where he
fell on a stone.[83] Here he is. Open the door!

[*Enter* LAMACHUS, *wounded, supported by two* SOLDIERS,
and lamenting in tragic style.]

LAMACHUS:
                    Alas, alack,
            Hateful and bloody woes!
                    Sorry my lot,
            Stricken by furious foes!
                    But worse than all
            If that old peasant should see
                    My wretched fate,
            And then should laugh at me!

[*Enter* DIKAIOPOLIS, *crowned, with a girl on each arm.*]

DIKAIOPOLIS:

> What perfect breasts,
> How good and firm to nuzzle!
> A kiss, my sweet,
> A real lascivious snuzzle!
> I've won the prize,
> The victory is mine;
> I've come here now
> To claim my skin of wine!

LAMACHUS:

> O culmination dire of all my woes!
> O wounds of dismal pain!

DIKAIOPOLIS: Well, well, hullo again!

LAMACHUS: A stranger I to bliss!

DIKAIOPOLIS [*to one of the girls*]:

> That *was* a gorgeous kiss.

LAMACHUS: I'm lost in endless night!

DIKAIOPOLIS [*to the other girl*]:

> Watch out that you don't bite!

LAMACHUS: O fatal charge! O fatal stake-filled hollow –

DIKAIOPOLIS [*speaking*]: Who ever heard of *charging* for anything on Pitcher Day?

LAMACHUS: Save me, I beg thee, save me, great Apollo!

DIKAIOPOLIS: It's not *his* feast today, you fool.

LAMACHUS:

> Friends, take me up and mind my leg:
> Attend a soldier sick.

DIKAIOPOLIS:

> Girls, take me up and get a grip
> On my rejoicing prick.

LAMACHUS:

> The stone has shaken up my brains:
> How dizzy is my head!

DIKAIOPOLIS:

> Another part of me stands up
> And says it's time for bed.

LAMACHUS:

        The sight of Doctor Pittalus[84]
        Will cheer my ailing eyes.

DIKAIOPOLIS:

        Where are you, judges? Where's the King?[85]
        I've come to claim the prize.

LAMACHUS:

        The hostile spear has pierced my bones:
        I wail with piteous cries.

[LAMACHUS *is carried off.* DIKAIOPOLIS *disentangles himself from the girls and crosses to the King-Archon's seat in the front row, where he displays his empty jug.*]

DIKAIOPOLIS [*recitative*]:

        Behold the empty jug. Will you acclaim me
        As champion of Bacchus' festival?

LEADER: Indeed we will. Hail to the champion!

CHORUS: Hail to the champion!

DIKAIOPOLIS:

        True to the rules, I drank the wine unmixed
        And drained the whole in one continuous draught.

LEADER: A noble deed. Hail to the champion!

CHORUS: Hail to the champion!

[*The* KING-ARCHON, *shaking his head at this highly irregular procedure, presents* DIKAIOPOLIS *with a wine-skin.*]

DIKAIOPOLIS:

        I've got the skin; there's time at least
        To give ourselves another feast.
        Let's have this toast with three times three –
        'Hail to the champion' – that's me.

CHORUS [*chairing* DIKAIOPOLIS *and the girls off the stage*]:

        We're hoping for another win
        To give us more to revel in.
        Meantime we're with you through and through –
        'Hail to the champion' – that's you.
        Hail to the champion!!!

The Clouds

or

The School for Sophists

Introductory Note to *The Clouds*

In the 420s Greece, and in particular Athens, was in an intellectual ferment. The eternal verities were being questioned. New forms of education were coming into existence, and new kinds of morality too. The young, men like Alcibiades, took all this up with enthusiasm. The old were suspicious: would not these new-fangled ideas destroy the cohesiveness of society and lead to anarchy or despotism? And how about the new teachers, the sophists as they were called? Why couldn't they work for a living like everybody else? Aristophanes, though in years a contemporary of Alcibiades, believed (at least for the purposes of his comedy) that the old were right; and *The Clouds* is his exposure of what the 'new learning' stands for and what it leads to.

It had all started, as far as Athens was concerned, with Protagoras, who had spread the gospel that it did not matter whether the gods existed and that all values were relative. Then there had been Anaxagoras, who had meddled in geology, astronomy, and heaven knows what else, had declared the sun to be a stone and not a god, and finally had been sent into exile by an Athenian court. More recently the Sicilian Gorgias and others had arrived in town and begun to teach the new art of rhetoric, training their disciples to concentrate not on being right, but on getting people to believe that they were right. And already there were many who proclaimed that all previous codes of morality had been superseded, and that from now on might was right. These four elements – atheism, scientific inquiry and speculation, rhetoric, and the new morality – all appear in *The Clouds*, and all are ascribed to Socrates.

Socrates himself was forty-five when *The Clouds* was originally written. A few months before he had behaved with notable courage during the Athenian retreat from Delium in Boeotia – which perhaps did not endear him to his comrades, who thought of him as swaggering and conceited. In Athens he had gathered round him a circle of rich young men, who listened eagerly as he questioned those who thought themselves clever, and proved that they had never worked out the grounds on which their opinions were based. But he had nothing to do with atheism, physical science or rhetoric, and his moral inquiries were directed not at setting up a new morality, but at providing foundations for the old one to stand on. Why then did Aristophanes attribute to him all the (in his view) least desirable characteristics of rival teachers?

It is quite likely that Aristophanes did not know the difference. Socrates gave young men an unconventional education, and that was enough. Besides, Socrates was easily the best known of the various 'sophists'. The others were mostly foreigners who came to Athens from time to time. Socrates was an Athenian citizen and, except for military service and other public duties, never left the city. So, if one wished to caricature an individual 'sophist', Socrates was the obvious choice.

Mud, however, once thrown, has a tendency to stick; and, if we are to believe Plato (and it seems unlikely that his account is false in essentials), the mud thrown at Socrates by Aristophanes and other comic poets stuck so well that when Socrates was charged in 399 with 'corrupting the young' and with 'not believing in the City's gods but in other strange deities', his accuser said in court that Socrates believed the sun to be a stone and the moon to be earth (which were Anaxagoras' views, not his). It was not just *The Clouds*, of course. Quotations preserved from other comedies show clearly that Socrates was always being got at in them, and being presented very much as he is presented in *The Clouds*. The Athenians who sat on the jury in 399 would have been superhuman if twenty-five years of this had not prejudiced them, quite apart from other considerations Aristophanes must bear his share of the responsibility.

Although Aristophanes unreservedly condemns the new learning, that does not mean that he uncritically approves of the older generation. Strepsiades (whose name means 'Twister') is quite ready to get out of paying his debts by dishonest means, and Right, the champion of the old education, has an interest in young boys which is overdone even for fifth-century Athens. Strepsiades takes his revenge on Socrates, but not before he has been suitably punished himself. The play, indeed, could almost be described as a tragedy showing how wickedness recoils on itself; and the Clouds behave very much as gods do in tragedy: they lead Strepsiades down the primrose path of evil, which is also the way he wants to go himself, and let him fall over the cliff at the end of it.

The Clouds, in fact, is an unusually serious comedy, and it was too serious for its original audience. When it was originally produced, in the spring of 423, the judges placed it third and last. As we can see from *The Wasps*, Aristophanes was very bitter about this. Some time between 420 and 417 he set to work revising *The Clouds*, but the revision was never completed and the play was never produced again. Despite this, it is the revised version that we possess, and it bears marks of its incomplete state. These, however, are not such as would be noticed in a modern production.

CHARACTERS

STREPSIADES *an elderly farmer*
PHEIDIPPIDES *his son*
SLAVE
TWO STUDENTS *at Socrates' school*
SOCRATES *the philosopher*
RIGHT *an Argument*
WRONG *an Argument*
FIRST CREDITOR
SECOND CREDITOR
CHAEREPHON *the philosopher*
CHORUS OF CLOUDS

WITNESS *brought by First Creditor*
STUDENTS *at the school*
SLAVES *to Strepsiades*

ACT ONE

SCENE ONE: *Inside* STREPSIADES' *house. Two bedrooms are separated by a partition down the centre of the stage, with a door in it.*

[*In one room* PHEIDIPPIDES *is sound asleep under an enormous weight of blankets. In the other* STREPSIADES *is restlessly tossing and turning. Finally he abandons all attempts at sleep and sits up with a yawn.*]

STREPSIADES: Lord Zeus, how long the nights are! Will they never end? When will it be day? Come to think of it, I heard the cock ages ago. And the servants are still snoring! They'd never have dared to in the old days. Damn this war! One can't lay a hand on one's own slave now, in case he runs away to the enemy. Still, it's not only them: what about my dutiful son in there? Do you think he's going to wake up before it's day? Not he; he's still farting merrily away, wrapped up in his five blankets. Well, there's nothing for it: best cover up and try to get to sleep. [*He does so, but is soon sitting up again.*] It's no good, I can't. I'm being bitten all over by horses. And forkings out. And debts. All on account of that boy. He grows his hair long, rides around in his chariot and pair – do you know, he actually dreams of horses. Result, every time it comes to the twenty-fourth or twenty-fifth of the month, I die of terror. That's the time when things grow on you – like interest.[1] Boy!

[*A* SLAVE *appears.*]

Light a lamp and bring in my accounts. I want to see how many people I owe to and how much the interest has got to now.

[*The* SLAVE *goes out, and shortly returns with the lamp and a number of waxed tablets. He holds the lamp behind* STREPSIADES *while the latter consults the tablets.*]

Let me see now: what have we? To Pasias, one thousand two hundred drachmas. What's that for? Let me think . . . Oh yes, that was when I bought the horse with the Q brand. Ha! Rather than that I should have been branded myself.[2]

PHEIDIPPIDES [*in his sleep*]: Watch it, Philon, you're cheating. Keep in your lane.

STREPSIADES: You see? That's what's ruining me. Even at night it's always horses, horses, horses.

PHEIDIPPIDES: How many laps is the next race?

STREPSIADES [*speaking at the door*]: I don't know, but not as many bends as you've driven me round. [*Looking at the accounts again*] Who came after Pasias? Mm – to Ameinias, three hundred for a small chariot – what's this? – complete with wheels.

PHEIDIPPIDES: Let him have a roll, groom, and take him home.

STREPSIADES: I can tell you what you've been rolling in. Money – and it's my money. Already because of you I've been dragged into court more than once and ordered to pay up or else. Now some of them are even threatening to have my goods seized if I don't. [*By this time he is shouting.* PHEIDIPPIDES *stirs, rubs his eyes, gets up, shuffles sleepily to the door and pokes his head through.*]

PHEIDIPPIDES: Really, dad, what's wrong with you? Why do you keep tossing and turning and talking to yourself all night?

STREPSIADES: Oh, it's just something in the bed-clothes been biting me. A bailiff, I think.

PHEIDIPPIDES: Well, do let a fellow get a bit of shut-eye. [*He goes back to bed and is soon asleep again.*]

STREPSIADES [*with venom*]: Yes, you do that. But remember that all my debts will be yours one day! Gods, I wish I could strangle the matchmaker who put the idea in my head of marrying your mother! I had a life without worries out in the country: none of your grooming or hot baths for me, no, I was happy with my bees and my sheep and my olives. Then I married this city girl, the niece of Megacles, no less, very classy – a right Coesyra!³ So I went to bed that night smelling as usual of bad wine, drying-racks, fleeces, profits, that kind of thing: while she positively oozed perfume and saffron, not to mention sex, money, sex, over-eating, and, well, sex. Don't imagine I'm saying she didn't ever do anything else. Oh, she could sew all right, though, as I used to say when I showed her my coat here, all she ever did sew was the seed of bankruptcy.⁴

[*He gets out of bed and dresses. Just as he puts on the coat referred to – an exceedingly threadbare object – the lamp goes out.*]

SLAVE: We seem to be out of oil in the lamp, sir.

STREPSIADES: Well, did I ask you to use the thirsty one? Come here – I'll make you regret it.

SLAVE [*making a dash for it*]: Why should I?

[STREPSIADES *makes a grab at him but he gets away.*]

STREPSIADES: [*calling after him*] Because you put in such a fat wick, that's why. What was I talking about? – Well, when me and my [*with heavy sarcasm*] very good wife had this boy, we had a great row about what to call him. She insisted on getting something into the name that would remind him of those damn horses and hippodromes – Xanthippus she liked, or maybe Charippus or Callippides. Myself I wanted to name him Pheidonides after his grandad. Well, we argued a lot, you know, until in the end we split the difference and called him Pheidippides. But that wasn't the end of the story. When she was holding him and fondling him she used to say something like, 'When you're a big boy and ride in procession to the Acropolis in your chariot, wearing a lovely yellow coat, like your Uncle Megacles . . .' I did what I could; when it was my turn, I said, 'No, my son, when you're a big boy and drive the goats home from the hills, like your daddy did before you, wearing your good old leather smock . . .' – but it was no good. He never took any notice of anything his father said. So now we've an epidemic here – horsitis. Well, anyway, I've been hunting all night for a way out, and I think I see one. Not easy, but wonderful if it works. If I can only get that boy to help, I think I'm saved! He! he! First, to wake him up. [*Goes into* PHEIDIPPIDES' *room. In a whisper*] Now what's the nicest possible way? Hm ... [*Bending over* PHEIDIPPIDES] Pheidippides! My sweet little Pheidippikins!

PHEIDIPPIDES [*waking up, seeing that it is now daylight, and getting sluggishly out of bed*]: Wharrisiddad?

STREPSIADES: I want you to kiss me and put your right hand in mine.

PHEIDIPPIDES [*doing so*]: Okay. What's up?

STREPSIADES [*looking him full in the eyes*]: Tell me the truth: do you love your father?

PHEIDIPPIDES [*pointing to a statue in the corner of his room*]: I do, I swear it, by Poseidon the god of horses.

STREPSIADES: Please, not the god of horses! He's the one that's brought all this trouble on me. Well, dear, if you really love me from your heart – will you do something for me?

PHEIDIPPIDES [*getting irritated*]: What?

STREPSIADES: I want you to reform – to change your ways [PHEIDIPPIDES, *who has heard this many times before, sighs audibly*] – and go and learn what I'm going to ask you to.

PHEIDIPPIDES: Yes, but what?

STREPSIADES [*anxiously*]: You'll do what I ask?

PHEIDIPPIDES: I will, I swear it by Po – [*hastily checking himself*] by – by – Di – Dionysus.

STREPSIADES: You know the house next door?

PHEIDIPPIDES: Yes. What is it?

STREPSIADES: That, my son, is the Thinkery. For clever brains only, they say. It's where the scientists live, the ones who try to prove that the sky is like one of those round things you use to bake bread.⁵ They say it's all around us and we're –

PHEIDIPPIDES: And we're the lumps of coal, I suppose?

STREPSIADES: Exactly – you've got the idea. Anyway, if you pay them well, they can teach you how to win your case – whether you're in the right or not.

PHEIDIPPIDES [*guardedly*]: Who are these people?

STREPSIADES: I don't remember their name, but they're very fine – what do they call themselves? – philosophers.

PHEIDIPPIDES: Ugh! I know the buggers. You mean those stuck-up white-faced barefoot characters – like that bloody Socrates and Chaerephon.⁶

STREPSIADES: Really, you shouldn't talk so childishly! My boy [*emotionally*], if you care at all whether your poor father gets his daily bread, will you forget about horses for a bit and go and join them? Just for me!

PHEIDIPPIDES: I wouldn't, by – Dionysus, not if you gave me all the pheasants in Athens.

STREPSIADES [*on his knees*]: My – my beloved son – I beg of you – do go and study with them.

PHEIDIPPIDES: What am I supposed to learn?

STREPSIADES [*raising himself to his feet*]: They say they have two Arguments in there – Right and Wrong, they call them – and one of them, Wrong, can always win any case, however bad. Well, if you can learn this Argument or whatever it is, don't you see, all those debts I've run into because of you, I needn't pay anyone an obol of them ever.

PHEIDIPPIDES: No, I won't. How could I ever look my cavalry friends in the eye again, with a face looking like it had been covered in chalk?

STREPSIADES: Then, holy Demeter! you'll never eat anything of mine again, not you nor any of your damn thoroughbreds. I'll throw you out of the house – you can go anywhere so long as it's hell.

PHEIDIPPIDES: I know Uncle Megacles will see I'm not without horse and home. Anyway, I don't believe you. [*He goes out of the room but, needless to say, not out of the house.*]

STREPSIADES: Come on, Strepsiades, this can't be the knock-out punch. Please the gods, I'm going to go to the Thinkery and get taught there myself. [*He wraps his old coat around him and goes out by a side passage down left. Scene Two follows immediately.*]

SCENE TWO: *Outside the Thinkery. The stage is curtained, and there is a door down right, approached by steps.*

[STREPSIADES *enters by a side passage down right. At the bottom of the steps he hesitates.*]

STREPSIADES [*to himself*]: How can I? How can I study all this logic-chopping and hair-splitting? I'm an old man; I never was brainy, and now I've hardly got any memory at all. [*Remembering something that seems to be an overriding consideration*] I've got to. No more dilly-dallying. [*He resolutely climbs the steps and knocks.*] Boy! My little boykins!

STUDENT [*from inside*]: Go to blazes! Who's that making all that racket?

STREPSIADES: Strepsiades is my name, son of Pheidon, from Cicynna.

[*The* STUDENT, *looking angry, comes out.*]

STUDENT: What kind of fool are you? Do you realize that by your violent and unphilosophical kicking of the door you have precipitated the abortion of a discovery?

STREPSIADES: I do apologize. I'm only a countryman. But do tell me, what was this thing that got aborted?

STUDENT [*mysteriously*]: It is not lawful to divulge it to non-members.

117

STREPSIADES: Well, that's all right. I want to join the Thinkery, that's why I've come.

STUDENT: Very well; but remember, your lips must be sealed. It was like this: Socrates just asked Chaerephon how many of its own feet a flea could jump – do you see? – because one of them had just bitten Chaerephon's eyebrow and jumped over on to Socrates' head.

STREPSIADES: Well, how did he find out?

STUDENT: He used a most elegant method. He melted some wax and put the flea's feet into it, so that when it set the flea had a stylish pair of slippers on. And then he took them off its feet and measured the distance out, like this, you see [*taking a step or two, toe touching heel*].

STREPSIADES: Gosh, what an intellectual brain!

STUDENT: Like to hear another?

STREPSIADES: Yes I would, please, do tell me.

STUDENT [*as repeating a story learned by heart*]: Chaerephon of Sphettus once asked Socrates whether he was of the opinion that gnats produced their hum by way of the mouth or – the other end.

STREPSIADES: Well, well, what did he say?

STUDENT: 'The intestinal passage of the gnat,' he replied, 'is very narrow, and consequently the wind is forced to go straight through to the back end. And then the arse, being a hole forming the exit from this narrow passage, groans under the force of the wind.'

STREPSIADES: Like a trumpet, you mean. I must say that's a marvellous feat of intestinology. I can see getting acquitted is going to be child's play for a chap who knows all there is to know about gnats' guts.

STUDENT: Then the day before yesterday Socrates was robbed of a great thought by a lizard.

STREPSIADES: How on earth did that happen?

STUDENT: Well, he was studying the path of the moon, or its orbit as we call it, and he was gazing up at the sky with his

mouth open, in the dark, you see, and this lizard [*trying to
keep himself from laughing*] – this lizard on the roof shitted
right in his face!

STREPSIADES [*half collapsed with laughter*]: Oh, I liked that
one! The lizard shitted in Socrates' face! Ha! ha! ha!

STUDENT [*when he has recovered*]: And then yesterday, we
found we had nothing to eat at dinner-time. So Socrates –

STREPSIADES: What did he bring off this time?

STUDENT: I was just going to tell you. He sprinkled a little ash
on the table, bent round a skewer to serve as a pair of
compasses, and then –

STREPSIADES: Yes, yes, what did he do then?

STUDENT: He whipped somebody's coat while they were
wrestling.

STREPSIADES: And we still think Thales[7] was the wisest man
that ever lived! Come on, come on, open the door and let
me see the great man now. I don't think my blad – I mean
my brain can hold out much longer. Come on, open it up,
can't you?

[*The* STUDENT *flings open the door. At the same moment the
curtain rises revealing the interior of the stage, on which are a
number of other* STUDENTS, *gazing intently at the ground –
some bending over, some kneeling with their heads touching the
ground, all motionless, utterly absorbed in scientific thought.*]

STREPSIADES: In Heracles' name, where did you catch these
creatures?

STUDENT: What are you so surprised about? What did you
think they were?

STREPSIADES: Spartan prisoners from Pylos,[8] if you ask me.
Why on earth are they all staring at the ground?

STUDENT: They are investigating phenomena under ground.

STREPSIADES: Roots to eat, you mean? Oh, you needn't
worry about investigating for them; I know where you can
find lovely big ones. But what about that lot [*pointing*]?
They're completely doubled up!

STUDENT: Yes, they're examining the lowest reaches of hell.

STREPSIADES: That, I suppose, explains why their third eye [*poking one of the* STUDENTS *in the backside with his stick so that he falls over*] is looking at the sky! [*Very pleased with his own joke.*]

STUDENT [*rescuing the poked one; with perfect seriousness*]: That's right; we're teaching it to do astronomy all by itself, you see. Economy – one man, two jobs. [*To the other* STUDENTS] Go inside; what'll *he* say if he sees you out here?

STREPSIADES: No! – not yet! Can't they stay a bit? I want to tell them about a little problem I have.

STUDENT: Can't do that. Too much fresh air is very bad for the brain, you know – they mustn't stay outside any longer.

[*The other* STUDENTS *go into the school. They leave behind a number of instruments and a map.*]

STREPSIADES [*examining some of the instruments*]: What on earth are these things?

STUDENT: Well, this one's for astronomy, and that one's for geometry, and –

STREPSIADES: Geometry – what's that useful for?

STUDENT: Well – for – for – sharing out allotments of land, for example.

STREPSIADES: Oh, you mean in a new settlement?9

STUDENT: Any land you want.

STREPSIADES: That's delightful! I never heard of a more democratic invention.

STUDENT: And this, you see, is a map of the whole world. Look, here's Athens.

STREPSIADES [*inspecting the map*]: Can't be; if it's Athens, where are the jurymen?

STUDENT: No, I assure you, it is, and all this area is Attica.

STREPSIADES: Well, what's happened to my own village, Cicynna?

STUDENT: It's in there somewhere. Anyway, here's the island of Euboea, look, lying stretched out opposite us, all along here.

STREPSIADES: Yes, I knew that already. It's been lying like that ever since me and Pericles and the rest of us knocked it out.[10] Where's Sparta?

STUDENT [*pointing*]: Right here.

STREPSIADES: Too near, too near! You'd better have another thought or two about that – get it to be a heck of a lot further away from us.

STUDENT: We can't do that, silly.

STREPSIADES: Can't you? Then take that! [*He begins to belabour the* STUDENT *with his stick. As he does so* SOCRATES *swings into view like a god in tragedy, suspended in a contrivance like the gondola of a balloon. On seeing him* STREPSIADES *is so amazed that he drops the stick.*] Who in heaven's name is that hanging from the meathook?

STUDENT: Why, it's him, of course.

STREPSIADES: Him? Who's him?

STUDENT: Socrates.

STREPSIADES [*in religious awe*]: Socrates! Could you give him a shout for me?

STUDENT: No, I haven't got time, you do it yourself. [*Exit hastily and fearfully into the school.*]

STREPSIADES [*looking up at* SOCRATES, *who is now almost directly above him*]: Socrates! My sweet little Socrakins!

SOCRATES: Why call'st me, O thou creature of a day?

STREPSIADES: Well, for a start, I'd be very interested to know what you're doing up there.

SOCRATES: I am walking upon air and attacking the mystery of the sun.

STREPSIADES: Well, if you *must* attack the Mysteries of the gods why can't you do it on the ground?

SOCRATES: Why, for accurate investigation of meteorological phenomena it is essential to get one's thoughts into a state of, er, suspension by mixing small quantities of them with air – for air, you know, is of very similar physical constitution to thought – at least, to mine. So I could never make any discoveries by looking up from the ground – there is a powerful attractive force between the earth and the moisture contained in thought. Something similar may be observed to happen in the case of watercress.

STREPSIADES [*scratching his head*]: I don't understand all this about thought attracting moisture to watercress. Come down to me, Socrakins, please do, and teach me what I've come for.

SOCRATES [*as his gondola is lowered to the ground and he climbs out*]: Well, what have you come for?

STREPSIADES: I want to be made an orator. Heartless usurers and creditors are laying me waste with fire, the sword, and bailiffs.

SOCRATES: How did you manage to get so much in debt without realizing it?

STREPSIADES: It was all because of a violent attack of a terrible disease called horsitis. But anyway, Socrates, will you teach me that Argument of yours – you know, that one that always pays off and never pays up? It doesn't matter what your fees are; I'll pay them, I swear it by the gods.

SOCRATES: Ah, but what gods? The first thing you'll have to learn is that with us the gods are no longer current.

STREPSIADES: Well, what *is* the currency you swear by? Iron coins like they have at Byzantium?

SOCRATES: Do you want to see with your own eyes the real truth about the gods and all that?

STREPSIADES: By Zeus, yes, if you can show me.

SOCRATES: And to talk face to face with the Clouds whom we worship?

STREPSIADES: Yes, please.

SOCRATES [*leading him over to a bed which stands only a few inches from the ground*]: Then first of all, please sit on the sacred bed.

Flowery-speak

STREPSIADES [*doing so*]: All right.

[SOCRATES *dances in ungainly fashion around the bed.*]

SOCRATES [*giving him a wreath of unattractive-looking vegetation*]: Now put this on your head.

STREPSIADES [*alarmed*]: What's this? You're not going to make a sacrifice of me, like Athamas in the play?[11]

SOCRATES: No, this is just part of our normal initiation ceremony.

STREPSIADES: But what good will it do me?

SOCRATES [*who is taking some flour from a bag on the bed*]: You'll become a really fine-grained first-rate flowery speaker. Now keep very still. [*Begins to sprinkle the flour over* STREPSIADES.]

STREPSIADES [*trying to dodge the flour*]: You needn't think you can fool me – I'm becoming floury already!

SOCRATES:

Keep silence all, and hear my prayer.
O Lord, O King, O boundless Air,
On whom the earth supported floats,
And Ether bright, hear these my notes;

And you who send the thunder loud,
Almighty Goddesses of Cloud,
Behold your Thinker waiting here:
Arise and in the sky appear!

STREPSIADES [*hastily pulling his coat over his head*]:

Not yet, not yet, don't let them soak
Me till I'm covered with my cloak.
Why was I such a silly chap
That I forget to take my cap?

SOCRATES:

Come, holy Clouds, and show your power.
Come, leave your father Ocean's bower
(If there you be), or where Nile flows,
Or high Olympus crowned with snows

(If there you be) or Mimas' peak,
Or distant lakes in Scythia bleak:
Where'er you be, my prayers now hear,
Accept my offerings, and appear!

[*Silence. The* CHORUS *is heard singing in the distance.*]

CHORUS:

Rise, my sisters, Clouds eternal,
   Shining bright with morning dew,
From the roaring Ocean's bosom
   To the sky, the world to view.

p Let us see the distant mountains
   And the holy earth below,
Where we irrigate the cornfields
   And the babbling rivers flow,

ff While far off the breakers thunder
p   'Neath the sun's unwearied rays:
Make yourselves like human beings
   And to earth direct your gaze.

SOCRATES [*recitative*]:

       Almighty Clouds, you heard my
          prayer indeed.

[*To* STREPSIADES] Mark'd you their voice, how like the
          thunder 'twas?

STREPSIADES:

       Their glory I revere, and in reply
       I fain would blow a fart, I'm so afraid.
       If heaven's law permits it – matter of
          fact,
       Even if not – I badly need to crap.

SOCRATES:

       Jest not nor do as those comedians base;
       The gods like bees are swarming: hark
          again!

CHORUS [*nearer*]:
> Come, my sisters, where Athena
>   Rules the loveliest land in Greece,
> Where reside the glorious Mysteries[12]
>   That to troubled hearts bring peace;
>
> Where stand lofty, beauteous temples
>   Full of gifts beyond all price;
> Where no season lacks its share of
>   Festival and sacrifice;
>
> Where they hold to Dionysus
>   Joyous feast at start of spring,
> Hear the flute and hear the chorus
>   In melodious contest sing.

STREPSIADES: Who are those women who sing like the Muses themselves? Do tell me, Socrates. They're not ancestral heroines, are they, or anything like that?

SOCRATES: No, indeed. They are the celestial Clouds, the patron goddesses of the layabout. From them come our intelligence, our dialectic and our reason; also our speculative genius and all our argumentative talents.

STREPSIADES: Now you say that, I feel I could fly. I want to be a real subtle thinker, like you, and be able to split the thinnest hair going, and deflate my opponent with a pointed little argument and still have another up my sleeve for my own speech, and – Oh, I do so want to see these Clouds, if I can, Socrates.

SOCRATES [*pointing*]: Look over there, towards Mount Parnes. I can see them coming now.

STREPSIADES: Where, where?

SOCRATES: Yes, here they come through the glens and woods, a whole host of them – [*to* STREPSIADES, *who is looking vainly at the blue sky*] no, over *here*, coming in by the side.

STREPSIADES: What are you talking about? I can't see a thing.

SOCRATES: They're coming on to the stage now, for heaven's sake!

[*As he says this the* CHORUS *enter: unmistakably young women, but with dresses shaped and coloured like clouds.*]

STREPSIADES [*continuing to squint hard at the entry-way after they have passed*]: Ah yes, I see them now.

SOCRATES [*turning round* STREPSIADES' *head to face the* CHORUS]: So you should, unless you've got pumpkins where your eyes should be.

STREPSIADES: Yes – and how wonderful! The place is full of them!

SOCRATES: And you mean to say you didn't use to think they were goddesses?

STREPSIADES: Heavens, no – I thought they were mist, dew, smoke, vapour, something like that.

SOCRATES: Well, well! Then you can't have known that they nourish the brains of the whole tribe of sophists? No? And the prophets and teachers of medicine and other such dirty long-haired weirdies – anyone in fact, so long as he doesn't do any useful work? They're especially fond of writers of dithyrambs.[13] For one thing, they see a lot of them, since those chaps never have a foot on the ground; and for another, aren't they always talking about clouds and things?

STREPSIADES: That's right, isn't it? 'Deadly lightning, twisted bracelet of the watery Clouds' – and 'Locks of the hundred-headed Typhon' – and 'Conflagrating storms' – and 'Airy nothings' – and 'Crook-talon'd birds, the swimmers of the air' – and – let me think – yes! – 'Showers of moisture from the dewy Clouds'. That's right! And for that rubbish they're feasted after the performance on – wait a bit – on vast conger-eels and thrushes' avian flesh!

SOCRATES: All thanks to these ladies, and quite right too.

STREPSIADES: Socrates – one thing I'm puzzled about. You did say these were Clouds?

SOCRATES: Yes.

STREPSIADES: Well, how come they look so like women?
The other clouds – I mean, well, the real ones, look quite
different.

SOCRATES: Oh, how do they look?

STREPSIADES: Well, it's hard to say exactly – well, I suppose
like fleeces when they're laid out to dry, but anyway, not in
the least like women. And [*pointing to a member of the*
CHORUS] I never yet saw a cloud with a nose!

SOCRATES: Ah, but look at it this way. You've seen clouds,
haven't you, shaped like centaurs and leopards and lions
and such like?

STREPSIADES: Yes – well?

SOCRATES: They can take any shape they fancy. So if they see
a wild man walking around, one of those hairy sex maniacs,
like what's his name, Xenophantus' son,[14] well, they take
their cue from him and turn into wolves.

STREPSIADES: And if they catch sight of someone who rifles
the public funds, like Simon,[15] what do they do?

SOCRATES: Turn into foxes, of course.

STREPSIADES: Ah, now I understand why they looked like
deer yesterday! They must have seen Cleonymus[16] and
wanted to remind him how cowardly he'd been that time
when –

SOCRATES: I think we know all about that, [*to the audience*]
don't we? But you've got the idea; and anyway, they had
one look at Cleisthenes[17] just now, and naturally, on the
spot, as you can see, they turned into women.

STREPSIADES [*to the* CHORUS]: Well, welcome, holy
Clouds; I wonder if, just for me, you'd show me the power
of your wonderful heavenly voices?

CHORUS [*in close harmony*]:

> Hail, grey-headed hunter of phrases artistic!
>   Hail, Socrates, master of twaddle!
> Out of all of the specialists cosmologistic
>   We love for the brains in his noddle

Only Prodicus;[18] you we admire none the less
For the way that you swagger and cuss,
And never wear shoes, and don't care how you dress,
And solemnly discourse of us.

STREPSIADES [*in raptures*]: How fantastic! How divine!

SOCRATES: Yes, these are the only truly divine beings – all the rest is just a lot of fairy tales.

STREPSIADES: What on earth – ! You mean you don't believe in Zeus?

SOCRATES: Zeus? Who's Zeus?

STREPSIADES: Zeus who lives on Olympus, of course.

SOCRATES: Now really, you should know better. [*Confidentially*] There is no Zeus.

STREPSIADES: What? Well, who sends the rain, then? Answer me that.

SOCRATES: Why, our friends here do that, and I'll prove it. Have you ever seen it raining when the sky was blue? Surely Zeus, if it was him, would be able to send rain even when the Clouds were out of town.

STREPSIADES: That certainly backs your argument. I wonder why I was so naive as to think that rain was just Zeus pissing into a sieve. Well, that's one thing; but who is it that thunders and sends shivers up my spine?

SOCRATES: The Clouds do that too – when they get in a whirl.

STREPSIADES: I can see I'm never going to trip you. But what do you mean, a whirl?

SOCRATES: Well, being suspended in the air, you see, when they get swollen with rain they are necessarily set in motion, and of course they collide with one another, and because of their weight they get broken and let out this great noise.

STREPSIADES: 'Necessarily set in motion', you say. Ah, but who sets them in motion? Now *that's* got to be Zeus!

SOCRATES: Not a bit of it; as I say, it's a whirl in the sky.

STREPSIADES: Awhirl! – ah, I get you. That I must say I hadn't been told before. I get it. Zeus is dead, and now Awhirl is the new king. But you still haven't told me what causes the thunder.

SOCRATES: Didn't you hear? I said that it occurs when Clouds swollen with rain collide with one another, and is caused by their density.

STREPSIADES: Ha! Do you expect me to believe that?

SOCRATES: You yourself are a living proof of it. You have no doubt at some time – say, at the Pan-Athenian Festival – had a bit too much soup for dinner?

[STREPSIADES *nods guiltily*.]

Well, didn't that make your tummy grumble, not to say rumble?

STREPSIADES: It certainly does, straight away, a terrible noise, just like thunder. Gently at first [*imitates the noise*], then like this [*again, a little louder*], and when I crap, it really lets fly [*tries to imitate the noise again, but finds himself breaking wind in very truth*] – just like they do [*indicating the* CHORUS].

SOCRATES [*approvingly*]: Well, if a little tummy like yours [*pats it*] could let off a fart like that, what do you think an infinity of air can do? That's how thunder comes about. In point of fact, I happen to know that in Phrygian – the oldest language on earth　they actually call thunder 'phartos'.[19]

STREPSIADES: Very well: how about the thunderbolt? Tell me how that gets its fire – and hits us and burns us to a cinder, or maybe singes us alive – I don't know which is worse. Obviously that's Zeus' weapon against people who perjure themselves.

SOCRATES: Who are you, Methuselah? If Zeus strikes down perjurers, why hasn't he ignited Simon, Cleonymus and Theorus?[20] Why? [*Waits for an answer; protests from the audience*.] Yes, I know what I'm talking about. [*To* STREPSIADES] And why does he strike his own temple and his brother Poseidon's at Sunium, not to mention any number of his own oak trees? Or have you ever heard of a perjured oak tree?

STREPSIADES: I don't know. But what you say does seem to make sense. What is the thunderbolt, in that case?

SOCRATES: It's when a dry wind in the sky gets shut up in a cloud. It blows it up like a bladder and the inevitable result is that it bursts; so the wind rushes out, owing to the density of the cloud, and the rapidity and violence of its motion cause it to set itself on fire.

STREPSIADES: Why, that's exactly what happened to me last month.[21] I was roasting a haggis for the family, left it unattended for a time, and sure enough it got puffed up and – bang! – it plastered itself all over my eyes. I got a bad burn or two.

CHORUS [*to* STREPSIADES]:
If you're ready to work and your memory's good,
    If you've got the ability to think,
If you laugh at the cold and at shortage of food,
    Wrestling, dice, sex, fresh air, even drink,
If you honour the art of defeating your foe
    By stratagems deft of the tongue –
Then we'll make you so smart that wherever you go
    Strepsiades' praise will be sung.

STREPSIADES: Well, nobody can say I'm not tough and can't stay awake at night thinking. And as far as a penny-pinching spartan digestion is concerned that is quite prepared to live on nothing but onions – I'm your man – here I am – get to work on me.

SOCRATES: I assume, then, that you now believe in only the gods that we believe in, that is, Chaos, our friends the Clouds here, and the Tongue?

STREPSIADES: I will never sacrifice or pour libation or burn incense to any other god. And if I met one in the street I wouldn't speak to him.

LEADER: Well, now that you're a worshipper of ours, you'll never come to any harm. Just tell us what you want us to do for you.

STREPSIADES: Just one tiny little thing, holy Clouds: I want to be the best orator in Greece – Strepsiades first, the rest nowhere.

LEADER: We'll see to that. In future there will be nobody carries more resolutions in the Assembly than you do.

STREPSIADES: Not resolutions, that's not what I'm interested in. I just want to be able to twist and turn my way through the forest of the law so as to give my creditors the slip.

LEADER: Well, that's certainly not much to ask. We'll see you get it. Just put yourself in the hands of our high priest here [*indicates* SOCRATES], have confidence, and we'll do the rest.

STREPSIADES: I have confidence all right. I've got to. It's the inevitable result [*glances at* SOCRATES *to show he is already picking up some of the jargon*] of horse force and wife pressure.

So I give myself entirely to the school – I'll let it beat
    me,[22]
It can starve me, freeze me, parch me, it can generally
    ill-treat me,
If it teaches me to dodge my debts and get the reputation
Of the cleverest, slyest fox that ever baffled litigation.
Let men hate me, let men call me names, and over and
    above it
Let them chase me through each court, and I assure you
    that I'll love it.
Yes, if Socrates can make of me a real forensic winner,
I don't mind if he takes out my guts and has them for his
    dinner.

CHORUS:
If he has them for his dinner –
SOCRATES:
If I have them for my dinner –

131

ALL:
  Yes, if Socrates, etc.

LEADER:
  I can see you're not a coward, and you've got the
      disposition
  To become, if taught by us, a great and famous
      rhetorician.

STREPSIADES:
  This I really can't believe; is it the truth that you are
      telling?

LEADER:
  Men will stand all night in queues before the entrance to
      your dwelling,
  To consult you and to pick your brains and find a
      quibble shifty
  To escape from paying damages of forty thou. or fifty;
  And so grateful will they be at winning by a margin
      healthy
  That in no long time your expertise will make you really
      wealthy.

SOCRATES:
  It will make you really wealthy –

STREPSIADES:
  It will make me really wealthy?

ALL:
  Yes, so grateful, etc.

LEADER: Time now, Socrates, to take your pupil through the
  preliminaries. You must shake up his mind a bit, test his
  intelligence.

SOCRATES [*to* STREPSIADES]: Tell me, what kind of a mind
  do you have? I must know that in order to be able to bring
  the latest devices to bear on your most strongly fortified
  prejudices.

STREPSIADES: What do you mean? I came here to be educated, not to be besieged, and I haven't got any fortified precipices anyway.

SOCRATES: Don't be silly; I only want to ask you a few questions. Do you have a good memory?

STREPSIADES: Yes and no. Yes if somebody owes me something – no if I owe it to someone else.

SOCRATES: I see. Do you think you're a natural speaker?

STREPSIADES: No, not a natural speaker. A natural cheat, yes.

SOCRATES: Well then, how on earth do you expect to learn anything?

STREPSIADES: I'll manage.

SOCRATES: Well, anyway, if I put a choice bit of cosmology in front of you, I assume I can be sure that you will snap it up?

STREPSIADES: I'm not going to be treated like a dog!

SOCRATES [*aside*]: He's so stupid it's not true! [*To* STREPSIADES] I am afraid that in your education I may well be compelled to resort to the use of force. [*An anxiety strikes him.*] By the way, what do you do when you get hit?

STREPSIADES: Well, without an instant's delay I wait a little, and then raise a cry of assault, and then I wait a *very* little – like about two seconds – and go to law.

SOCRATES: All right; take off your coat, please. [*Lays his hand on* STREPSIADES' *coat.*]

STREPSIADES [*wriggling free*]: Why? You can't beat me. I haven't done anything wrong.

SOCRATES: I wasn't going to; but the rule is that no-one may enter the Thinkery wearing his coat.

STREPSIADES [*still clinging to the coat*]: What do you think I'm planning to do? Plant something here and then accuse you of stealing it?

SOCRATES: Oh, do stop talking nonsense and take the thing off.

[STREPSIADES *reluctantly complies, leaving the coat on the ground.*]

133

STREPSIADES: Tell me, if I'm a really hard-working keen student, will I become like your other pupils here?

SOCRATES: Nobody will be able to tell you from Chaerephon.

STREPSIADES: I might as well be dead in that case!

SOCRATES [*going to the inner door of the school, snapping up* STREPSIADES' *coat on the way*]: Will you stop blethering and get a move on in here?

STREPSIADES: I will if you give me a honey-cake to feed the snakes with. I'm frightened of going into that cave of yours.[23] [*Goes gingerly towards the door, eyeing the ground for snakes.*]

SOCRATES: Come in, for heaven's sake!

[STREPSIADES *goes in, followed by* SOCRATES.]

CHORUS:

> Go in, brave pilgrim, and be sure
> That Fortune will be gracious,
> And blessing in profusion pour
> On your attempt audacious.
> Rejoice that, though advanced in years,
> Your problems monetary
> Have brought you here to learn ideas
> Quite revolutionary.

[*The* CHORUS *advance and their* LEADER *addresses the audience.*]

I swear by Dionysus, my protector in my youth,
Athenians, that I'll tell you now the frank and simple truth.
So may I lose my wits and may I finish last again,
If I don't think my audience consists of clever men.
I thought that I had never written any play so witty
As this; that's why I let it first be tasted by this city.
A lot of sweat went into it; and yet this play retreated
By vulgar works of vulgar men unworthily defeated.

To all this trouble I went for you, and this was all your gratitude!

But you need have no fear that I will take a similar
    attitude
To you, or ever let you down. For ever since the year [24]
That certain persons praised the first of my productions
    here,
The moral and immoral chap, *The Banqueters* I mean,
Which like an unwed mother I abandoned on the green
For someone to adopt [25] – and when the infant caught
    your eyes
You kindly brought it up (and gave the play a worthy
    prize) –
Well, at that time, as I submit, you made a promise sworn
To look with favour on all plays that might of me be born.

So here's my latest, like Electra [26] looking here and there
To find an audience that's a lock cut from her brother's
    hair.
My Comedy's a modest girl: she doesn't play the fool
By bringing on a great thick floppy red-tipped leather tool
To give the kids a laugh, or making fun of men who're
    bald;
Requests to dance a cordax [27] simply leave the lass
    appalled.
And no old man with walking-stick applies a well-aimed
    poke
In hopes to drown the groaning at another feeble joke.
No torches, shouts, or violence, or other weak
    distraction: [28]
She comes before you trusting in her words and in her
    action.

And I am not a long-haired fop, nor yet a smooth-faced
    cheat
Who pretends that something's new when it is really a
    repeat:
I always think up new ideas, not one of which is ever

The same as those that went before, and all of them are
  clever.
I went for Cleon, hard and low, when he was at his
  height,
But only once: why punch when you've already won the
  fight?
But now you see Hyperbolus[29] is butt of all the others:
They have him down, but still assail his weak spots and
  his mother's.
The first of them was Eupolis, the stinking thief, who
  bashed
Hyperbolus in *Maricas*,[30] which was my *Knights* rehashed
(He also plundered Phrynichus, though on a smaller scale:
A cordax and a drunk old woman gobbled by a whale).
Hermippus then and all the rest on one another's heels
Kept on at him (and plagiarized *my* joke about the eels).[31]
If anyone still laughs at them, well, I can't say I mind
If fools like that to humour such as I provide are blind;
But if you now accept my work with ready ears and eyes,
Posterity will reckon you a generation wise.

CHORUS:
  Zeus, thou almighty Ruler of the heavens,
    Thee first we call, accept our dance, we pray;
  Thou too who wield'st the stern and savage trident,
    Lord of the Earthquake, hear our song today.

  Father renowned who nourishest all creatures,
    Ether, most holy, thee we also praise;
  And him who drives the fiery solar chariot,
    Mortals and gods refreshing with his rays.

LEADER:
  We Clouds, my dear spectators, feel we must
  Say that the way you treat us is unjust.
  More blessings than all other gods we bring
  To you; yet you make us no offering

136

Nor even pour libation. Just reflect
What care we take your city to protect.
Suppose you make a great strategic blunder:
Then we send omens bad, like rain or thunder,
And send you home while it's not yet too late.
Then, when you chose the fellow the gods hate,
The Paphlagonian trafficker in leather,[32]
As general, we gave warning through the weather:
With knitted brow we thundered, lightning flared,
The moon forsook her path,[33] the sun declared
That, if that villain won, he'd quench his flame.
And you elected Cleon just the same!
But still the gods, although they cannot cure
Your foolishness political, make sure
You always get a second opportunity
To rectify your blunders with impunity.
What! you don't have this second chance, say you,
Now you've elected him? Oh yes, you do.
That shark takes bribes and public money steals,
Doesn't he, now? Well, catch him by the heels
And dump him in the stocks, and all will prove
Well for the state, despite your first false move.

CHORUS:
Thou who art throned on Cynthus' rocky summit,
  Graciously hear us, Phoebus, Delian Lord;
Thou too, blest Maid,[34] who dwell'st in the Ephesians'
  Temple of gold, by Lydian maids adored.

Thou our Protectress, wielder of the aegis,
  Stay of this city, Pallas, hear our song;
Last but not least the reveller of Parnassus,
  Bacchus, we call, amid his Maenad throng.

LEADER:
Before we started on our journey here
We met the Moon, who said she wished good cheer

To Athens and to all her allies true,
But had a bone or two to pick with you.
She says you wrong her, seeing she has blessed
You always in a fashion manifest.
For instance, each of you a drachma saves
Each month, which else you'd have to give to slaves
Torches to buy when you went out at night:
So much you profit by the lunar light,
And more; for which, she says, your thanks are scurvy –
You've turned the calendar all topsy-turvy.³⁵
And when the gods from meals are turned away
Because you've sacrificed on the wrong day,
It's her they blame – they make quite dreadful threats;
Meanwhile you squabble over little debts
And go to law on days which should be feasts
And working days for none except the priests.
On other days, when we in mourning fast
For some great fallen hero of the past,
You down on earth unseasonably rejoice.
Some of our ire we vented on your choice
As delegate to Delphi – you know who –
Hyperbolus: his wreath away we blew,
Hurting his pride to make him mend his ways
And teach you by the moon to count your days.

[*Re-enter* SOCRATES *from the school, looking exasperated.*]
SOCRATES: In the name of Respiration and Chaos and Air and all that's holy – ! I have never met such a clueless stupid forgetful bumpkin in all my life. The pokiest little thing I teach him, he forgets before he's even learnt it! Never mind, I'll see if a bit of daylight does him any good. [*Calling towards the door*] Strepsiades! Where are you? Can you bring your bed out here?
STREPSIADES [*from inside, grumpily*]: What with all the bugs it's walking back in again. [*He comes out carrying the bed.*]

SOCRATES: Come over here and put it down, and then pay attention.

STREPSIADES [*doing so*]: All right.

SOCRATES: Now what do you want to be taught first? Something that you haven't ever been taught before. Come on. Words? Rhythms? Verse measures?

STREPSIADES [*eagerly*]: Measures, yes, that's what I want to know about. Only the other day a corn-dealer cheated me with an oversized quart measure.

SOCRATES [*impatiently*]: I'm not talking about that. What measure do you consider the most attractive? Iambic trimeters? Trochaic tetrameters?

STREPSIADES: Well ... let me see ... I think I prefer the gallon.

SOCRATES: The gallon? What on earth are you blethering about?

STREPSIADES: I thought you said tetrameters. That means four, doesn't it? Well, I certainly prefer four quarts to three, if that's what you wanted to know.

SOCRATES: Damn your quarts, you stupid peasant. Let's try rhythms, perhaps you'll understand them better.

STREPSIADES: I will if they'll help me sell my corn.

SOCRATES: Well, I don't know about that, but you'll certainly be a better conversationalist, knowing what an anapaest is and a dactyl and all the other kinds of feet.[36]

STREPSIADES: Come off it. I know all about feet already.

SOCRATES: Tell me what you know about them.

STREPSIADES [*waving his foot at* SOCRATES]: Why, this is a right one, and [*changing feet*] this is a left one. I've known that since I was a baby.

SOCRATES: Idiot!

STREPSIADES: Well, my good man, why should I learn about any of these things? I don't want to, anyway.

SOCRATES: Well, what *do* you want to learn about?

STREPSIADES: That arg – argument, the one you call Wrong.

SOCRATES: Ah, there are many other things you have to learn first. For instance, which animals are male?

STREPSIADES: Well, I know that, if I haven't gone potty. A ram, a he-goat, a bull, a jackass, a chicken –

SOCRATES: See what you do? You call the male and female by the same name 'chicken'.

STREPSIADES: Eh?

SOCRATES [*very slowly, as to a child*]: You just called the male 'chicken', and you call the female 'chicken' too.

STREPSIADES [*after some thought*]: By Poseidon, so I do. What ought I to call them?

SOCRATES: Say 'chickeness', and the male you can call 'chicker'.[37]

STREPSIADES: Chickeness! Holy Air, that's wonderful! Just for telling me that I'll fill your trough with barley.

SOCRATES: Hold it again. You called it a trough. Much too masculine a name for such a feminine object.

STREPSIADES: What do you mean, a masculine name for a feminine object?

SOCRATES: Sort of like Cleonymus.

STREPSIADES: That foxy fellow, you mean?

SOCRATES: That's right: fox, trough, they're just the same.

STREPSIADES: But that's impossible. Cleonymus hasn't got a trough, masculine *or* feminine – he does his kneading with a round mortar [*illustrates his meaning with a handy implement*]. No, but what should I call a trough from now on?

SOCRATES: Well, as I was saying, it's just like a fox. Fox – vixen; trough – triffen.[38]

STREPSIADES: Triffen will be feminine?

SOCRATES: That's right.

STREPSIADES: I've got it now. Triffen – vixen – Cleonymē.

SOCRATES: But you've still got to learn which names are masculine and which feminine.

STREPSIADES: No, I know which are feminine.

140

SOCRATES: Which?

STREPSIADES: Lysilla – Philinna – Cleitagora – Demetria –

SOCRATES [*interrupting*]: Yes; and which are masculine?

STREPSIADES: Millions. [*Thinks hard.*] Well, there's Philoxenus – and Melesias – and Alexander –[39]

SOCRATES: Silly, they aren't masculine.

STREPSIADES: You don't think they are?

SOCRATES: Not a bit. If you met Alexander, what would be
the first thing you'd say to him?

STREPSIADES: I'd say – I'd say 'Hullo, Sandie!'[40]

SOCRATES: There you are; you've called him a woman.

STREPSIADES: And rightly too – the way *she* manages to
dodge the call-up. But what's the point of my learning all
these things? Everybody knows them already.

SOCRATES [*bitterly*]: There certainly doesn't seem to be much
point in trying to teach you them. Now [*pointing to the bed*]
just get in there –

STREPSIADES [*apprehensively*]: And?

SOCRATES: And have some thoughts about one of your own
problems.

STREPSIADES: Please, not in there! If I must think, do let me
lie on the ground and do it.

SOCRATES: I'm afraid there is no alternative.

STREPSIADES [*getting into the bed*]: You're sending me into the
bugs' torture chamber, you know that.

[SOCRATES *goes into the school.*]

CHORUS:
>   Think closely, follow every track,
>   And twist and turn and double back,

[STREPSIADES *begins to writhe in agony.*]

>   And when you know not how
>   To come to a conclusion true,
>   Jump to another point of view,
>   And never sleep, but –

STREPSIADES: Yow!!

CHORUS:
> What ails thee, friend? Why criest so?

STREPSIADES: I'm being ravaged by a foe,
> A vast Phlee-asian host;[41]
> They've gnawed my ribs and now they'll
>   pass
> To driving tunnels up my arse –
> They'll make of me a ghost.

CHORUS:
> Nay, bear it not so grievously.

STREPSIADES: That's fine advice to offer me!
> In debt up to my brow,
> Without my shoes, without my tan,
> Uncertain if I'm still a man,
> And tortured by these – Yowww!!!

[*He returns to his private agony.* SOCRATES *looks out of the door.*]

SOCRATES: Hey, what are you up to? Are you thinking or not?

STREPSIADES: Certainly I am.

SOCRATES: Well, what are you thinking about?

STREPSIADES: Whether when the bugs have finished with me there'll be any of me left. Ouch!

SOCRATES: Oh, go to blazes! [*Goes back inside.*]

STREPSIADES [*calling after him*]: I'm not sure I'm not there already. [*He moves as if intending to get out of bed.*]

LEADER: Now, now, don't be a coward: cover yourself up. You've got to get yourself a few juicy ideas to cheat those creditors.

STREPSIADES [*meekly retreating under the bedclothes*]: I wish these bedclothes would produce one for a change – or even a juicy something else, I wouldn't mind that either.

[SOCRATES *comes out.*]

SOCRATES: Let's have a look what this one is doing. [*Kicking* STREPSIADES *through the bedclothes.*] You there, are you asleep?

142

STREPSIADES [*muffled*]: No.

SOCRATES: Well, have you got anything yet?

STREPSIADES: No. [*By this time there is a remarkable bulge in the bedclothes.*]

SOCRATES: What, nothing?

STREPSIADES: Well, I've got my prick in my hand, if that's what you – No, I suppose you don't.

SOCRATES: Enough of that. Cover up and get thinking.

STREPSIADES [*sitting up*]: What about? Tell me that.

SOCRATES: You tell me what. Think of something you want to know about.

STREPSIADES: If I've told you once I've told you a million times. I want to know about interest – how not to pay it.

SOCRATES: All right; cover up, give your brain a little more play, and reflect on the matter. Make sure you draw the correct distinctions.

STREPSIADES [*pulling the bedclothes over his head*]: Yow! It's those bugs again!

SOCRATES: Now don't wriggle. And if an idea gets you into any difficulty, let go of it, withdraw for a bit, and then get your brain to work again shifting it around and weighing it up. [*He is about to go off when a shout calls him back.*]

STREPSIADES [*getting eagerly and thankfully out of bed*]: Socrates! Socrates, my very own!

SOCRATES: Yes, what is it?

STREPSIADES: I've got an idea for dodging interest.

SOCRATES: Tell me what it is.

STREPSIADES: Tell me –

SOCRATES [*after a moment*]: Yes?

STREPSIADES: Suppose I bought a Thessalian slave, a witch, and got her to draw down the moon one night, and then put it in a box like they do mirrors and kept a close watch on it.

SOCRATES: What good would that do you?

STREPSIADES: Well, if the moon never rises, I never pay any interest.

143

SOCRATES: Why not?

STREPSIADES: Why not? Because it's reckoned by the month, of course.

SOCRATES: That's very good. Here's another one for you. Say someone sues you for 30,000 drachmas. How do you get out of it?

STREPSIADES: How – do – I – I don't know. But I'd better find a way.

SOCRATES: Don't keep your thought penned up inside you all the time. Let it out into the air for a bit, keeping it under control, of course, like a yo-yo.[42]

STREPSIADES [*after some thought*]: I've found a marvellous way of stopping that lawsuit. I think you'll think so too.

SOCRATES: Like what?

STREPSIADES: Have you seen that stone the druggists sell – the beautiful transparent one you can light fires with?

SOCRATES: You mean a burning-glass?

STREPSIADES: That's right. Well, suppose when the clerk is entering the case on one of his tablets, I stand like this with the glass between him and the sun and melt the wax where the particulars of the case against me are?

SOCRATES: Beautiful, by the Graces!

STREPSIADES: Whew! Glad I managed to strike that 30,000-drachma case off the list.

SOCRATES: See if you can get this one. You're the defendant – and you've nearly lost the case – and your witnesses are nowhere to be found. How do you get out of that one?

STREPSIADES: That's child's play.

SOCRATES: Go on.

STREPSIADES: Well – assuming there is still one case to be heard before mine – well, before they called on my case – I'd run away and hang myself.

SOCRATES: Oh, you're talking nonsense.

STREPSIADES: No, I'm not. Once I'm dead nobody can sue me.

144

SOCRATES: You just babble. Get out. I'm not going to teach you any more.

STREPSIADES: Oh, why? Do, please, Socrates, for the gods' sake.

SOCRATES: But look, anything you do learn you forget straight away. For instance, tell me now, what was the first thing I taught you?

STREPSIADES: Let me see now, what came first? – what – came – Knead – something we were kneading in – but what on earth was it?

SOCRATES: Oh, to hell with you, you amnesiac old fool! [*He walks furiously away, but remains in earshot during the following conversation.*]

STREPSIADES [*in despair*]: Gods, what will happen to me now? If I can't learn tongue-wrestling, I'm done for. Holy Clouds, can you give me any advice?

LEADER: Well, what we advise is this: do you have a grown-up son? If so, send him here to be a student instead of you.

STREPSIADES: Yes, I've a son, [*sarcastically*] a fine fellow. What am I to do, though? He doesn't want to learn anything.

LEADER: And you can't make him?

STREPSIADES: No. He's strong, good-looking, and descended from a long line of stinking rich women. Never mind, though, I'll go and get him; and if he doesn't come, make no mistake, I'll throw him out of my house. [*To* SOCRATES] Go inside and wait till I come back; I won't be long. [*Exit.*]

CHORUS [*to* SOCRATES]:
>We only of the heavenly band
>   Look with grace on you:
>This fellow's clay within your hand –
>   What you say he'll do.
>Observe the way his heart's uplifted,
>   Make your profit fast;
>For favouring winds ere now have shifted –
>   Luck don't always last.

SCENE THREE: *The street outside* STREPSIADES' *house and the Thinkery. The* CHORUS *are present as before.*

[STREPSIADES, *very angry, comes out of his house, dragging a bewildered* PHEIDIPPIDES *after him.*]

STREPSIADES: In the name of Mist, leave this house. Go and nibble at your uncle's pillared portico.

PHEIDIPPIDES: What on earth's happened to you, dad? Why, Zeus in heaven, you act like you were out of your mind!

STREPSIADES: Zeus in heaven! Hah! How stupid can you get? Believing in Zeus, a big boy like you! Ha! ha! ha!

PHEIDIPPIDES: What's so funny about that?

STREPSIADES: That you could be such a baby – so naive. Never mind. Come to daddy and he'll tell you something a grown-up needs to know. [PHEIDIPPIDES *comes over, and* STREPSIADES *whispers, audibly, in his ear.*] Promise you'll never tell this to anyone?

PHEIDIPPIDES: Promise. What is it?

STREPSIADES: You were swearing by Zeus just now, weren't you?

PHEIDIPPIDES: Yes.

STREPSIADES: Well, now, isn't education a wonderful thing? Pheidippides – there *is* no Zeus.

PHEIDIPPIDES: No Zeus? Who's taken over?

STREPSIADES: Awhirl is king now; he's driven Zeus into exile.

PHEIDIPPIDES: What are you blethering about?

STREPSIADES: I assure you, it's perfectly true.

PHEIDIPPIDES: Who says so, anyway?

STREPSIADES: Diag – I mean Socrates,[43] and Chaerephon, you know, the expert on fleas' feet.

PHEIDIPPIDES: You believe nuts like that? You must be off your head.

STREPSIADES: Hush! I won't have anything rude said about

146

them. They're brilliant men and so sensible too – so frugal: they never do extravagant things like getting their hair cut or putting on oil, and they would never dream of taking a hot bath. You, you're never out of the bath – it's as if you were always getting ready for my funeral; except that I'm still alive, lad, and you're doing it at my expense. Now get along there quickly and let them teach you instead of me.

PHEIDIPPIDES: Huh! What that's any use can that lot teach anyone?

STREPSIADES: What a thing to ask! They teach you everything that's worth knowing. They'll soon teach *you* how dense and stupid you are. Here, just wait a moment, will you? [*Goes into the house.*]

PHEIDIPPIDES: Gods help me, my father really is mad. What am I going to do? Get the court to certify him, or just get in touch with the undertaker?

[*His reflections are interrupted by the return of* STREPSIADES, *followed by a* SLAVE *carrying two chickens, one male and one female.*]

STREPSIADES [*pointing to the male bird*]: Tell me now, what do you call this?

PHEIDIPPIDES [*in the tone of one who humours a lunatic*]: A chicken.

STREPSIADES: That's very good. And this one [*pointing to the other bird*]?

PHEIDIPPIDES: A chicken.

STREPSIADES: What, both the same? You *have* made a fool of yourself. You'd better not do it again. In future call this one a chickeness and the other one a chicker.

PHEIDIPPIDES: Chickeness? Was that the kind of bright idea you were taught in that creeps' academy?

STREPSIADES: Yes, and a great deal more too; but every time I was taught anything I forgot it straight away – I'm too old, Pheidippides, too old.

PHEIDIPPIDES: That's why you lost your coat?

STREPSIADES: I didn't lose it, I – I – thought it away. You get that? I thought it away.

PHEIDIPPIDES: And your shoes? What did you do with them, you old fool?

STREPSIADES: Oh, put them down as 'essential expenditure', Pericles style.⁴⁴ Come on now, let's go. Do what I ask you now, and in future you can do what you like, all right? I remember [*emotionally*] that I was already doing what *you* were asking me when you were a babbling six-year-old. I spent my very first obol of jury pay to get you a little toy cart to play with!

PHEIDIPPIDES: I swear you'll be sorry for this one day. [*Reluctantly follows* STREPSIADES *over to the door of the Thinkery.*]

STREPSIADES: Good for you, my boy! Socrates! Come out and see what I've got! Here's my son. He didn't want to come, but I persuaded him.

SOCRATES [*coming out*]: I see. He must be immature. It's clear he doesn't yet know the ropes here.

PHEIDIPPIDES: [*under his breath*] I'd like to see you on the end of one.

STREPSIADES: Damn you, what do you mean cursing your teacher?

SOCRATES: Listen to his slack pronunciation – the drawl, the open mouth – did you hear? It's not going to be easy to teach him to win cases and make good debating points that don't actually mean anything. And yet [*reflectively*] for 6,000 drachmas, Hyperbolus did manage to learn it.

STREPSIADES [*much relieved*]: Fine, fine, teach him. He's really quite precocious. Do you know, when he was a little boy, so high [*indicating with his hand*], he was building toy houses at home, and ships too and little carts of figwood – and what do you think? – he made little frogs out of pomegranate peel! Well, anyway, see that he learns your

two Arguments, whatever you call them – oh yes, Right
and Wrong – the one that takes a bad case and defeats Right
with it. If he can't manage both, then at least Wrong – that
will do – but that he must have.

SOCRATES: Well, I'll go and send the Arguments here in
person, and they'll teach him themselves.

STREPSIADES [*calling after* SOCRATES *as he goes out*]: Don't
forget, he's got to be able to argue against any kind of
justified claim at all.45

[*Enter* RIGHT, *dressed in the good old Attic style. He is
followed by the smirking figure of* WRONG, *dressed similarly
to* PHEIDIPPIDES *except that his tunic is embroidered with
tongues.*]

RIGHT: This way. Let the audience see you. You may be
brazen but you're not *that* brazen.

WRONG: Sure, go wherever you like. The more of an
audience we have, the more soundly I'll trounce you.

RIGHT: Trounce me? What do you think you are?

WRONG: An Argument, like you.

RIGHT: Yes, a *wrong* Argument.

WRONG: Maybe, but I'll still beat you, Right though you call
yourself.

RIGHT: What sort of trick will you use?

WRONG: Oh, just a few new ideas.

RIGHT: Yes, they're in fashion now, aren't they, [*to the
audience*] because of you idiots.

WRONG: Idiots indeed! They're extremely intelligent.

RIGHT: Anyway, I'll wallop you.

WRONG [*unconcerned*]: How?

RIGHT: Simply by putting my just case.

WRONG: It'll crumble as soon as I open my mouth. Anyway,
there isn't any such thing as Justice.

RIGHT: No Justice?!

WRONG: You think there is? Where is she?

RIGHT: Where the gods are, of course.

WRONG: Very well; in that case, why didn't she destroy Zeus for putting his father in chains?[46]

RIGHT: Ugh, you make me puke. A bowl, somebody!

WRONG: You're just a fogbound out-of-tune old bag-pipe.

RIGHT: And you're just a shameless out-of-condition young bugger.

WRONG: I'm terribly flattered.

RIGHT: And a pickpocket.

WRONG: Another bouquet! No, I mean it.

RIGHT: And what's more, you beat your father.

WRONG: You know, you're showering me with gold.

RIGHT: Lead, more like – at least my generation would have thought so.

WRONG: To mine all those words you used are really exquisite compliments.

RIGHT [*disgusted*]: You're the absolute limit.

WRONG: And you're the absolute prehistoric survival.

RIGHT: You're the one that teaches our teenagers not to go to school. One day Athens will wake up to what you've been doing to our youth.

WRONG [*sniffing*]: Do you ever wash?

RIGHT: You're not doing so badly, are you? Considering you used to be a beggar, pretending to be that Mysian Telephus[47] and living on little scraps of ideas you got from your bag and shared with every down-and-out in Athens.[48]

WRONG: Yes, wasn't I clever?

RIGHT: Yes, weren't you mad? And madder yet the city that bred you to ruin its own youth.

WRONG: You don't mean to be this boy's teacher, do you, Methuselah?

RIGHT: Yes, I do, if he wants to be made a decent person and know how to do something besides talk.

WRONG [*to* PHEIDIPPIDES]: Come here and leave him to rant.

RIGHT: Lay a hand on him and I'll wallop you! [*Rushes at*
WRONG, *but is restrained by the* LEADER.]

LEADER:

Cease your wrangling now, I pray;
Tell us, Right, the way you taught
Athens' boys in bygone years;
You then, Wrong, will have your say,
Give this lad some food for thought,
Make him marvel as he hears.
When he's heard your clashing views,
He himself his path will choose.

RIGHT [*recitative*]:

To this proposal I agree.

WRONG: And I.

LEADER: But which will open this debate momentous?

WRONG:

He can start for all I care;
Doesn't matter how he speaks,
Modern thought will clip his wings.
Yes, I promise, if he dare
Say one word, his eyes and cheeks
I'll make black with hornet-stings
Made of words – so just you wait!
I'll consign him to his fate.

CHORUS:

As you battle in words and in thoughts of the mind,
Let us see which is better and which lags behind;
We're concerned in this contest for Socrates' sake;
For the future of Learning, no less, is at stake.

LEADER:

Now, you who fostered by your education
The glorious old traditions of our nation,
Break into speech with Aeschylean voice,
Explain why you should be this stripling's choice.

RIGHT: I'll tell you about the way boys were brought up in the old days – the days when I was all the rage and it was actually fashionable to be decent. First of all, children were supposed to be seen and not heard. Then, all the boys of the district were expected to walk together through the streets to their music-master's, quietly and decorously, and without a coat, even when it was snowing confetti – and they did. And when they got there he made them learn some of the old songs by heart – like 'Pallas, great sacker of cities' or 'Let the glad chorus re-echo' – singing them to the traditional tunes their fathers used, and on *no* account pressing their thighs together. And if any of them did anything disreputable such as putting in chromatic bits, all tied up in knots, the sort Phrynis[49] introduced and they all do now, why, he was given six of the best for insulting the Muses. Then in the gymnasium, when they sat down, they were expected to keep their legs well up, so as not to – so as not to torment us with desire; and when they got up, to smooth down the sand, so as not to leave any lovely – I mean provocative marks on it for their lovers to gaze at. What's more, [*sternly*] they never put on oil below the belt, [*dreamily*] and their pricks looked like peaches, all velvety and dewy and – [*recollecting who he is*] and you didn't see a boy being his own pimp, walking along making eyes at his lovers and putting on a beautiful soft voice, oh no! They weren't allowed to grab the best vegetables at dinner either, like the dill and parsley – those were always reserved for their elders and betters. In fact they ate no fancy stuff at all. And they never giggled, they never stood like this with one foot over the other, and they never –

WRONG: How very archaic! How quaint! How fit for history's dustbin, along with boring minor festivals, grasshopper brooches, and Ceceides![50]

RIGHT: Yes, you can laugh. But that's the sort of discipline that I used to rear the men who fought at Marathon. What

does *your* kind do for our young men? They wrap themselves in coats these days up to the eyebrows. And when I
saw one of them in the Pan-Athenian dance,[51] so feeble he let
his shield drop to his haunches, why, I nearly choked – the
insult to our beloved goddess! [*To* PHEIDIPPIDES] So
choose Right, my lad, choose me, you can be sure of success. Keep away from the Market Square, and the public
baths too. Be ashamed when you ought to be ashamed. Turn
bright red when people make fun of you. Stand up when
someone older than you comes in. Respect your parents.
Don't do anything disgraceful or fly in the face of the great
goddess Modesty. Don't run after dancing-girls; you never
know what may happen – suppose some little whore chucks
an apple at you as a come-and-get-me? – your reputation's
gone in an instant. Don't ever contradict your father or call
him an antediluvian; he brought you up before you could
fly by yourself; be grateful.

WRONG: Watch out, lad! If you listen to him, Dionysus
knows, you'll end up just like Hippocrates' sons and be
called a vegetable, and rightly too.

RIGHT: Don't take any notice of him. Spend your time in the
gymnasium – get sleek and healthy. You don't want to be
the sort of chap who's always in the Market Square telling
stories about other people's sex lives, or in the courts
arguing about some piffling quibbling filthy little dispute.
No, you'll run off to Academe's Park and relax under the
sacred olive trees, a wreath of pure white flowers on your
head, with a decent well-mannered companion or two;
[*almost lyrical*] and you'll share the fragrance of leafy poplar
and carefree convolvulus, and the joys of spring, when the
plane tree whispers her love to the elm!

If my sound advice you heed, if you follow where I
    lead,
    You'll be healthy, you'll be strong and you'll be sleek;

You'll have muscles that are thick and a pretty little
   prick –
   You'll be proud of your appearance and physique.

If contrariwise you spurn my society and turn
   To these modern ways, you'll get a pale complexion,
And with two exceptions, all of your limbs will be too
   small –
   The exceptions are the tongue and the e-lection;

You will sing the trendy song, 'Wrong is right and right
   is wrong,
   There's no difference, there's no Justice, there's no
   God',
And you'll catch the current craze for Antimachus'⁵²
   ways –
   Or in plainer language, you'll become a sod.

CHORUS:
   O how sweet are your words and how modest your
   thought!
   How we envy the happiness of those whom you taught!
   [*To* WRONG]
   He impresses us so, we advise you to choose
   Your best armaments verbal, your sexiest Muse.
LEADER:
   Come, Wrong, and set your wits to win this fight
   Against the argument we've heard from Right;
   You'll need the newest weapons of your school,
   Or else you'll be the butt of ridicule.

WRONG: Don't worry, ever since he began his speech I've
been bursting to blow it to bits. That's why the people here
at the Thinkery call me Wrong; I was the one who invented ways of proving anything wrong, laws, prosecutors,
anything. Isn't that worth millions – to be able to have a
really bad case and yet win? Well, let's have a look at this

educational system you're so proud of. We'll dispose of it pretty quickly. For example, you say you won't let him have any hot baths. What have you got against them?

RIGHT [*dogmatically*]: Hot baths cause cowardice.

WRONG: Hold it, I've got you first time, and there's no wriggling away. Tell me, of the sons of Zeus, who would you say was the bravest man and performed the greatest number of labours?

RIGHT: Well, obviously Heracles.

WRONG: And have you ever heard of Heracles having a *cold* bath?[53]

  [RIGHT *is speechless.*]

Well, was he the bravest of them all, or wasn't he?

RIGHT [*spluttering*]: He's – he's – he's just like all the young men! They always say that sort of clever thing, at least they think it's clever, and flock to the public baths and leave the wrestling-schools empty.

WRONG: Then you object to their hanging around the Market Square. Why, don't you know that for Homer the word 'marketeer' is a term of praise – he applies it to Nestor and all his other fountains of wisdom?[54] How can it possibly be a bad thing? And the tongue – you say it's bad for the young to exercise it too much; well, I refute that. And then he talks about modesty or decency or something – another curse of our time! Come on, prove me wrong; tell me of anything good that your modesty or decency has ever done.

RIGHT: Well – that was what got Peleus his knife in the story.[55]

WRONG: A knife! Well, well! What a rich haul, I must say! Even Hyperbolus, the lamp man – yes, I must admit, even if his crimes *have* made him a mint – he never got a knife! Poor fellow!

RIGHT: You know that's not all. It was because of Peleus' virtue that Thetis married him.

WRONG: Yes, and that was why she deserted him as well. If

he'd been a bit less virtuous he might have been a more satisfactory performer under the blankets. Women do *like* a man who shows a bit of imagination in bed, you know, Methuselah! [*To* PHEIDIPPIDES] Listen to all the things that virtue can't do for you, my lad – all the pleasures you'll forfeit. No boys. No women. No gambling. No fancy stuff to eat. No booze. No belly laughs. Could you live without all these? [PHEIDIPPIDES *shakes his head.*] I thought not. Let me turn now to – to the demands of Nature. Suppose you fall in love with a married woman – have a bit of fun – and get caught in the act. As you are now, without a tongue in your head, you're done for. But if you come and learn from me, then you can do what you like and get away with it – indulge your desires, laugh and play, have no shame. And then supposing you do get caught with somebody's wife, you can say to him, cool as a cucumber, 'What have I done wrong? Look at Zeus; wasn't he always the slave of his passions, sexwise? And do you expect a mere mortal like me to do any better than a god?'

RIGHT: Ah, but suppose the man doesn't take any notice? Suppose he starts applying the carrot and ashes treatment? Then you'll have bugger's arse for the rest of your life. [*To* WRONG] Get out of that one, clever guy!

WRONG: Why, what is there to get out of?

RIGHT: Well, I mean, being taken for a bugger – what could be worse than that?

WRONG: Suppose I prove you wrong about this, will you admit defeat?

RIGHT: Certainly I will – if you can.

WRONG: Very well then. Not to use your crude language – would you say our advocates, for example, are, or are not, on the whole, well, gay?

RIGHT: Yes, they are.

WRONG: I agree with you. And our poets – tragic ones, I mean, of course?

RIGHT: Yes, they're – gay too.

WRONG: Right again. What about our politicians?

RIGHT: Them too.

WRONG: Then don't you see you were talking nonsense? Why, look at the audience; what do you think most of them are?

RIGHT: I'm looking.

WRONG: And what do you see?

RIGHT: Good gods, the bug – the gay ones have it! At least, I know *he* is [*pointing*] and him, and him there with the long hair. Heavens, they're almost *all* gay!

WRONG: Well then?

RIGHT: You win. [*To the audience*] Hey, you sods out there! I'm deserting – I'm going over to your side – [*throws his coat at* STREPSIADES *and* PHEIDIPPIDES] here, for the gods' sake, take this, will you? [*Rushes off the stage and accidentally-on-purpose lands in the arms of one of the gentlemen he has just pointed out.*]

WRONG [*to* STREPSIADES]: Well, now, which do you want – shall I take your son, or do you want to be taught yourself?

STREPSIADES: Oh, teach him – give him a bit of stick, he could do with it – but in any case, make sure you give his teeth a good cutting edge. I want him to be able to get a snap victory in a small case or two with the left side of his mouth and leave the right side free for the bigger ones.

WRONG: All right; I promise you, when you get him back, he'll be a real genius.

PHEIDIPPIDES: All I know is I'll be a real bloody paleface.

CHORUS [*as* WRONG *leads* PHEIDIPPIDES *into the school and* STREPSIADES *turns towards his house*]:
    Farewell; [*to* STREPSIADES] but I divine that soon
    You'll sing a less ecstatic tune.
    You've sowed the wind, and we can see
    Your harvest will the whirlwind be.

[STREPSIADES, *taking no notice, dances into his house in an
ecstasy of joy. The* LEADER *watches him till he is out of sight,
then advances and addresses the audience.*]

We would like to tell you, judges, of the blessings we'll
accord

Those who give to both this chorus and this play their
just reward.

If you want to put the ploughshare to some fallow land
you've got,

Then we'll see that even in time of drought there's rain
upon your plot.

If you keep a vineyard, we'll protect it from the double
bane

Both of soaking with too much and parching with too
little rain.

But if any mortal treats the Clouds of heaven with
despite,

We have power to reduce him to a miserable plight;

Both his olives and his vines and all his other crops will
fail:

From our powerful slings we'll smite them with those
missiles you call hail,

Which we'll also do in case he builds a house: we'll give
him proof

Of our anger by destroying every tile upon his roof.

And if he should give a wedding for a friend or a relation,

We will ruin the festivities with our precipitation:

Then just watch him as he beats his breast and penitently
sighs

'Would to heaven I were in Egypt[56] – or had given *The
Clouds* first prize!'

ACT TWO

SCENE: *The same.*

[*Enter* STREPSIADES, *from his house, anxiously counting the days on his fingers.*]

STREPSIADES: Twenty-sixth, twenty-seventh, twenty-eighth, twenty-ninth – four more days before it comes to that day I fear and hate above all others, the last day of the month, 'Old and New'![57] All my creditors have taken the oath, paid their deposits into court, and now say they're going to get me. I ask them for a reasonable little favour or two – 'Please don't call the loan in now' – 'Give me some more time' – 'Couldn't we forget it?' – and so on – but they all say that's not their idea of getting paid and call me a villain and say they'll sue. [*Changing his mood*] Well, let them. If Pheidippides has been properly taught, they can't hurt me. I'll soon know if he has been. [*Knocking on the school door.*] Boy! Here, I say! Boy! [*As he delivers another thunderous knock* SOCRATES *opens the door and* STREPSIADES *falls flat on his face.*]

SOCRATES [*helping him to his feet*]: Glad to see you, Strepsiades.

STREPSIADES: Same to you. [*Producing a tattered tunic*] I wonder if you'd accept this? Just as a token of my appreciation. But my son – has he learnt that Argument we were listening to a moment ago?

SOCRATES: Yes, he has.

STREPSIADES: Holy Fraud, how wonderful!

SOCRATES: Yes, you'll be able now to win any case at all.

STREPSIADES: Even if the witnesses were actually there when I was borrowing the money?

SOCRATES: Even if there were a thousand of them.

STREPSIADES [*adopting a tragic pose*]:
> Then raise aloft the cry of long-sought joy!
> I triumph! Weep, ye moneylenders, weep,
> Yourselves, your capital, and your interest's interest!
> No longer can ye work on me your mischief,
> Such is the son that's reared within my house,
> A shining star wielding a two-edged tongue,
> My shield and guardian, saviour of my fortunes,
> Bane of my foes, disperser of my griefs!
> Run, run, and bring him forth from out thy halls.
> [SOCRATES *goes into the school.*]
> Thy father calls, beloved son; appear.

SOCRATES [*re-emerging with* PHEIDIPPIDES]:[58]
>   Behold your offspring.

STREPSIADES: Beloved boy!

SOCRATES: Good-bye and thank you.

STREPSIADES [*dancing, embracing his son, etc.*]:
>   Unmingled joy!
> [SOCRATES *goes into the school.* STREPSIADES *has a good
> look at* PHEIDIPPIDES *and lets out a cry of rapture.*]

STREPSIADES: What a gorgeous complexion, son! You've got 'Not guilty' written all over your face – and your cheeks have that special Athenian bloom – grows nowhere else – the did-you-really-mean-that. I can see injured innocence shining out next time you're caught red-handed! Now at last you can be some use to your old father. You were his ruin; now be his salvation.

PHEIDIPPIDES: Why, what are you afraid of?

STREPSIADES: The last day of the month – Old and New.

PHEIDIPPIDES [*with mock naivety*]: What, you mean there's a day that's (a) old and (b) new?

STREPSIADES: Of course there is – and that's when everyone says they're going to pay their deposits into court.

PHEIDIPPIDES: Well, they're going to lose their money. It's not possible for one day to be two days.

STREPSIADES: How not possible?

PHEIDIPPIDES: Not unless it's possible for the same woman to be (a) old and (b) young at the same time.

STREPSIADES: Still, that's what the law says – to put down the deposits on the Old and New.

PHEIDIPPIDES: Ah, you see, people don't understand what the law is aimed at.

STREPSIADES: Well, what is it aimed at?

PHEIDIPPIDES: Well, our lawgiver Solon was a good democrat, right?

STREPSIADES: Yes, but I don't see what that has to do with the Old and New.

PHEIDIPPIDES: So he fixed the summonses for *two* days – the Old, you see, and the New – with the intention that the deposits should be put in on the second of those days – that is, the *New* Moon – the first of the month.

STREPSIADES: Well, in that case, why mention the Old at all?

PHEIDIPPIDES: To give the defendant a day to reach a settlement; then if he failed he could always get a stomach-ache or something on the morning of the New Moon.

STREPSIADES [*still not convinced*]: Then why on earth don't the magistrates accept the deposits on the New Moon? They only take them on the day before.

PHEIDIPPIDES: They're acting like the people who taste the food for festivals. They always do that on the day before the festival starts, right? So the magistrates, in order to make away with as much of the deposit money as possible – as quickly as possible –

STREPSIADES: I see! Here [*to the audience*], why are you poor blighters out there just sitting like stones, not even laughing? Ah, they're just fodder for us clever ones – we can treat them like sheep. But I do wish they wouldn't be quite such a heap of earthenware. Well, anyway, the two of us have never had it so good, and I think someone ought to write a song about it. Like this.

> 'How happy is Strepsiades,
>> How wondrous wise his sonny!'
> So all will say when your brave tongue
>> Has saved for me my money.

Come home. This is an occasion to celebrate! [*They go into* STREPSIADES' *house.*]

[*Enter* FIRST CREDITOR *and* WITNESS.]

FIRST CREDITOR: Why should anyone want to make a loan? Better to harden one's heart at the outset rather than have all this trouble afterwards. Here I am, having to drag you into my problems because I need a witness, and having to make an enemy in my own deme. Well, I must not put Athens to shame. [*Knocks*] Strepsiades!

STREPSIADES [*coming out*]: Who's there?

FIRST CREDITOR: I summon you to appear in court on the Old and New.

STREPSIADES: Witness everybody, that he named *two* days. – What about?

FIRST CREDITOR: The twelve hundred drachmas you borrowed to buy the ash-coloured horse.

STREPSIADES: Horse! Hark at that! And me that hates everything to do with horses!

FIRST CREDITOR: You know you borrowed it, and you gave an oath that you would pay.

STREPSIADES: Ah, well, that was before Pheidippides had learnt his invincible Argument.

FIRST CREDITOR: And now he has, you intend to refuse to pay?

STREPSIADES: Well, you don't think I sent him to school for nothing, do you?

FIRST CREDITOR: Are you prepared to swear by the gods, in a place of my choice, that you do not owe me the money?

STREPSIADES: Swear by which gods?

FIRST CREDITOR: Zeus, Hermes and Poseidon.

STREPSIADES: Delighted. I'd give you three obols to be allowed to.

FIRST CREDITOR [*purple-faced*]: Well, of all the shameless –!

STREPSIADES [*poking him in the stomach*]: You know, you'd make quite a good wine-skin if we salted you.

FIRST CREDITOR: I'll –

STREPSIADES: Four gallons it would hold, I think.

FIRST CREDITOR: By Zeus and all the gods, you'll pay for this.

STREPSIADES [*feigning uncontrollable laughter*]: Oh, oh, the gods – and Zeus – ! How funny the way you swear – for those of us in the know!

FIRST CREDITOR: You'll pay for this, never fear. And I'm not going till you tell me whether I can expect to get my money back.

STREPSIADES: Wait a moment and I'll tell you. [*Goes into the house.*]

FIRST CREDITOR [*to* WITNESS]: What do you think he's going to do? Pay, or what?

STREPSIADES [*returning with a kneading-trough*]: Where's the man who was demanding that money from me? [*To* FIRST CREDITOR] Look, what's this?

FIRST CREDITOR: That? A trough, of course.

STREPSIADES: And an ignorant person like you dares to ask me for money? Do you expect me to pay so much as an obol to someone who thinks a triffen is called a trough?

FIRST CREDITOR: So you're not going to pay?

STREPSIADES: You'll have to steal it if you want it. Now clear off, will you? Get away from my door! Hurry up!

FIRST CREDITOR: All right, I'm going. But let me tell you, I'm going to see you in court or be damned.

STREPSIADES [*as* FIRST CREDITOR *and* WITNESS *leave*]: Then you'll lose your deposit as well; and I wouldn't like that to happen to you just because you didn't know what to call a triffen.

[*Enter* SECOND CREDITOR, *dusty, with a limp.*]

SECOND CREDITOR: Alas! Alas!

STREPSIADES: Who's this singing laments? Not one of Carcinus' gods,[59] is it?

SECOND CREDITOR:
    Why wishest thou to know who I may be?
    I am a man of sorrows.

STREPSIADES: Well, keep them to yourself – I don't want to catch them.

SECOND CREDITOR:
    O cruel goddess, O my chariot smashed!
    Pallas, thou hast destroyed me utterly.[60]

STREPSIADES: Why, what has Tlepolemus ever done you wrong?

SECOND CREDITOR:
    Mock not at me, but bid thy son repay
    The cash he borrowed of me, as is just
    Especially in my present low estate.

STREPSIADES: What's all this about money?

SECOND CREDITOR: The money, I tell you, the money he borrowed.

STREPSIADES [*in mock sympathy*]: You *are* in a bad way.

SECOND CREDITOR: Yes, by the gods, I fell off my chariot.

STREPSIADES: The way you blether suggests what you fell off was the proverbial donkey.[61]

SECOND CREDITOR: Blether?! All I want is my money.

STREPSIADES: I'm sure you're ill. Had your brain shaken up, probably.

SECOND CREDITOR: *I'm* sure, by Hermes, that I'll sue if you don't pay.

STREPSIADES: Tell me now: do you think that when Zeus

rains, it's new rain every time, or do you think the sun sucks up water from the ground so that he can use it again?

SECOND CREDITOR: I don't know and I don't care.

STREPSIADES: What right have you to be paid, if you don't know any meteorology?

SECOND CREDITOR: Are you short of cash? If you are, I'll be satisfied with the interest for the time being.

STREPSIADES [*innocently*]: Interest? Could you tell me what that is?

SECOND CREDITOR: Why – it's simply – the fact that – well, if somebody owes you money, the debt keeps growing and growing, month by month, day by day, as time runs on.

STREPSIADES: Quite right. Now then: do you think the sea has any more water in it now than it used to?

SECOND CREDITOR: No, it's the same size; there would be something wrong if it wasn't.

STREPSIADES: Well, then, if the sea doesn't get any bigger as the rivers run into it, what business have you pretending that money grows as time runs on, or whatever you said? Go and chase yourself! Get out of my sight! Boy! fetch me a goad.

[*A slave runs and brings him one.*]

SECOND CREDITOR [*as* STREPSIADES *pricks him with the goad*]: Assault! Help! Witness, somebody!

STREPSIADES [*continuing to ply the goad*]: Gee up! What are you waiting for? Get along there, you gelding!

SECOND CREDITOR: Assault! And battery! Help!

STREPSIADES: Move! Move! Or else I'll stick this up your thoroughbred arse!

[*The* CREDITOR *takes to his heels.*]

Yes, I thought I'd get rid of you that way – you and your chariots and wheels and all.

[STREPSIADES *goes in, in a feasting mood. A short pause; then the music of the* CHORUS's *entrance-song is heard again, and they sing solemnly.*]

CHORUS:

> Is he not in love with evil?
>   See the way he tries to cheat
> Honest men who've lent him money –
>   This he thinks a noble feat!
>
> But before this day is ended
>   He will sure be made distraught,
> And will make the great Professor
>   Rue the wickedness he taught.
>
> For his son's a rhetorician
>   (Which is what his dad desired)
> Armed with Wrong to vanquish every
>   Argument by Right inspired.
>
> Brief, Strepsiades, the season
>   Fate allows you to rejoice:
> Soon, yea, soon you will be praying
>   For your son to lose his voice.

[*Sounds of heated argument from the house, followed by a yell.* STREPSIADES *rushes out clutching his face and in extreme agitation;* PHEIDIPPIDES *follows him, looking totally unconcerned.*]

STREPSIADES: Help, neighbours! Help, cousins! Help, Cicynnians! I'm being assaulted! Rescue me! Zeus, my head! And look what he's done to my cheeks! [*To* PHEIDIPPIDES] You abominable villain, do you realize what you're doing hitting your father?

PHEIDIPPIDES: Yes, I do.

STREPSIADES [*to the* CHORUS]: Do you hear him? He admits it!

PHEIDIPPIDES: Of course I do.

STREPSIADES: You're a disgusting young criminal.

PHEIDIPPIDES: More, more! I love being called that sort of thing.

STREPSIADES [*after a moment's thought*]: Sack-arse!!!

PHEIDIPPIDES: I do like these compliments.

STREPSIADES [*baffled*]: How dare you hit your father?

PHEIDIPPIDES: I was perfectly justified, and by Zeus, I'll prove it to you.

STREPSIADES: Justified! Hitting your father justified!

PHEIDIPPIDES: You argue your case, I'll argue mine, and I'll guarantee to prove it.

STREPSIADES: Prove it? Prove you're right to – ?

PHEIDIPPIDES: Easily. Now which of the Arguments do you want?

STREPSIADES: Arguments? What Arguments?

PHEIDIPPIDES: Forgotten already? Do you want Right or Wrong?

STREPSIADES: Well – if you can prove that it's right for a son to hit his father – then you certainly have been taught to defeat a just claim, as *I* wanted you to be. Hah!

PHEIDIPPIDES: I will all right, never mind; when you've heard me you won't have a word to utter against me.

STREPSIADES: I'll be very interested to hear what you have to say!

CHORUS:
    Search hard for ways this argument to win.
        The facts compel us to believe
        The boy has something up his sleeve:
    Observe the shameless frame of mind he's in!

LEADER:
    Come, tell us what contention this domestic strife
        upwhipped.
    – Of course, you know your cue comes here, you saw it
        in the script.

STREPSIADES: I'll explain right from the start, how it all began. You know I'd made a big dinner. Well, afterwards I just asked my son to take his lyre and sing something by Simonides – I asked for 'The Fleecing of Lamb-achus'.[62]

And straight away, would you believe it, he says, 'That's so out of date – playing a lyre and singing while people are drinking – what do you think we're doing, grinding corn or something?'

PHEIDIPPIDES: And quite right too. I should have given you one right then and there, and I don't mean a song either. Telling me to sing! – who did you think you were entertaining, a gang of crickets?

STREPSIADES: Do you hear him? That's the sort of thing he was saying at the time – 'and Simonides is a rotten poet anyway', he added. Well, I could barely restrain myself – but I did. I asked him if he would at least take a myrtle branch in his hand⁶³ and recite some Aeschylus for me. That started him off again – 'Oh, Aeschylus is a prince among poets, to be sure – a prince of hot air and barbarous bombast. He doesn't use words, he uses bloody mountains.' Well, by this time he was making me shake all over, and my heart was thumping. But I bit my lip hard and said 'All right, you win. Give us something from one of your clever modern chaps.' So he launched straight into a speech by Euripides, something about a man, the gods preserve us, a man sleeping with his sister – his sister on both sides!⁶⁴ Well, I couldn't bear it any longer. I pitched into him, called him all sorts of things. Then, you know what happens, we started throwing names at each other. And in the end he jumps up and starts giving me a dusting, choking me, punching me, you name it, he did it.

PHEIDIPPIDES: And you deserved it. Carping at Euripides! He's a genius!

STREPSIADES: A genius? What do you mean, you – I'd better not say it, I'll only be hit again.

PHEIDIPPIDES [*unrelenting*]: And you'll deserve it again, by Zeus.

STREPSIADES: Deserve it indeed! Who was it brought you up from a baby, you impudent child? [*Softening with reminis-*

cence] I always understood from your babbling what it was
you wanted. You had only to say 'broo' and I understood
and gave you something to drink. When you cried 'mam-
ma', there I'd be with a bit of bread. And the moment you
said 'kakka', I'd grab you, take you outside, and hold you
out where you could shit without messing the house up.
[*Becoming wrathful again with another reminiscence*] And now
what do you do, curse you? When you were throttling me,
didn't I yell 'Here, watch it, I want to crap'? And did you
take me outside? No, you just kept choking me, and then
yelled at *me* because I did a kakka on the spot!

CHORUS:
>   We're all agog to hear the other side.
>   For if he proves it wasn't bad
>   For him to suffocate his dad,
>   Soon all young men will flay their elders' hide.

LEADER:
>   It's up to you, the modernist, to use your youthful
>   thrust
>   To manage to persuade us that the things you did were
>   just.

PHEIDIPPIDES: It's delightful to be acquainted with the wisdom of today, and be able to look down on convention. Do
you know, there was a time when I thought about nothing
but horses, and in those days I couldn't say three words
together that made sense. But now my father has made sure
that's all behind me. I'm intimate with all the new ideas and
arguments, I can dance on the point of a needle. And I can
prove that it's right for me to punish my father.

STREPSIADES: I wish you'd go back to your horses. Better for
me you kept four of the damn things, rather than use your
surplus energy hitting me.

PHEIDIPPIDES: As I was saying before I was so rudely interrupted – yes, I want to ask you a question or two. When
I was a child, did you hit me?

STREPSIADES: Yes, of course I did – for your good – because I loved you.

PHEIDIPPIDES: Very well. You hit me for my good. Therefore, if it's for one's good to be hit, it was right for me to take thought for *your* good and hit you. Why should you be immune from being hit, when I'm not? I'm a free man, just like you. As Euripides forgot to say, 'The son gets thumped, do you think the father shouldn't?'⁶⁵ You'll say, I know, that it's the universal practice that only children should be beaten. But I should remind you that it is also universally agreed that old age is second childhood. In fact, seeing one expects a higher standard of behaviour from the old than the young, it's only right that they should be more severely punished when they fall short.

STREPSIADES: But look at the laws! Can you name a city where the law allows you to do this to your father?

PHEIDIPPIDES: But what is a law anyway? It must have been made at some time, and made by a man just like you or me; and he must have persuaded his people by argument to accept it. Why shouldn't I now make a new law allowing sons to beat their fathers in return? I'll be generous; the times we boys got hit before the law was changed, we'll renounce all claim to compensation for them. You can treat them as a free gift. And again, look at chickens and so on. They actually fight their fathers. And what difference is there between them and us, except that they don't move resolutions?

STREPSIADES: Well, if you're so keen on a chicken's life, why don't you go the whole hog? Why don't you eat manure and sleep in a henhouse?

PHEIDIPPIDES: It's not the same thing, silly. Not according to Socrates it isn't.

STREPSIADES: Well, in that case you'd better not hit me. If you do you'll live to regret it.

PHEIDIPPIDES: Never!

STREPSIADES: Oh yes, you will. I've got the right to beat you now; but one day you may have a son, and you'll have the right to beat him, and what will you say if he quotes your new law against you?

PHEIDIPPIDES: That's all very well; but supposing I don't have a son? I'll have been thumped already, and won't be able to hit *anybody* back – and you'll be laughing all over your dead face!

STREPSIADES [*to a group of elderly men in the audience*]: I think he's right, you know, old chaps, I think he's got a point. It's only reasonable that if we do wrong we should suffer for it.

PHEIDIPPIDES: Here's another point.

STREPSIADES: I've had enough of them. Any more and I'll most likely be dead.

PHEIDIPPIDES: Oh, I don't know. All this may hurt you less than you think.

STREPSIADES: Why, what possible good can I get out of this behaviour of yours?

PHEIDIPPIDES: Easy. Mum's next on the list for bashing.

STREPSIADES: What?! This is really too much!

PHEIDIPPIDES: Suppose I prove to you, with the help of my invincible Argument, that it's right to hit one's mother as well? If I do that, what will you do?

STREPSIADES: If you do that, I'll be very happy to let you throw yourself off the Acropolis. And you can take Socrates and that precious Argument of yours with you. [*To the* CHORUS] Clouds, this is your fault. I put my all in your hands, and this is what you've done to me.

LEADER:
No, not our fault: you brought it on yourself,
By making love to evil crookery.

STREPSIADES: But why didn't you tell me at the time? You know I'm only a countryman, and an old man too. Why did you deceive me?

LEADER:

    We do the same to everyone we see
    Surrender to seductive wickedness,
    Bringing him to disaster, so that he
    May learn that Heaven's laws must be obeyed.

STREPSIADES: Ah, holy Clouds, your verdict's hard but just. I shouldn't have tried to cheat my creditors out of their money. You're right. [*To* PHEIDIPPIDES] My dear, dear son – come with me and let's get that bloody Chaerephon and Socrates for diddling us.

PHEIDIPPIDES: What! – show disrespect to my teacher?

STREPSIADES: Aye, aye: revere the great paternal Zeus.

PHEIDIPPIDES: Zeus! Where have you been all these years? Does Zeus exist?

STREPSIADES [*defiantly*]: He does.

PHEIDIPPIDES: No, he doesn't. Awhirl is king now; he's driven Zeus into exile.

STREPSIADES: That he hasn't. I only believed that because those damn thinkers set my mind awhirl.[66] Good gods – a brainstorm I had – and I actually worshipped it!

PHEIDIPPIDES: I can't be bothered any longer with your blethering. [*Goes into the house.*]

STREPSIADES: How mad I was! I let Socrates persuade me to deny the gods! [*Addressing the statue of Hermes on a pillar outside his house*] Hermes, don't be cross with me. Don't destroy me. Forgive me – I was demented, I listened to too much blether. Give me some advice. Should I prosecute them, or what do you think? [*Pretending to see the statue indicating dissent*] You're right. I shouldn't have thought of trying to trip them in the courts. I'll go right off and burn the blighters' school. Xanthias!

    [XANTHIAS, *one of* STREPSIADES' *slaves, appears.*]
Fetch a ladder and a mattock, and come with me! And somebody bring a lighted torch!

    [XANTHIAS *and another* SLAVE *bring the articles requested.*]

Now, Xanthias [*pointing to the roof of the Thinkery*], get up there and take his roof off, if you love your master! Or better, throw it down on top of them!

[XANTHIAS *sets up the ladder, climbs on to the roof and gets to work.*]

Give me the torch; I'll make them pay for what they've done; not all their verbal wizardry will save them! [*He goes up the ladder. By now* XANTHIAS *has laid the roof-beams bare, and* STREPSIADES *proceeds to apply the torch to them.*]

FIRST STUDENT [*from inside*]: Hey! Hey! Help! Help!

STREPSIADES [*on the roof*]: Do your job, torch!

[CHAEREPHON *puts his head out of the school door. He is as white as a sheet, with enormous eyes, as if he has never seen daylight.*]

CHAEREPHON: What in heaven's name do you think you're doing?

STREPSIADES: Doing? Having an intellectual discussion with your roof-beams, of course.

SECOND STUDENT [*rushing out*]: Help! Who's burning our house?

STREPSIADES: Remember the last coat you pinched? That's who.

SECOND STUDENT: You'll burn us all alive!

STREPSIADES: That's just what I want to do – if my tools don't fail me, and if I [*looking apprehensively over his shoulder*] don't fall off and break my neck first.

SOCRATES [*coming out slowly and with dignity*]: You there on the roof, what are you doing?

STREPSIADES [*mimicking him*]: I am walking upon air and attacking the mystery of the sun.

SOCRATES [*coughing in the smoke*]: Help, I'm going to suffocate!

CHAEREPHON [*who is still inside*]: Help, I'm being prematurely cremated!

[CHAEREPHON *and all the* STUDENTS *rush out of the school, and stand for a moment bewildered.*]

STREPSIADES [*descending the ladder, followed by* XANTHIAS]: No more than you deserved; people who cock snooks at the gods and argue about the back side of the moon must pay for it. [*Kicks* SOCRATES *in the backside.*] On them! Stones!

[SOCRATES *and the rest take flight.* STREPSIADES *and his* SLAVES *pursue them with a volley of stones,* STREPSIADES *shouting*]

Revenge! Revenge for the injured gods! Remember what they did! Revenge!

[*He continues shouting until he and the pursuers as well as the pursued have disappeared.*]

[*The* LEADER *waits to see if anyone else is going to appear, then turns to her colleagues.*]

LEADER:
        Let's go: I think it's not unfair to say
        Our choral work has not been bad today.
[*The* CHORUS *files out.*]

Lysistrata

or

The Flight of the Swallows

Introductory Note to *Lysistrata*

The Acharnians is an appeal for peace. *Peace*, produced four years later, is a celebration of peace; for negotiations were nearing completion, and the Peace of Nicias, delusive end of a ten years' war, was concluded only a few days after the play was performed. *Lysistrata* is the third and last of Aristophanes' peace plays that we possess; it has much in common with the other two, but its spirit is different from either of them. It is a dream about peace, conceived at a time when Athens was going through the blackest, most desperate crisis she had known since the Persian War.

Late in 413 B.C. the news reached Athens of the total destruction of their expeditionary force in Sicily. They had no navy and, it seemed, no hope. Sparta had already occupied the strong point of Decelea in Attica, and the Athenians daily expected her naval forces, or those of Syracuse, to appear before the Piraeus; and Athens' subject allies (with some exceptions, notably Carystus in Euboea) seized the opportunity of changing sides.

But, as so often before, Athens reacted to disaster with energy, and Sparta squandered a victory by stupidity. No naval attack on the Piraeus was ever made, and meanwhile the Athenians built a whole new navy. For this they made use of the special reserve set aside twenty years before as an emergency naval fund and kept in one of the temples on the Acropolis. Moreover, feeling that the democracy needed to be protected from its own rash decisions, they set up a 'Committee of Ten for the Safety of the State' (the *probouloi*) who appear to have virtually taken over the functions of the democratic Council (though the latter continued to meet, and probably took the decisions and prepared the agenda for the Assembly in name but not in fact).

Lysistrata was produced at the beginning of 411. A year had passed since the disaster; but nothing had yet happened to raise any hopes of an honourable end to the war. Aristophanes had never been an advocate of peace at any price. Any peace must be satisfactory to both sides; and, in this play, the women of both sides have to cooperate in bringing it about. The play is not a plea to the Athenians to end the war. At the beginning of 411 they would not have been able to end it on tolerable terms. The idea is more like this: 'How on earth could this war be brought to an end, with honour satisfied on all sides? Well, suppose the women . . .'

It is striking that the play ends with two songs in praise of Sparta (which musically, as dialectally, is represented in this translation by Scotland). It says much for the archon's good sense and tolerance that he allowed it to be produced in this form. It could, of course, be that he was himself secretly pro-Spartan.

CHARACTERS

LYSISTRATA
CALONICE } *Athenian women*
MYRRHINE
LAMPITO *a Spartan woman*
CHORUS OF OLD MEN
CHORUS OF OLD WOMEN
STRATYLLIS *leader of the Women's Chorus*
A MAGISTRATE *member of the Committee of Ten for the Safety of the State*
FIVE YOUNG WOMEN
CINESIAS *husband to Myrrhine*
BABY *son to Cinesias and Myrrhine*
A SPARTAN HERALD
A SPARTAN AMBASSADOR
AN ATHENIAN NEGOTIATOR
TWO LAYABOUTS
DOORKEEPER *of the Acropolis*
TWO DINERS

ISMENIA *a Boeotian woman*
A CORINTHIAN WOMAN
RECONCILIATION *maidservant to Lysistrata*
FOUR SCYTHIAN POLICEMEN
A SCYTHIAN POLICEWOMAN
ATHENIAN CITIZENS, SPARTAN AMBASSADORS, ATHENIAN AND SPARTAN WOMEN, SLAVES, *etc.*

ACT ONE

SCENE: *In front of the entrance to the Athenian Acropolis. At the back of the stage stands the Great Gateway (the Propylaea); to the right, a stretch of the Acropolis wall with a little shrine to Athena Niké (Victory) built into it; to the left, a statue of the tyrannicides Harmodius and Aristogeiton. It is early morning.*

[LYSISTRATA *is standing in front of the Propylaea looking, with increasing impatience, to see if anyone is coming.*]

LYSISTRATA [*stamping her foot and bursting into impatient speech*]: Just think if it had been a Bacchic celebration they'd been asked to attend – or something in honour of Pan or Aphrodite – particularly Aphrodite! You wouldn't have been able to move for all the drums.[1] And now look – not a woman here!

[*Enter* CALONICE.]

Ah! here's one at last. One of my neighbours, I – Why, hello, Calonice.

CALONICE: Hello, Lysistrata. What's bothering you, dear? Don't screw up your face like that. It really doesn't suit you, you know, knitting your eyebrows up like a bow or something.

LYSISTRATA: Sorry, Calonice, but I'm furious. I'm disappointed in womankind. All our husbands think we're such clever villains –

CALONICE: Well, aren't we?

LYSISTRATA: And here I've called a meeting to discuss a very important matter, and they're all still fast asleep!

CALONICE: Don't worry, dear, they'll come. It's not so easy

for a wife to get out of the house, you know. They'll all be rushing to and fro for their husbands, waking up the servants, putting the baby to bed or washing and feeding it –

LYSISTRATA: Damn it, there are more important things than that!

CALONICE: Tell me, Lysistrata dear, what is it you've summoned this meeting of the women for? Is it something big?

LYSISTRATA: Very.

CALONICE [*thinking she detects a significant intonation in that word*]: Not thick as well?

LYSISTRATA: As a matter of fact, yes.

CALONICE: Then why on earth aren't they here?

LYSISTRATA [*realizing she has been misleading*]: No, not that kind of thing – well, not exactly. If it had been, I can assure you, they'd have been here as quick as you can bat an eyelid. No, I've had an idea, which for many sleepless nights I've been tossing to and fro –

CALONICE: Must be a pretty flimsy one, in that case.

LYSISTRATA: Flimsy? Calonice, we women have the salvation of Greece in our hands.

CALONICE: In our hands? We might as well give up hope, then.

LYSISTRATA: The whole future of the City is up to us. Either the Peloponnesians are all going to be wiped out –

CALONICE: Good idea, by Zeus!

LYSISTRATA: – and the Boeotians be destroyed too –

CALONICE: Not all of them, please! Do spare the eels.[2]

LYSISTRATA: – and Athens – well, I won't say it, but you know what might happen. But if all the women join together – not just us, but the Peloponnesians and Boeotians as well – then we can save Greece.

CALONICE: The women! – what could they ever do that was any use? Sitting at home putting flowers in their hair, putting on cosmetics and saffron gowns and Cimberian see-through shifts, with slippers on our feet?

LYSISTRATA: But don't you see, that's exactly what I mean to use to save Greece. Those saffron gowns and slippers and see-through dresses, yes, and our scent and rouge as well.

CALONICE: How are you going to do that?

LYSISTRATA: I am going to bring it about that the men will no longer lift up their spears against one another –

CALONICE: I'm going to get some new dye on my yellow gown!

LYSISTRATA: – nor take up their shields –

CALONICE: I'll put on a see-through right away!

LYSISTRATA: – or their swords.

CALONICE: Slippers, here I come!

LYSISTRATA: *Now* do you think the women ought to be here by now?

CALONICE: By Zeus, yes – they ought to have taken wing and flown here.

LYSISTRATA: No such luck, old girl; what do you expect? – they're Athenian, and everything they do too late. But really – for nobody to have come at all! None from the Paralia, none of the Salaminians[3] –

CALONICE: Oh, they'll have been on the go since the small hours. [*Aside*] They probably will too.[4]

LYSISTRATA: And the ones I was most counting on being here first – the Acharnians – they haven't come either.

CALONICE: Well, as to that, I did see Theagenes' wife consulting the shrine of Hecate in front of her door,[5] so I imagine she's going to come.

[*Enter, from various directions,* MYRRHINE *and other women.*] Ah, here are some coming – and here are some more. Ugh! [*puckering up her nose*] where do this lot come from?

LYSISTRATA: Ponchidae.[6]

CALONICE: I can well believe it!

MYRRHINE [*a little out of breath*]: We're not late, are we, Lysistrata?

[LYSISTRATA *frowns and says nothing.*]

Well? Why aren't you saying anything?

LYSISTRATA: Myrrhine, I don't think much of people who come this late when such an important matter is to be discussed.

MYRRHINE [*lamely*]: Well, I had some difficulty finding my girdle in the dark. If it is so important, don't let's wait for the rest; tell us about it now.

LYSISTRATA: Let's just wait a moment. The Boeotian and Peloponnesian women should be here any time now.

MYRRHINE: Good idea. Ah, here comes Lampito!

[*Enter* LAMPITO, *with several other Spartan women, their dresses fringed at the bottom with sheepskin, and with representatives from Corinth and Boeotia.*]

LYSISTRATA: Welcome, Lampito, my dear. How are things in Sparta? Darling, you look simply beautiful. Such colour, such resilience! Why, I bet you could throttle a bull.

LAMPITO: Sae cuid you, my dear, if ye were in training. Dinna ken, I practise rump-jumps every day.

LYSISTRATA [*prodding her*]: And such marvellous tits, too.

LAMPITO [*indignantly*]: I'd thank ye not tae treat me as though ye were just aboot tae sacrifice me.[7]

LYSISTRATA: Where's this other girl come from?

LAMPITO [*presenting* ISMENIA]: By the Twa Gudes,[8] this is the Boeotian Ambassadress that's come tae ye.

LYSISTRATA [*inspecting* ISMENIA]: I should have known – look what a fertile vale she's got there!

CALONICE: Yes, and with all the grass so beautifully cropped, too!

LYSISTRATA: And this one?

LAMPITO: Och, she's a braw bonny lass – a Corinthian.

CALONICE: Yes, I can see why you call her that! [*indicating a prominent part of the Corinthian's person*].

LAMPITO: Who's the convener of this female assembly?

LYSISTRATA: I am.

LAMPITO: Then tell us the noo what ye have tae say.

MYRRHINE: Yes, dear, tell us what this important business is.

LYSISTRATA: I will tell you. But before I do, I want to ask you just one little question.

MYRRHINE: By all means.

LYSISTRATA: The fathers of your children – don't you miss them when they're away at the war? I know not one of you has a husband at home.

CALONICE: I know, my dear. My husband has been away for five months, five months, my dear, in Thrace I think, keeping an eye on our general there.[9]

MYRRHINE: And mine has been in Pylos[10] for the last seven months.

LAMPITO: And as for my mon, if he ever turns up at home, it's anely to pit a new strap on his shield and fly off again.

LYSISTRATA: That's what it's like. There isn't anyone even to have an affair with – not a sausage! Talking of which, now the Milesians have rebelled, we can't even get our six-inch Ladies' Comforters which we used to keep as leather rations for when all else failed. Well then, if I found a way to do it, would you be prepared to join with me in stopping the war?

MYRRHINE: By the Holy Twain,[11] I would! Even if I had to take off my cloak this very day and – drink!

CALONICE: And so would I – even if I had to cut myself in two, like a flatfish, and give half of myself for the cause.

LAMPITO: And I too, if I had tae climb tae the top o' Taygetus,[12] so I cuid see the licht o' peace whenas I got there.

LYSISTRATA: Then I will tell you my plan: there is no need to keep it back. Ladies, if we want to force our husbands to make peace, we must give up – [*She hesitates.*]

CALONICE: What must we give up? Go on.

LYSISTRATA: Then you'll do it?

CALONICE: If need be, we'll lay down our lives for it.

LYSISTRATA: Very well then. We must give up – sex.

[*Strong murmurs of disapproval, shaking of heads, etc. Several of the company begin to walk off.*]

Why are you turning away from me? Where are you going?
What's all this pursing of lips and shaking of heads mean?
You're all going pale – I can see tears! Will you do it or
won't you? Answer!

MYRRHINE: I won't do it. Better to let the war go on.

CALONICE: I won't do it either. Let the war go on.

LYSISTRATA: Weren't you the flatfish who was ready to cut
herself in half a moment ago?

CALONICE: I still am! I'll do that, or walk through the fire, or
anything – but give up sex, never! Lysistrata, darling, there's
just nothing like it.

LYSISTRATA [*to* MYRRHINE]: How about you?

MYRRHINE: I'd rather walk through the fire too!

LYSISTRATA: I didn't know we women were so beyond
redemption. The tragic poets are right about us after all: all
we're interested in is having our fun and then getting rid of
the baby. My Spartan friend, will you join me? Even if
it's just the two of us, we might yet succeed.

LAMPITO: Well – it's a sair thing, the dear knows, for a
woman tae sleep alone wi'oot a prick – but we maun do it,
for the sake of peace.

LYSISTRATA [*enthusiastically embracing her*]: Lampito, darling,
you're the only real woman among the lot of them.

CALONICE: But look, suppose we did give up – what you
said – which may heaven forbid – but if we did, how would
that help to end the war?

LYSISTRATA: How? Well, just imagine: we're at home,
beautifully made up, wearing our sheerest lawn negligées and
nothing underneath, and with our – our triangles carefully
plucked; and the men are all like ramrods and can't wait to
leap into bed, and then we absolutely refuse – that'll make
them make peace soon enough, you'll see.

LAMPITO: Din ye mind how Menelaus threw away his sword
when he saw but a glimpse of Helen's breasties?[13]

CALONICE: But look, what if they divorce us?

185

LYSISTRATA: Well, that wouldn't help them much, would it? Like Pherecrates[14] says, it would be no more use than skinning the same dog twice.

CALONICE: [*misunderstanding her*]: You know what you can do with those imitation dogskin things. Anyway, what if they take hold of us and drag us into the bedroom by force?

LYSISTRATA: Cling to the door.

CALONICE: And if they hit us and force us to let go?

LYSISTRATA: Why, in that case you've got to be as damned unresponsive as possible. There's no pleasure in it if they have to use force and give pain. They'll give up trying soon enough. And no man is ever happy if he can't please his woman.

CALONICE: Well – if you really think it's a good idea – we agree.

LAMPITO: And we'll do the same thing and see if we can persuade oor men tae mak peace and mean it. But I dinna see how ye're ever going to get the Athenian riff-raff tae see sense.

LYSISTRATA: We will, you'll see.

LAMPITO: Not sae lang as their warships have sails and they have that bottomless fund o' money in Athena's temple.

LYSISTRATA: Oh, don't think we haven't seen to that! We're going to occupy the Acropolis. While we take care of the sexual side of things, so to speak, all the older women have been instructed to seize the Acropolis under pretence of going to make sacrifices.

LAMPITO: A guid notion; it soonds as if it will wark.

LYSISTRATA: Well then, Lampito, why don't we confirm the whole thing now by taking an oath?

LAMPITO: Tell us the aith and we'll sweir.

LYSISTRATA: Well spoken. Officeress!

[*Enter a* SCYTHIAN POLICEWOMAN, *with bow and arrows and a shield. She stares open-eyed about her.*]

186

Stop gawping like an idiot! Put your shield face down in front of you – so. Now someone give me the limbs of the sacrificial victim.

[*The severed limbs of a ram are handed to her.*]

CALONICE [*interrupting*]: Lysistrata, what sort of oath is this you're giving us?

LYSISTRATA: Why, the one that Aeschylus talks about some-where, 'filling a shield with blood of fleecy sheep'.[15]

CALONICE: But Lysistrata, this oath is about peace! We can't possibly take it over a shield.

LYSISTRATA: What do you suggest, then?

CALONICE: Well, if we could slaughter a full-grown cock . . .

LYSISTRATA: You've got a one-track mind.

CALONICE: Well, how *are* you going to take the oath, then?

MYRRHINE: I've got an idea, if you like. Put a large black cup on the ground, and pour some Thasian vine's blood[16] into it, and then we can swear over the cup that we won't – put any water in.

LAMPITO: Whew, that's the kind of aith I like!

LYSISTRATA: A cup and a wine-jar, somebody!

[*These are brought. Both are of enormous size.*]

CALONICE: My dears, isn't it a whopper? It cheers you up even to touch it!

LYSISTRATA: Put the cup down, and take up the sacrificial jar.

[*The attendant elevates the jar, and* LYSISTRATA *stretches out her hands towards it and prays.*]

O holy Goddess of Persuasion, and thou, O Lady of the Loving Cup, receive with favour this sacrifice from your servants the women of Greece. Amen.

[*The attendant begins to pour the wine into the cup.*]

CALONICE: What lovely red blood! And how well it flows!

LAMPITO: And how sweet it smells forby, by Castor!

MYRRHINE [*pushing to the front*]: Let me take the oath first!

CALONICE: Not unless you draw the first lot, you don't!

LYSISTRATA: Lampito and all of you, take hold of the cup.

187

One of you repeat the oath after me, and everybody else signify assent.

[*All put their hands on the cup.* CALONICE *comes forward; and as she repeats each line of the following oath, all the others bow their heads.*]

LYSISTRATA: I will not allow either boyfriend or husband –

CALONICE: I will not allow either boyfriend or husband –

LYSISTRATA: – to approach me in an erect condition. Go on!

CALONICE: – to approach me in an – erect – condition – help, Lysistrata, my knees are giving way! [*She nearly faints, but recovers herself.*]

LYSISTRATA: And I will live at home without any sexual activity –

CALONICE: And I will live at home without any sexual activity –

LYSISTRATA: – wearing my best make-up and my most seductive dresses –

CALONICE: – wearing my best make-up and my most seductive dresses –

LYSISTRATA: – to inflame my husband's ardour.

CALONICE: – to inflame my husband's ardour.

LYSISTRATA: But I will never willingly yield to his desires.

CALONICE: But I will never willingly yield to his desires.

LYSISTRATA: And should he force me against my will –

CALONICE: And should he force me against my will –

LYSISTRATA: I will be wholly passive and unresponsive.

CALONICE: I will be wholly passive and unresponsive.

LYSISTRATA: I will not raise my legs towards the ceiling.

CALONICE: I will not raise my legs towards the ceiling.

LYSISTRATA: I will not take up the lion-on-a-cheese-grater position.

CALONICE: I will not take up the lion-on-a-cheese-grater position.

LYSISTRATA: As I drink from this cup, so will I abide by this oath.

CALONICE: As I drink from this cup, so will I abide by this oath.

LYSISTRATA: And if I do not abide by it, may the cup prove to be filled with water.

CALONICE: And if I do not abide by it, may the cup prove to be filled with water.

LYSISTRATA [*to the others*]: Do you all join in this oath?

ALL: We do.

[CALONICE *drinks from the cup.*]

LYSISTRATA [*taking the cup*]: I'll dispose of the sacred remains.

MYRRHINE: Not all of them, my friend – let's share them, as friends should.

[LYSISTRATA *drinks part of the remaining wine and, with some reluctance, hands the rest to* MYRRHINE. *As she is drinking it off a shout of triumph is heard backstage.*]

LAMPITO: What was that?

LYSISTRATA: What I said we were going to do. The Citadel of Athena is now in our hands. Well then, Lampito, you'll be wanting to go and see to your side of the business at home; but you'd better leave your friends here [*indicating the other Peloponnesian women*] as hostages with us. We'll go up on to the Acropolis now and join the others – the first thing we must do is bar the doors. [*Exit* LAMPITO.]

CALONICE: Won't the men be coming soon to try to get us out?

LYSISTRATA: They can if they like – it won't bother me. Doesn't matter what they threaten to do – even if they try to set fire to the place – they won't make us open the gates except on our own terms.

CALONICE: No, by Aphrodite, they won't. We must show that it's not for nothing that women are called impossible.

[*All the women retire into the Acropolis, and the gates are closed and barred. Enter the* CHORUS OF MEN, *twelve in number, advanced in years, carrying heavy logs and pitchers – the latter containing, as we shall see, lighted embers.*]

LEADER [*recitative*]:
>Keep moving, Draces, even if the weight
>Of olive wood is hurting your poor shoulder.

CHORUS:
>>Incredible! Impossible!
>>>Our women, if you please!
>>We've kept and fed within our doors
>>>A pestilent disease!
>
>>They've seized our own Acropolis,
>>>With bars they've shut the gate!
>>They hold the statue of the Maid,[17]
>>>Protectress of our state!
>
>>Come on and let us hurry there
>>>And put these logs around,
>>Smoke out the whole conspiracy
>>>From Pallas' sacred ground!
>
>>With one accord we vote that all
>>>Have forfeited their life,
>>And first in the indictment-roll
>>>(Who else?) stands Lycon's wife.[18]

LEADER:
>And shall these females hold the sacred spot
>That mighty King Cleomenes[19] could not?

CHORUS:[20]
>>The grand old Spartan king,
>>>He had six hundred men,
>>He marched them into the Acropolis
>>>And he marched them out again.
>>And he entered breathing fire,
>>>But when he left the place
>>He hadn't washed for six whole years
>>>And had hair all over his face.

We slept before the gates;
　　We wore our shields asleep;
We all of us laid siege to him
　　In units twenty deep.
And the King came out half starved,
　　And wore a ragged cloak,
And 'I surrender – let me go!'
　　Were all the words he spoke.

Now the enemies of the gods
　　And of Euripides[21]
Have seized the Acropolis and think
　　They can beat us to our knees.
Well, we swear that they will not,
　　And we will take them on,
Or else we never fought and beat
　　The Medes at Marathon.

LEADER:

　　I doubt if I have any hope
　　Of hauling these logs up the slope.
　　　　My legs they are wonky,
　　　　I haven't a donkey,
　　But somehow I'll just have to cope.

　　And I'd better make sure that I've got
　　Some fire still left in my pot;
　　　　For it would be so sad
　　　　If I thought that I had
　　And I found in the end that I'd not.

[*He blows on the embers in the pitcher. A pungent smoke
arises, which hurts his eyes.*]
　　　　Yow!
　　This smoke is so stinging and hot.

I think a mad dog in disguise
Has jumped up and bitten my eyes!
   With precision more fine
   One might call it a swine,
'Cos just look what it's done to my styes.²²

But come, let us go to the aid
Of Pallas the Warrior-Maid;
   For now is the time,
   As to glory we climb,
And we must not, must not be afraid.
[*Blows on the embers again.*]
         Yow!
This smoke fairly has me dismayed.

Ah, that's woken the old flame up all right, the gods be praised! Now, suppose we put the logs down here, and put tapers into the pots, lighting them first of all of course, and then go for the door like a battering ram? We'll call on them to let the bars down, and if they refuse, then we'll set fire to all the doors and smoke them out. Let's put this stuff down first.

[*They lay down the logs. The* LEADER *has some difficulty in sorting out his logs and his pitcher.*]

Ugh! Can the generals in Samos hear us?²³ Will some of them come and help? Well, at least these things aren't crushing my backbone any longer. [*He puts a taper into his pitcher.*] It's up to you now, pot; let's have the coal burning, and let me be the first to have my taper alight. [*Turning towards the shrine of Victory*] Our Lady of Victory, be with us now, and may we set up a trophy to thee when we have conquered the audacious attempt of the women to occupy thy holy Acropolis.

[*The* CHORUS OF MEN *continue to make preparations. Just now, however, the voices of the* CHORUS OF OLD WOMEN, *also twelve in number, are heard in the distance.*]

STRATYLLIS [*off*]:
>   I think I see the smoke and vapour rising.
>   The fire has started, ladies; we must hasten.

CHORUS OF WOMEN [*off, approaching*]:[24]
>   Come, come and help
>   Before our friends are fried.
>   Some evil men
>   Have lit a fire outside.
>
>   Are we too late?
>   It's early in the day,
>   But at the spring
>   We suffered great delay.
>
>   The jostling slaves,
>   The crash as pitchers fall,
>   The crush, the noise –
>   It's no damn fun at all.
>
>   But now I come with water to the aid
>   Of thy beleaguered servants, holy Maid!

[*Hereabouts the* WOMEN *begin to enter, carrying pitchers full of water.*]
>   Some frail old men
>   Approach with limping gait,
>   And carry logs
>   Of an enormous weight.
>
>   Dire threats they make,
>   Our friends they hope to see
>   Roasted alive.
>   O Maid, this must not be!

No, may they save
All Greece from war insane,
For that is why
They occupy thy fane.

If seeds of fire around thy hill are laid,
Bear water with thy servants, holy Maid!

[STRATYLLIS, *at the* WOMEN's *head, almost collides with the* MEN, *who were just about to begin their rush at the doors.*]

STRATYLLIS: Hold it! What do you think you're up to, you scoundrels?

[*The* LEADER *tries to protest.*]

If you were honest, or had any respect for the gods, you wouldn't be doing what you're doing now.

LEADER: This is the end! A swarm of women come as reinforcements!

STRATYLLIS: What are you so frightened for? We don't outnumber you, after all. Still, remember you haven't seen the millionth part of us yet!

LEADER [*to his neighbour*]: Are we going to let them go on blethering like this? Shouldn't we be bringing down our logs on their backs rather? [*All the* MEN *put down their pitchers.*]

STRATYLLIS [*to her followers*]: Put down your jars too. We don't want any encumbrances in case it comes to a fight.

LEADER [*raising his fist*]: Someone ought to give them a Bupalus²⁵ or two on the jaw – that might shut them up for a bit.

STRATYLLIS [*presenting her cheek to him*]: All right; there you are; hit me; I won't shy away. Only, if you do, no dog will ever grab your balls again!

LEADER: If you don't shut up, you old crone, I'll knock the stuffing out of you!

STRATYLLIS: If you so much as touch me with the tip of your finger –

194

LEADER: All right, suppose I do; what then?

STRATYLLIS: I'll bite your chest and tear out your inside!

LEADER [*with calculated insolence*]: Euripides was right! 'There is no beast so shameless as a woman'!

STRATYLLIS [*with cold determination*]: Rhodippe! Everybody! Take up – jars! [*They do so.*]

LEADER: Damn you, what have you brought water for?

STRATYLLIS: Well, how about *you*, you warmed-up corpse? What's that fire for? Your funeral?

LEADER: No – those pals of yours, for their funeral.

STRATYLLIS: And we've got the water here to put your fire out!

LEADER: Put our fire out?

STRATYLLIS: You'll see!

   [*She prepares to throw the contents of her pitcher on the wood, but the* LEADER *keeps her off with his lighted taper.*]

LEADER: I'm just making up my mind whether to give *you* a roasting.

STRATYLLIS: You wouldn't happen to have any soap, would you? How would you like a bath?

LEADER: A bath, you toothless wonder?

STRATYLLIS: A bridal bath, if you like.[26]

LEADER: Of all the barefaced –

STRATYLLIS: I'm not a slave, you know.

LEADER: I'll shut your big mouth.

STRATYLLIS: If you try, you'll never sit on a jury again.

LEADER: Come on, let's set fire to her hair!

STRATYLLIS: Over to you, water!

   [*The* WOMEN *all empty their pitchers over the* MEN, *who are thus thoroughly drenched.*]

MEN:
         Help, I'm soaking!

WOMEN [*with affected concern*]:   Was it hot?

MEN: No, it certainly was not!
         What're you doing? Let me go!

WOMEN [*continuing to wet them*]:
>   We're watering you to make you grow.
MEN: Stop it! Stop! I'm numb with cold!
WOMEN: Well, if I may make so bold,
>   [*pointing to the* MEN's *fires*]
>   Warm yourselves before the grate.
MEN: Stop it! Help! Help! Magistrate!
>   [*As if in answer to their call, an elderly* MAGISTRATE *of
>   severe appearance enters, attended by four* SCYTHIAN
>   POLICEMEN. *The* WOMEN *put down their empty pitchers
>   and await developments. The* MAGISTRATE *has not, in fact,
>   come in answer to the* MEN's *appeal, and he at first takes no
>   notice of their bedraggled appearance. Of the* WOMEN *he
>   takes no notice at all.*]

MAGISTRATE: I hear it's the same old thing again – the
unbridled nature of the female sex coming out. All their
banging of drums in honour of that Sabazius[27] god, and
singing to Adonis on the roofs of houses,[28] and all that
nonsense. I remember once in the Assembly – Demostratus,
may he come to no good end, was saying we ought to send
the expedition to Sicily, and this woman, who was dancing
on the roof, she cried, 'O woe for Adonis!', and then he
went on and said we should include some heavy infantry
from Zacynthus, and the woman on the roof – she'd had a
bit to drink, I fancy – she shouted, 'Mourn for Adonis, all ye
people!' But the damnable scoundrel from Angeriae[29] just
blustered on and on. Anyway [*rather lamely*] that's the sort
of outrage that women get up to.

LEADER: Wait till you hear what this lot have done. We have
been brutally assaulted, and what is more, we have been
given an unsolicited cold bath out of these pots [*kicking one
of them and breaking it*], and all our clothes are wringing wet.
Anybody would think we were incontinent!

MAGISTRATE: Disgraceful. Disgraceful. But by Poseidon the
Shipbuilder, I'm not surprised. Look at the way we pander

to the women's vices – we positively teach them to be wicked. That's why we get this kind of conspiracy. Think of when we go to the shops, for example. We might go to the goldsmith's and say, 'Goldsmith, the necklace you made for my wife – she was dancing last night and the clasp came unstuck. Now I've got to go off to Salamis; so if you've got time, could you go down to my place tonight and put the pin back in the hole for her?' Or perhaps we go in to a shoemaker's, a great strapping well-hung young fellow, and we say, 'Shoemaker, the toe-strap on my wife's sandal is hurting her little toe – it's rather tender, you know. Could you go down around lunchtime perhaps and ease the strap off for her, enlarge the opening a little?' And now look what's happened! I, a member of the Committee of Ten, having found a source of supply for timber to make oars,[30] and now requiring money to buy it, come to the Acropolis and find the women have shut the doors in my face! No good standing around. Fetch the crowbars, somebody, and we'll soon put a stop to this nonsense. [*To two of the* POLICE- MEN] What are you gawping at, you fool? And you? Dreaming about pubs, eh?

[*Crowbars are brought in.*]

Let's get these bars under the doors and lever them up. I'll help.

[*They begin to move the crowbars into position, when* LYSIS- TRATA, CALONICE *and* MYRRHINE *open the gates and come out.*]

LYSISTRATA: No need to use force. I'm coming out of my own free will. What's the use of crowbars? It's intelligence and common sense that we need, not violence.

MAGISTRATE: You disgusting creature! Officer! – take her and tie her hands behind her back.

LYSISTRATA: By Artemis, if he so much as touches me, I'll teach him to know his place!

[*The* POLICEMAN *hesitates.*]

197

MAGISTRATE: Frightened, eh? Go on, the two of you, up-end her and tie her up!

CALONICE [*interposing herself between* SECOND POLICEMAN *and* LYSISTRATA]: If you so much as lay a finger on her, by Pandrosus,³¹ I'll hit you so hard you'll shit all over the place.

MAGISTRATE: Obscene language! Officer! [*To* THIRD PO-LICEMAN] Tie this one up first, and stop her mouth.

MYRRHINE [*interposing herself between* THIRD POLICEMAN *and* CALONICE]: By the Giver of Light, if you touch her, you'll soon be crying out for a cupping-glass!

MAGISTRATE: What's all this? Officer! [*To* FOURTH PO-LICEMAN] Get hold of her. I'm going to stop this relay some time.

STRATYLLIS [*intervening in her turn*]: By the Bull Goddess, if you go near her, I'll make you scream! [*Giving an exemplary tug to* FOURTH POLICEMAN's *hair.*]

MAGISTRATE: Heaven help me, I've no more archers! Well, we mustn't let ourselves be worsted by women. Come on, officers, we'll charge them, all together.

LYSISTRATA: If you do, by the Holy Twain, you'll find out that we've got four whole companies of fighting women in there, fully armed.

MAGISTRATE [*calling her bluff*]: Twist their arms behind them, officers.

[*The* POLICEMEN *approach the four women with intent to do this.*]

LYSISTRATA [*to the women inside*]: Come out, the reserve! Lettuce-seed-pancake-vendors of the Market Square! Inn-keepers, bakers and garlic-makers! Come to our help!

[*Four bands of women emerge from the Acropolis.*]

Drag them along! Hit them! Shout rude words in their faces!

[*The* POLICEMEN *are quickly brought to the ground, and punched and kicked as they lie there.*]

All right – withdraw – no plunder will be taken.

[*The women retire into the Acropolis.*]

MAGISTRATE [*his hand to his head*]: My bowmen have been utterly defeated!

LYSISTRATA: Well, what did you expect? Did you think we were slaves? – or that women couldn't have any stomach for a fight?

MAGISTRATE: I must admit I thought they only had one for booze.

LEADER:
> Our noble magistrate, why waste you words
> On these sub-human creatures? Know you not
> How we were given a bath when fully clothed,
> And that without the benefit of soap?

STRATYLLIS:
> Well, he who uses force without good reason
> Should not complain on getting a black eye.
> We only want to stay at home content
> And hurting no-one; but if you provoke us,
> You'll find you're stirring up a hornets' nest!

CHORUS OF MEN:
> Monsters, enough! – our patience now is gone.
> It's time for you to tell
> Why you are barricaded here upon
> Our hallowed citadel.

LEADER [*to* MAGISTRATE]:
> Now question her, and test her out, and never own she's right:
> It's shameful to surrender to a girl without a fight.

MAGISTRATE [*to* LYSISTRATA]: Well, the first thing I want to know is – what in Zeus' name do you mean by shutting and barring the gates of our own Acropolis against us?

LYSISTRATA: We want to keep the money safe and stop you from waging war.

MAGISTRATE: The war has nothing to do with money –

LYSISTRATA: Hasn't it? Why are Peisander[32] and the other office-seekers always stirring things up? Isn't it so they can take a few more dips in the public purse? Well, as far as we're concerned they can do what they like; only they're not going to lay their hands on the money in there.

MAGISTRATE: Why, what are you going to do?

LYSISTRATA: Do? Why, we'll be in charge of it.

MAGISTRATE: *You* in charge of *our* finances?

LYSISTRATA: Well, what's so strange about that? We've been in charge of all your housekeeping finances for years.

MAGISTRATE: But that's not the same thing.

LYSISTRATA: Why not?

MAGISTRATE: Because the money here is needed for the war!

LYSISTRATA: Ah, but the war itself isn't necessary.

MAGISTRATE: Not necessary! How is the City going to be saved then?

LYSISTRATA: We'll save it for you.

MAGISTRATE: You!!!

LYSISTRATA: Us.

MAGISTRATE: This is intolerable!

LYSISTRATA: It may be, but it's what's going to happen.

MAGISTRATE: But Demeter! – I mean, it's against nature!

LYSISTRATA [*very sweetly*]: We've got to save you, after all, Sir.

MAGISTRATE: Even against my will?

LYSISTRATA: That only makes it all the more essential.

MAGISTRATE: Anyway, what business are war and peace of yours?

LYSISTRATA: I'll tell you.

MAGISTRATE [*restraining himself with difficulty*]: You'd better or else.

LYSISTRATA: I will if you'll listen and keep those hands of yours under control.

MAGISTRATE: I can't – I'm too livid.

STRATYLLIS [*interrupting*]: It'll be you that regrets it.

MAGISTRATE: I hope it's you, you superannuated crow! [*To* LYSISTRATA] Say what you have to say.

LYSISTRATA: In the last war[33] we were too modest to object to anything you men did – and in any case you wouldn't let us say a word. But don't think we approved! We knew everything that was going on. Many times we'd hear at home about some major blunder of yours, and then when you came home we'd be burning inside but we'd have to put on a smile and ask what it was you'd decided to inscribe on the pillar underneath the Peace Treaty.[34] – And what did my husband always say? – 'Shut up and mind your own business!' And I did.

STRATYLLIS: *I* wouldn't have done!

MAGISTRATE [*ignoring her – to* LYSISTRATA]: He'd have given you one if you hadn't!

LYSISTRATA: Exactly – so I kept quiet. But sure enough, next thing we knew you'd take an even sillier decision. And if I so much as said, 'Darling, why are you carrying on with this silly policy?' he would glare at me and say, 'Back to your weaving, woman, or you'll have a headache for a month. "Go and attend to your work; let war be the care of the menfolk." '[35]

MAGISTRATE: Quite right too, by Zeus.

YSISTRATA: Right? That we should not be allowed to make the least little suggestion to you, no matter how much you mismanage the City's affairs? And now, look, every time two people meet in the street, what do they say? 'Isn't there a man in the country?' and the answer comes, 'Not one'. That's why we women got together and decided we were going to save Greece. What was the point of waiting any longer, we asked ourselves. Well now, we'll make a deal. You listen to us – and we'll talk sense, not like you used to – listen to us and keep quiet, as we've had to do up to now, and we'll clear up the mess you've made.

MAGISTRATE: Insufferable effrontery! I will not stand for it!

LYSISTRATA [*magisterially*]: Silence!

MAGISTRATE: You, confound you, a woman with your face veiled, dare to order me to be silent! Gods, let me die!

LYSISTRATA: Well, if that's what's bothering you –

[*During the ensuing trio the women put a veil on the* MAGISTRATE's *head, and give him a sewing-basket and some uncarded wool.*]

LYSISTRATA:
>With veiling bedeck
>Your head and your neck,
>And then, it may be, you'll be quiet.

MYRRHINE: This basket fill full –

CALONICE: By carding this wool –

LYSISTRATA: Munching beans – they're an excellent diet.

>So hitch up your gown
>And really get down
>To the job – you could do with some slimmin'.
>And keep this refrain
>Fixed firm in your brain –

ALL: That war is the care of the *women*!

[*During the song and dance of the women the* MAGISTRATE *has been sitting, a ludicrous figure, with not the least idea what to do with the wool. During the following chorus, fuming, he tears off the veil, flings away wool and basket, and stands up.*]

STRATYLLIS:
>Come forward, ladies: time to lend a hand
>Of succour to our heroine's brave stand!

CHORUS OF WOMEN:
>I'll dance for ever, never will I tire,
>To aid our champions here.
>For theirs is courage, wisdom, beauty, fire;
>And Athens hold they dear.

STRATYLLIS [*to* LYSISTRATA]:
  Now, child of valiant ancestors of stinging-nettle stock,
  To battle! – do not weaken, for the foe is seized with
    shock.

LYSISTRATA: If Aphrodite of Cyprus and her sweet son Eros
  still breathe hot desire into our bosoms and our thighs, and
  if they still, as of old, afflict our men with that distressing
  ailment, club-prick – then I prophecy that before long we
  women will be known as the Peacemakers of Greece.

MAGISTRATE: Why, what will you do?

LYSISTRATA: Well, for one thing, there'll be no more people
  clomping round the Market Square in full armour, like
  lunatics.

CALONICE: By Aphrodite, never a truer word!

LYSISTRATA: You see them every day – going round the
  vegetable and pottery stalls armed to the teeth. You'd think
  they were Corybants![36]

MAGISTRATE: Of course: that's what every true Athenian
  ought to do.

LYSISTRATA: But a man carrying a shield with a ferocious
  Gorgon on it – and buying minnows at the fishmonger's!
  Isn't it ridiculous?

CALONICE: Like that cavalry captain I saw, riding round the
  market with his lovely long hair, buying a pancake from an
  old stallholder and stowing it in his helmet! And there was a
  Thracian too – coming in brandishing his light-infantry
  equipment for all the world as if he were a king or something. The fruiteress fainted away with fright, and he
  annexed everything on her stall!

MAGISTRATE: But the international situation at present is in a
  hopeless muddle. How do you propose to unravel it?

LYSISTRATA: Oh, it's dead easy.

MAGISTRATE: Would you explain?

LYSISTRATA: Well, take a tangled skein of wool for example.
  We take it so, put it to the spindle, unwind it this way, now

that way [*miming with her fingers*]. That's how we'll unravel this war, if you'll let us. Send ambassadors first to Sparta, this way, then to Thebes, that way –

MAGISTRATE: Are you such idiots as to think that you can solve serious problems with spindles and bits of wool?

LYSISTRATA: As a matter of fact, it might not be so idiotic as you think to run the whole City entirely on the model of the way we deal with wool.

MAGISTRATE: How d'you work that out?

LYSISTRATA: The first thing you do with wool is wash the grease out of it; you can do the same with the City. Then you stretch out the citizen body on a bench and pick out the burrs – that is, the parasites. After that you prise apart the club-members who form themselves into knots and clots to get into power, and when you've separated them, pick them out one by one. Then you're ready for the carding: they can all go into the basket of Civic Goodwill – including the resident aliens and any foreigners who are your friends – yes, and even those who are in debt to the Treasury! Not only that. Athens has many colonies. At the moment these are lying around all over the place, like stray bits and pieces of the fleece. You should pick them up and bring them here, put them all together, and then out of all this make an enormous great ball of wool – and from that you can make the People a coat.

MAGISTRATE: Burrs – balls of wool – nonsense! What right have you to talk about these things? What have you done for the war effort?

LYSISTRATA: Done, you puffed-up old idiot! We've contributed to it twice over and more. For one thing, we've given you sons, and then had to send them off to fight.

MAGISTRATE: Enough, don't let's rub the wound.

LYSISTRATA: For another, we're in the prime of our lives,

and how can we enjoy it? Even if we've got husbands, we're war widows just the same. And never mind us – think of the unmarried ones, getting on in years and with never a hope – that's what really pains me.

MAGISTRATE: But for heaven's sake, it's not only women that get older.

LYSISTRATA: Yes, I know, but it's not the same thing, is it? A man comes home – he may be old and grey – but he can get himself a young wife in no time. But a woman's not in bloom for long, and if she doesn't succeed quickly, there's no one will marry her, and before long she's going round to the fortune-tellers to ask them if she's any chance.

MAGISTRATE: That's right – any man who's still got a serviceable –

[*Whatever he was going to say, it is drowned by music. During the following trio the women supply him with two half-obols, a filleted head-dress and a wreath, and dress him up as a corpse.*]

LYSISTRATA:
Shut up! It's high time that you died.
You'll find a fine coffin outside.
Myself I will bake
Your Cerberus-cake,[37]
And here is the fare for the ride.[38]

CALONICE: Look, here are your fillets all red –
MYRRHINE: And here is the wreath for your head –
LYSISTRATA: So why do you wait?
You'll make Charon late!
Push off! Don't you realize? You're dead!

MAGISTRATE [*spluttering with rage*]: This is outrageous! I shall go at once and show my colleagues what these women have done to me.

LYSISTRATA: What's your complaint? You haven't been properly laid out? Don't worry; we'll be with you early the day after tomorrow to complete the funeral!

[*The* MAGISTRATE *goes out.* LYSISTRATA, CALONICE *and* MYRRHINE *go back into the Acropolis.*]

LEADER:
>No time to laze; our freedom's now at risk;
>Take off your coats, and let the dance be brisk!

CHORUS OF MEN:
>There's more in this than meets the eye,
>>Or so it seems to me.
>The scum will surface by and by:
>>It stinks of Tyranny!
>
>Those Spartan rogues are at their games
>>(Their agent's Cleisthenes)³⁹ –
>It's them that's stirring up these dames
>>To seize our jury fees!⁴⁰

LEADER:
>Disgraceful! – women venturing to prate
>In public so about affairs of State!
>They even (men could not be so naive)
>The blandishments of Sparta's wolves believe!
>The truth the veriest child could surely see:
>This is a Monarchist Conspiracy.
>I'll fight autocracy until the end:
>My freedom I'll unswervingly defend.
>As once our Liberators⁴¹ did, so now
>'I'll bear my sword within a myrtle bough',
>And stand beside them, thus.

[*He places himself beside the statue of Harmodius and Aristogeiton, imitating the attitude of the latter.*]

>>>>>>And from this place
>I'll give this female one upon the face!

[*He slaps* STRATYLLIS *hard on the cheek.*]

STRATYLLIS [*giving him a blow in return that sends him reeling*]:
>Don't trifle with us, rascals, or we'll show you
>Such fisticuffs, your mothers will not know you!

CHORUS OF WOMEN:
>   My debt of love today
>   To the City I will pay,
> And I'll pay it in the form of good advice;
>   For the City gave me honour
>   (Pallas' blessing be upon her!),
> And the things I've had from her deserve their price.

>   For at seven years or less
>   I became a girl priestess
> In the Erechthean temple of the Maid;
>   And at ten upon this hill
>   I made flour in the mill
> For the cakes which to our Lady are displayed.

>   Then I went to Brauron town
>   And put on a yellow gown
> To walk in the procession as the Bear;[42]
>   To complete my perfect score
>   I the sacred basket bore[43]
> At Athena's feast when I was young and fair.

STRATYLLIS:
>   See why I think I have a debt to pay?
>   'But women can't talk politics,' you say.
>   Why not? What is it you insinuate?
>   That we contribute nothing to the State?
>   Why, we give more than you! See if I lie:
>   We cause men to be born, you make them die.
>   What's more, you've squandered all the gains of old,
>   The Persians' legacy, the allies' gold;[44]
>   And now, the taxes you yourselves assess
>   You do not pay. *Who's* got us in this mess?
>   Do you complain? Another grunt from you,
>   And you will feel the impact of this shoe!
> [*She takes off her shoe and hits the* MEN'S LEADER *with it.*]

MEN:

> Assault! Assault! This impudence
> Gets yet more aggravated.
> Why don't we act in self-defence?
> Or are we all castrated?

LEADER:

Let's not be all wrapped up, let's show we're men,
Not sandwiches! Take off your cloaks again!

CHORUS OF MEN:

> Come, party-sandalled men of war,[45]
> The tyrants' foes in days of yore,
>   Those days when we were men;
> The time has come to grow new wings
> And think once more of martial things;
>   We must be young again.

LEADER:

If once we let these women get the semblance of a start,
Before we know, they'll be adept at every manly art.
They'll build a navy, quickly master strategy marine,
And fight against the City's fleet, just like that Carian
    queen.[46]
And if to form a cavalry contingent they decide,
They'd soon be teaching *our* equestrian gentry how to
    ride!
For riding on cock-horses suits a woman best of all;
Her seat is sure, and when it bolts she doesn't often fall.
Just look at Micon's painting,[47] and you'll see the sort of
    thing:
The Amazonian cavalry engaging Athens' king.
I think that we should seize them now, that's what we
    ought to do,
And shove them in the stocks – and I will start by seizing
    you!
[*He grabs* STRATYLLIS *by the scruff of the neck but is forced
to let her go by a well-aimed bite.*]

208

WOMEN:

> Our anger now is all afire,
>   And, by the Holy Twain,
> We'll give you such a dose of ire
>   You'll scream and scream again.

STRATYLLIS:

> Take off your coats and feel the heart beneath:
> We're women, and our wrath is in our teeth!

CHORUS OF WOMEN:

> The man who lays a hand on me
> Will never more eat celery
>   Or beans – he won't be able.
> I burn with anger: I will strike
> And smash his bloody eggs, just like
>   The beetle in the fable.[48]

STRATYLLIS:

Friend Lampito from Sparta and Ismenia from the north
Are still alive, and so I scorn the threats you vomit forth.
You cannot hurt us, though you pass your motions six
    times o'er:
[*Pointing at a well-known politician in the audience*]
You're hated by the People here and by the folks next door.
The other day I asked a friend to share a sacred meal
To Hecate; my friend (she is a rich Boeotian eel)
Sent word to say, 'I cannot come, my dear; forgive me,
    please;
I can't get through to Athens 'cause of You Know Who's
    decrees.'
These damn decrees will never stop, until we make a
    frontal
Assault on you and grab your legs and make you
    horizontal!
[*Each of the women grabs a man by the leg and brings him to
the ground. The* MEN, *defeated, retire down stage; the*
WOMEN *move closer to the Acropolis gates.*]

ACT TWO

SCENE ONE: *The same. It is five days later.*

[LYSISTRATA *comes out of the Acropolis, in great agitation.*]
STRATYLLIS [*in tragic tones*]:
  Lady who did this daring plot invent,
  Why from thy fortress com'st thou grim-look'd out?
LYSISTRATA:
  It is the thoughts of evil women's minds
  That makes me wander restless to and fro.
WOMEN: What sayest thou?
LYSISTRATA: 'Tis true, 'tis true.
STRATYLLIS:
  But what hath caused it? Speak; we are thy friends.
LYSISTRATA:
  Silence is hard, but it were shame to speak.
STRATYLLIS:
  Hide not the ill that we are suffering from.
LYSISTRATA:
  I will but one word speak: 'tis sex-starvation.
WOMEN: Alas, great Zeus!
LYSISTRATA: Why cry to Zeus? for 'tis but natural. [*In her
  ordinary voice*] I just can't keep them to their vow of abstin-
  ence any longer. They're deserting. One I caught clearing
  out the stopped-up hole in the wall near Pan's Grotto –
  another letting herself down by a rope – another leaving her
  post as sentry – and there was even one yesterday who was
  trying to fly down on sparrow-back – aiming straight for
  the nearest pimpshop!49 I was able to grab her by the hair
  and pull her back. And they invent every kind of excuse just

to be allowed to go home. Here's one now. [*To* FIRST WO-
MAN, *who is trying to leave the Acropolis swiftly and stealthily*]
Hey, you, where do you think you're going?

FIRST WOMAN: I want to go home. I've got some fleeces
there from Miletus, and the moths will be eating them
up.

LYSISTRATA: No nonsense about moths! Go back inside.

FIRST WOMAN: But I promise you, I swear, I'll come right
back. I'll only spread it out on the bed.

LYSISTRATA: No you won't; you're not going anywhere.

FIRST WOMAN: Am I to leave my fleeces to be destroyed,
then?

LYSISTRATA [*unyielding*]: If necessary, yes.

SECOND WOMAN [*rushing out of the Acropolis*]: Help! My flax,
my Amorgian flax! I left it at home without taking the bark
off!

LYSISTRATA: Here's another – flax this time. [*To* SECOND
WOMAN] Come back.

SECOND WOMAN: But by Artemis I will, as soon as I've
stripped it off!

LYSISTRATA: No. Once I let you strip anything off, they'll all
be wanting to.

THIRD WOMAN [*coming out as if heavily pregnant*]: Not yet,
holy Eilithuia,⁵⁰ not yet! Wait till I've got somewhere
where it's lawful to give birth!⁵¹

LYSISTRATA: What's all this nonsense?

THIRD WOMAN: Can't you see? I'm in labour!

LYSISTRATA: But you weren't even pregnant yesterday!

THIRD WOMAN: Well, I am today! Lysistrata, let me go home
right away. The midwife's waiting.

LYSISTRATA: What do you think you're talking about?
[*Pokes her stomach.*] Rather hard, isn't it? What have you got
there?

THIRD WOMAN: Hard? – yes, of course – it's – it's a baby, a
boy.

LYSISTRATA [*tapping it*]: Nonsense! It's made of bronze – and hollow – Let's have a look at it. [*Dives under* THIRD WOMAN'S *dress and emerges with an enormous bronze helmet.*] Athena's sacred helmet![52] What were you trying to kid me, saying you were pregnant?

THIRD WOMAN: But I am, I swear.

LYSISTRATA: What's this, then?

THIRD WOMAN: Well, I thought – if I found it coming upon me before I got out of the Acropolis – I could nest in the helmet like the pigeons do, and give birth there.

LYSISTRATA: No good trying to get out of it. You're caught. You can stay here until the day your baby [*pointing to the helmet*] is named.[53]

[*Two more women rush out of the Acropolis.*]

FOURTH WOMAN: I can't sleep in there any longer! I've seen the Guardian Serpent![54]

FIFTH WOMAN: I can't either! Those owls[55] are keeping me awake with their infernal hooting!

LYSISTRATA [*stopping them firmly*]: Tall tales will get you nowhere, ladies. I know you miss your husbands; but don't you realize they miss you as well? Think of the sort of nights they'll be spending! Be strong, sisters; you won't have to endure much longer. There is an oracle [*unrolls a scroll*] that we will triumph if only we don't fall out among ourselves. I have it here.

[*The women all gather round.*]

FIFTH WOMAN: What does it say?

LYSISTRATA: Listen. [*Reads*]

'When that the swallows escape from the hoopoes[56] and
    gather together,
Keeping away from the cock-birds, then trouble and
    sorrow will perish,
Zeus will make high into low – '

THIRD WOMAN: What, will we be on top when we do it?

LYSISTRATA:
  'But if the swallows rebel and fly from the sacred
    enclosure,
  Then will it manifest be that there is no creature more
    sex-mad.'
FIFTH WOMAN: Pretty blunt, isn't it? So help us the gods, we
  won't give up the fight now. Let's go inside. It would be
  disgraceful, my dears, wouldn't it, to flag or fail now we've
  heard what the oracle says.
  [*They all go into the Acropolis. The two* CHORUSES *move to
  the centre of the stage, facing each other.*]
MEN:
            I feel a rather pressing need
              To exercise my tongue:
            I'll tell a little fairy tale
              I heard when I was young.

            Well, once upon a time there was
              A wise young man who fled
            From women and from marriage, and
              He roamed the hills instead.

            He hunted hares with nets, and had
              A faithful little hound,
            And hated girls so much he ne'er
              Came back to his native ground.

            Yes, he was truly wise, this lad,
              Loathed women through and through,
            And following his example we
              Detest the creatures too.
LEADER [*to* STRATYLLIS]: Give us a kiss.
STRATYLLIS [*slapping him*]: You can take this!
LEADER [*raising his tunic and kicking her*]:
                          That's got you there.
STRATYLLIS [*giggling*]: Look at that hair!

                          213

MEN:

> A sign of valour is such hair
>> Upon the crotch, you know;
> Myronides[57] had lots of it,
>> And so had Phormio.[58]

WOMEN:

> I'll tell a little tale myself
>> (I like this little game)
> About a man who had no home,
>> And Timon[59] was his name.

> He lived among the thorns and briars,
>> And never served on juries;
> Some said his mother really was
>> A sister of the Furies.

> This Timon went away and lived
>> So far from mortal ken
> Not out of hate for women but
>> Because of hate for men.

> He loathed them for their wickedness,
>> Their company abhorred,
> And cursed them loud and long and deep –
>> But *women* he adored.

STRATYLLIS [*to* LEADER]:
>> One on the cheek! [*Slaps him.*]

LEADER [*in mockery*]: Oh, how I shriek!

STRATYLLIS: Let's have a go! [*Prepares to kick him.*]

LEADER: Think what you'll show!

> [STRATYLLIS *hastily lets her skirt fall again.*]

WOMEN:

> At least, despite our age, it's not
>> With hirsute mantle fringed:
> With utmost care and frequently
>> Our triangles are singed.

[LYSISTRATA *appears on the battlements. She looks away to the right, and cries out.*]

LYSISTRATA: Women! Women! Come here, quickly!

[*Several women join her, among them* CALONICE *and* MYRRHINE.]

CALONICE: What is it dear? What are you shouting for?

LYSISTRATA: A man! There's a man coming – and by the look of him he's equipped for the Mysteries of Aphrodite!

CALONICE: Aphrodite, Lady of Cyprus, Paphos and Cythera, as thou hast gone with us till now, so aid us still! – Where is he, whoever he is?

LYSISTRATA: There, down by the shrine of Chloe.

CALONICE: So he is; but who on earth is he?

LYSISTRATA: Have a look, all of you. Does anyone know him?

MYRRHINE: Yes, by Zeus! It's Cinesias, my husband!

LYSISTRATA: Well, dear, you know what you have to do: keep him on toast. Tantalize him. Lead him on. Say no, say yes. You can do anything – except what you swore over the cup not to do.

MYRRHINE: Don't worry, I'll do as you say.

LYSISTRATA: I'll stay here and start the process of toasting. Off you go.

[*All go within except* LYSISTRATA.]

[*Enter, right,* CINESIAS *and a* SLAVE, *the latter carrying a* BABY.]

CINESIAS: Gods help me, I'm so bloody stretched out I might just as well be on the rack!

LYSISTRATA: Who goes there?

CINESIAS: Me.

LYSISTRATA: A man?

CINESIAS: I certainly am!

LYSISTRATA: Well, off with you.

CINESIAS: Who do you think you are, sending me away?

LYSISTRATA: I'm on guard duty.

CINESIAS: Well – for the gods' sake – ask Myrrhine to come out to me.

LYSISTRATA: You want me to get you Myrrhine? Who might you be?

CINESIAS: Her husband – Cinesias from Paeonidae.

LYSISTRATA: Cinesias! That name we know well. It's for ever in your wife's mouth. She can't eat an egg or an apple but she says, 'Here's to my love Cinesias.'

CINESIAS [*breathing more rapidly*]: Gods!

LYSISTRATA: It's true, I swear by Aphrodite. And if we happen to get talking about our husbands, she always says, 'The rest are nothing to my Cinesias!'

CINESIAS: Bring her to me! Bring her to me!

LYSISTRATA: Well, aren't you going to give me anything?

CINESIAS: If you want. Look, this is all I've got; catch.
[*Throws up a purse of silver.*]

LYSISTRATA: Thanks. I'll go and get her. [*She disappears.*]

CINESIAS: Quickly, please! I've no joy in life any longer since she left home. It pains me to enter the place, it all seems so empty – and my food doesn't agree with me. I'm permanently rigid!

MYRRHINE [*appearing on the battlements, pretending to talk to somebody within*]: I love him, I love him! But he won't love me. Don't ask me to go out to him.

CINESIAS: Myrrie darling, why on earth not? Come down here.

MYRRHINE: No, I won't.

CINESIAS: Aren't you going to come down when I call you, Myrrhine?

MYRRHINE: You don't really want me.

CINESIAS: What! I'm dying for love of you.

MYRRHINE: I'm going. [*Turns to go back inside.*]

CINESIAS: No – don't – listen to your child!
[*The* SLAVE *caresses the* BABY *without result.*]
Come on, damn you – say 'mama'! [*Strikes the* BABY.]

BABY: Mama, mama, mama!

CINESIAS: What's wrong with you? Surely you can't harden your heart against your baby! It's five days now since he had a bath or a feed.

MYRRHINE: I pity him all right. His father hasn't looked after him very well.

CINESIAS: For heaven's sake, won't you come down to your own child?

MYRRHINE: How powerful motherhood is! My feelings compel me. I will come down. [*She leaves the battlements.*]

CINESIAS: I think she looks much younger and more beautiful than she was! And all this spurning and coquetting – why, it just inflames my desire even more!

MYRRHINE [*coming out and taking the* BABY *in her arms*]: Come on there, darling, you've got a bad daddy, haven't you? Come on, do you want a little drink, then? [*She feeds him.*]

CINESIAS: Tell me, darling, why do you behave like this and shut yourself up in there with the other women? Why do you give me pain – and yourself too? [*Attempts to caress her breast.*]

MYRRHINE: Keep your hands off me!

CINESIAS: And our things at home – they belong to you as well as me – they're going to ruin!

MYRRHINE [*playing with the* BABY]: I don't care!

CINESIAS: What, you don't care if the chickens are pulling all your wool to pieces?

MYRRHINE: No, I don't.

CINESIAS: And what about the rites of Aphrodite? How long is it since you performed them? [*Puts his arm around her.*] Come along home.

MYRRHINE [*wriggling free*]: No, I won't. Not until you stop the war and make peace.

CINESIAS: Then, if you want, we'll do that.

MYRRHINE: *Then*, if you want, I'll go home. Till then, I've sworn not to.

CINESIAS: But won't you let me make love to you? It's been such a long time!

MYRRHINE: No. Mind you, I'm not saying I don't love you . . .

CINESIAS: You do, Myrrie love? Why won't you let me, then?

MYRRHINE: What, you idiot, in front of the baby?

CINESIAS: No – er – Manes, take it home.

[*The* SLAVE *departs with the* BABY.]

All right, darling, it's out of the way. Let's get on with it.

MYRRHINE: Don't be silly, there's nowhere we can do it here.

CINESIAS: What's wrong with Pan's Grotto?

MYRRHINE: And how am I supposed to purify myself before going back into the Acropolis? It's sacred ground, you know.

CINESIAS: Why, there's a perfectly good spring next to it.

MYRRHINE: You're not asking me to break my oath!

CINESIAS: On my own head be it. Don't worry about that, darling.

MYRRHINE: All right, I'll go and get a camp bed.

CINESIAS: Why not on the ground?

MYRRHINE: By Apollo – I love you very much – but not on the ground! [*She goes into the Acropolis.*]

CINESIAS: Well, at least she does love me, that I can be sure of.

MYRRHINE [*returning with a bare camp bed*]: Here you are. You just lie down, while I take off my – Blast it! We need a – what do you call it? – a mattress.

CINESIAS: Mattress? I certainly don't!

MYRRHINE: In the name of Artemis, you're not proposing we should do it on the cords!

CINESIAS: At least give us a kiss first.

MYRRHINE [*doing so*]: There. [*She goes.*]

CINESIAS: Mmmm! Come back quickly!

MYRRHINE [*returning with a mattress*]: There. Now just lie down, and I'll – But look, you haven't got a pillow!

CINESIAS: I don't want one. [*He lies down on the mattress.*]

MYRRHINE: But I do! [*She goes in.*]

CINESIAS: This is a Heracles' supper and no mistake![60]

MYRRHINE [*returning with a pillow*]: Lift up your head. So.

CINESIAS: That's everything.

MYRRHINE: Everything?

CINESIAS: Yes. Come to me now, precious.

MYRRHINE [*her back to him*]: I'm just undoing my bra. Remember, don't let me down on what you said about making peace.

CINESIAS: May Zeus strike me dead if I do!

MYRRHINE: But look now, you haven't got a blanket!

CINESIAS: But I don't want one! All I want is you, darling!

MYRRHINE: In a moment, love. I'll just pop in for the blanket. [*Goes into the Acropolis.*]

CINESIAS: These bedclothes will be the end of me!

MYRRHINE [*returning with a blanket and a box of ointment*]: Lift yourself up.

CINESIAS: You can see very well I did that long ago.

MYRRHINE: Do you want me to anoint you?

CINESIAS: No, dammit, I don't!

MYRRHINE: Too bad, then, because I'm going to anyway.

CINESIAS [*aside*]: Zeus, make her spill the stuff!

MYRRHINE: Hold out your hand and you can rub it on.

CINESIAS [*smelling the ointment*]: I don't care for it. I only like sexy ones, and besides, this positively reeks of prevarication!

MYRRHINE [*pretending to sniff it in her turn*]: Why, silly me, I brought the wrong one!

CINESIAS: Well, never mind, darling, let it be.

MYRRHINE: Don't talk such nonsense. [*She goes in with the box.*]

CINESIAS: Curse whoever invented these ointments!

MYRRHINE [*returning with another unguent in a bottle*]: Here you are, take this bottle.

CINESIAS: I've got one already and it's fit to burst! [*indicating what he is referring to.*] Come here and lie down, damn you, and stop this stupid game.

MYRRHINE: I will, I swear it by Artemis. I've got both my shoes off now. But darling, don't forget about making peace.

CINESIAS: I'll –

[MYRRHINE *runs off into the Acropolis and the gates slam behind her.*]

She's gone! She's been having me on! Just when I was all ripe for her, she ran away! [*Bursts into sorrowful song.*[61]]

Oh what, tell me what, can this woeful laddie do?
And who, tell me who, can this woeful laddie screw?
Philostratus,[62] I need you, do come and help me quick:
Could I please hire a nurse for my poor young orphan
    prick?

CHORUS OF MEN:
It's clear, my poor lad, that you're in a baddish way.
And I pity you – O alack and well-a-day!
What heart, what soul, what bollocks could long endure
    this plight,
Having no one to screw in the middle of the night?

CINESIAS:
O Zeus! Hear me, Zeus! I am suffering tortures dire.

MEN:
It's that female's fault; she inflamed you with false fire.
I think she is a villain and deserves to suffer death!

WOMEN:
She's a heroine, and I will praise her while I've breath.

MEN:
A heroine you call her? – to that I'll ne'er agree.
I'll tell you just what I would really like to see:

994] *Lysistrata*

To see a whirlwind catch her, just like a heap of hay,
And to waft her aloft, take her up, up and away.

Then let the whirlwind drop, after tossing her around
Till giddy and dizzy she falls back to the ground,
Where suddenly she finds that there still is more in store:
We'd be queuing and screwing a dozen times or more.

SCENE TWO: *The same.*

[*Enter severally a* HERALD *from Sparta and the Athenian* MAGISTRATE *we met before. Both appear to be suffering from acute priapism but the* HERALD *is ineffectually endeavouring to conceal the fact.*]

HERALD: Where are the lairds o' the Athenian council, or the Executive Committee? I wuid hae words wi' them.

MAGISTRATE [*guffawing*]: Ha! ha! ha! What are you – a man or a phallic symbol?

HERALD: My dear lad, I'm a herald, and I'm come frae Sparta tae talk aboot peace.

MAGISTRATE [*pointing*]: Which is why you've got a spear under your clothes, I suppose?

HERALD [*turning his back on him*]: No, I hanna.

MAGISTRATE: What have you turned round for, then? Why are you holding your cloak in that funny way? Did you get a rupture on the way here?

HERALD [*to himself*]: By Castor, the man's senile!

MAGISTRATE: Why, you rascal, you've got prickitis!

HERALD: No, I hanna. Dinna be stupid.

MAGISTRATE: Well, what's that, then?

HERALD: It's a standard Spartan cipher rod.⁶³

MAGISTRATE [*indicating his counter-part*]: Yes, and so is this. You needn't think I'm a fool; you can tell me the truth. What is the present situation in Sparta?

HERALD: Tae be colloquial, things ha' reached a total cock-up. All our allies ha' risen, and we canna get hold o' Pellene.[64]
[*Looks longingly at the* WOMEN'S CHORUS.]

MAGISTRATE: What's the cause of it all? Do you think Pan was responsible?

HERALD: Pan? Och, no, it was Lampito, and then a' the ither women – almost as though there were some kind of plot in it – they a' pit up a Keep Oot notice over their whatnots.

MAGISTRATE: So how are you getting on?

HERALD: Verra badly, verra badly. We a' bend double as we walk roond the toon, as though we were carrying lamps.[65] D'ye ken, the women won't even let us sae much as touch their knobs, till we a' consent tae mak a general peace for the whole of Greece.

MAGISTRATE: Ah, now I see the plot! They're all in it – all the women everywhere. Tell your people at once to send delegates here with full powers to negotiate for peace. I'll go and tell the Council to choose delegates to represent Athens. When they see my – my cipher rod I don't think they'll hesitate a moment.

HERALD: That's a' fine by me. I'll fly.
[*Exeunt severally.*]
[*The two* CHORUSES *advance.*]

LEADER:
> There is no beast more stubborn than a woman,
> And neither fire nor leopard is more shameless.

STRATYLLIS:
> If you know that, why do you hate us so?
> We would be faithful friends, if you would let us.

LEADER:
> Women I loathe, both now and evermore.

STRATYLLIS:
> Well, as you please. But really, you look stupid
> Without your coat. Come on now, put it on.
> Or no, I know, I'll put your coat on for you.

LEADER [*when she has done so*]:
    That was a good turn that you did to me,
    And I was wrong to yield to wrath and doff it.

STRATYLLIS:
    There, you look better now, and not so comic.
    And now, if you'll keep still, I'll take that gnat
    Out of your eye.

LEADER:
               A gnat! that's what it was
    Was biting me! Come, dig it out and show me.
    I've had these bites for hours and hours and hours.

STRATYLLIS:
    All right. [*She explores his eye carefully; he winces.*]
           You *are* a difficult old man.
    Great Zeus, it's monstrous! Look, just look at it!
    It must be from the Marsh of Marathon!

LEADER:
    Thank you so much. The gnat was digging deep,
    And now the tears are streaming from my eyes.

STRATYLLIS:
    Don't worry, I've a handkerchief to wipe them –
    You *are* a bad old man, you know – and now
    I'll kiss you.

LEADER:
           No, you don't.

ALL THE WOMEN: Oh, yes, we do!
[*And each of them kisses one of the* MEN.]

LEADER:
    Damn you, you wheedlers! Still the saying's true –
    We can't live with you, we can't live without you!
    Let us make peace, that's what we ought to do;
    You won't hit us, we promise not to flout you;
      Let us all form a single happy ring
      And in that union our next number sing.

[*The two* CHORUSES *join hands and are from now on united in a single chorus. They sing the following two songs together.*]

No citizen need fear that we
    Will dent his reputation;
We rather think you've had enough
    Of toil and tribulation.

So what we'll do is not to jest
    Or try to be buffoons;
Instead we'd like to publicize
    Some unexpected boons.

If anyone is short of drachs,
    Two hundred (say) and twenty,
Just call on us, because we've got
    Good money-bags in plenty.

It's true they have no cash inside;
    Still, I should not complain:
That means that you will never need
    To pay it back again!

I'm entertaining some friends from Carystus tonight,
    tonight,
The table's prepared and you'll find the menu just right,
    just right.
There's plenty of soup and I've sacrificed a sow, a sow,
And – I think I can smell it – the pork should be roasting
    now, 'sting now.

You'd best be quick; it's a well-attended affair, affair,
So bath the kids and then get along right there, right
    there.
Walk in – no questions – pretend that you're in your
    own place, own place;

There's just one thing: the door will be shut in your face,
your face.

[*Enter a group of* SPARTAN AMBASSADORS, *again looking
very distended.*]

LEADER:

Here come our bearded Spartan friends. Why, anyone
would swear

That each of them was carrying a pig-pen under there!
Welcome, gentlemen. How are you?

AMBASSADOR: I dinna need tae answer that in words; ye can
see for yersel's how we are.

LEADER: Whew! You're certainly under severe tension – I
should say things were quite inflammatory.

AMBASSADOR: And that's no lie. We dinna mind where, we
dinna mind how, but we maun hae peace!

[*Enter several* ATHENIAN NEGOTIATORS.]

LEADER: Ah, here are our true-born Athenian representatives. Look as if they'd dropped from a great height
and broken their backs, the way they're bending over.
Yes, definitely a case of dropsy, I'd say. And look how
they're holding their clothes miles away from their
bodies!

NEGOTIATOR: Will somebody tell us where Lysistrata is?
We're at the *point* of collapse.

LEADER: You've both got the same thing, I think. When does
it get you worst? In the small hours?

NEGOTIATOR: Not just then – all the time – and it's killing us.
If we don't make peace right away, we shall all end up
screwing Cleisthenes.⁶⁶

[*The* SPARTAN AMBASSADORS *take off their coats.*]

LEADER: I shouldn't do that if I were you. You wouldn't want
your sacred emblems mutilated, would you?⁶⁷

NEGOTIATOR [*to* AMBASSADOR]: They're right, you know.

AMBASSADOR: I'm thinking so too. Here, let's pit them on
again.

225

NEGOTIATOR: Well now, old chap, this is a pretty pass we've all come to!

AMBASSADOR: Not sae bad as it wuid be, my dear fellow, if one of those amateur sculptors[68] saw us like this.

NEGOTIATOR: Anyway, to business. What are you here for?

AMBASSADOR: Tae mak peace.

NEGOTIATOR: That's good to hear. So are we. Why don't we ask Lysistrata to come out? She's the only one who can reconcile us properly.

AMBASSADOR: Ay, by the Twa Gudes, Lysistratus, Lysistrata, Lysistratum, masculine, feminine or neuter, I couldna care less, sae we can bring this war to an end!

[*Music. The Propylaea opens wide, and* LYSISTRATA *appears, magnificently arrayed.*]

NEGOTIATOR: No need to summon her, it seems; here she is!

CHORUS:[69]

> Mighty lady with a mission –
> Paragon of common sense –
> Running fount of erudition –
> Miracle of eloquence!
>> Greece is torn, and would be healed;
>> War is rife – let peace be sealed;
>> Thou hast conquered by thy charm;
>> Make the cities all disarm.
> Mighty lady with a mission –
> Paragon of common sense –
> Running fount of erudition –
> Miracle of eloquence!

LYSISTRATA: It's not hard, if you catch them when they're aroused but not satisfied. We'll soon see. Reconciliation!

[*An extremely beautiful and totally unclothed girl enters from the Acropolis.*]

Bring the Spartans to me first of all. Don't be rough or brusque; handle them very gently, not in the brutal way men lay hold on us, but the way a lady should – very civilized.

[RECONCILIATION *goes up to one of the* SPARTAN AMBASSADORS *and offers him her hand. He refuses.*]
Well, if he won't give you his hand, try that leather thing. That's right. Now the Athenians. You can take hold of anything they offer you. Now you, Spartans, stand on this side of me, and you, Athenians, on the other side, and listen to what I have to say.

[*The* AMBASSADORS *and* NEGOTIATORS, *guided by* RECONCILIATION, *take their places on either side of* LYSISTRATA.]

 I am a woman, but I am not brainless:[70]
 I have my share of native wit, and more,
 Both from my father and from other elders
 Instruction I've received. Now listen, both:
 Hard will my words be, but not undeserved.
 You worship the same gods at the same shrines,
 Use the same lustral water,[71] just as if
 You were a single family – which you are –
 Delphi, Olympia, Thermopylae –
 How many other Panhellenic shrines
 Could I make mention of, if it were needed!
 And yet, although the Mede is at our gates,
 You ruin Greece with mad intestine wars.
 This is my first reproach to both of you.

NEGOTIATOR [*who has been eyeing* RECONCILIATION *all through this speech*]: I hope she doesn't take much longer. I doubt if this giant carrot will stand it.

LYSISTRATA:
 The next is for the Spartans. Know you not
 How Pericleidas came to Athens once,
 And sat a suppliant at our holy altar,
 In scarlet uniform and death-white face,
 Beseeching us to send a force to help you?

For then two perils threatened you at once:
The Helots, and Poseidon with his earthquake.[72]
So Cimon took four thousand infantry
And saved the Spartan people from
    destruction.
This, Spartans, the Athenians did for you:
Is it then just to ravage Athens' land?

NEGOTIATOR: Yes, Lysistrata, they're in the wrong.

AMBASSADOR: We are. But by the Twa Gudes, she's a fine bottom.

LYSISTRATA:

Think not, Athenians, you are guiltless
    either.
Remember once you had to dress like
    slaves,
Until the Spartans came in force, and slew
The foreign mercenaries of Hippias[73]
And many of his allies and confederates.
They fought for you alone upon that day
And set you free, removed your servile
    cloak
And clothed you with Democracy again.

AMBASSADOR [*still intent on* RECONCILIATION]: I havena seen a bonnier lass.

NEGOTIATOR: Nor I a shapelier cunt.

LYSISTRATA:

So why on fighting are your hearts so set?
For each of you is in the other's debt.

Why don't you make peace? What's the problem?

AMBASSADOR [*who has got hold of* RECONCILIATION; *both he and his opposite number map out their demands on her person*]: We will, if ye'll give us back this little promontory.

NEGOTIATOR: Which one, sir?

AMBASSADOR: Pylos. We've set oor hearts on it and been prod-prodding at it for years.

NEGOTIATOR: By Poseidon, you shan't have it!

LYSISTRATA: Give it them.

NEGOTIATOR: Who will we have left to stimulate, then? To revolt, I mean.[74]

LYSISTRATA: Well, you ask for somewhere else in exchange.

NEGOTIATOR: Very well . . . give us [*mapping the areas out*] first of all the Echinian Triangle here, then the Malian Gulf – I mean the one round behind, of course – and lastly – er – the Long Legs – I mean the Long Walls of Megara.

AMBASSADOR: Are ye crazy? There's naething left!

LYSISTRATA: Come now, don't quarrel over a pair of legs – I mean walls.

NEGOTIATOR: I'm ready to go back to my husbandry now.

AMBASSADOR: And I'm wanting tae do some manuring.

LYSISTRATA: Time enough for that when you've made peace. If that's what you want to do, go and have a conference with your allies and agree it with them.

NEGOTIATOR: Allies, ma'am? – look at the state we're in! We know what the allies will say – the same as we do: 'Peace! Peace! Bed! Bed!'

AMBASSADOR: And oors the same.

NEGOTIATOR: And we certainly needn't ask the Carystians.[75]

LYSISTRATA: Fine then. Now we had better ratify the treaty in the usual way. The women will entertain you in the Acropolis; they have plenty of good food in their picnic baskets. And over that you can clasp hands and take the oaths. And then, let everyone take his wife and live happily ever after!

NEGOTIATOR: Let's go right away.

AMBASSADOR: Lead the way, my dear.

NEGOTIATOR: Yes, and quickly.

[*All except the* CHORUS *go inside.*]

CHORUS:

> Embroidered upholstery – magnificent cloaks –
> Fine ornaments fashioned of gold:

If your daughter is chosen the Basket to bear,[76]
   Don't ask where these items are sold.

For all that I've got for the taking is yours;
   The seals on the boxes are weak;
Remove them, and then from whatever's inside
   Take just what it is that you seek.

There's one little thing I should warn you of first,
   For if not, I'd be being unfair:
That unless you have got sharper eyesight than me,
   You'll find there ain't anything there!

    If anyone who's short of bread
    Has slaves and kids that must be fed,
    I've got some loaves of finest milling,
    Quadruple size, and very filling.

    Let any who provisions lack
    Come round to me with bag or sack;
    My servant is enjoined by me
    To give them all these loaves for free.

    One thing I should have said before –
    They'd better not come near the door;
    I have a dog who at the sight
    Of strangers will not bark but bite.

[*Some* LAYABOUTS *come in, and begin pounding on the Acropolis gates.*]

FIRST LAYABOUT: Open up! Open up!

DOORKEEPER [*coming to the door*]: Get away from here!

FIRST LAYABOUT [*to his companions*]: What are you waiting for? [*To the* DOORKEEPER *and others inside*] Do you want me

to burn you up with my torch? No, on second thoughts,
that's an absolute comic cliché and I won't do it.

[*Protests from the audience.*]

Oh – very well – to please you, I'll go through with it.

SECOND LAYABOUT: And we'll be with you.

DOORKEEPER [*coming out*]: Get off with you! I'll pull your
long hair out! Shoo! Get out of the way of the Spartans –
the banquet's nearly over, and they'll soon be coming out!

[*He drives them away and goes back inside. Presently the door
opens, and two well-fed* ATHENIAN DINERS *emerge.*]

FIRST DINER: Never known a party like it. The Spartans were
the life and soul of it, weren't they? And we were pretty
clever, considering how sozzled we were.

SECOND DINER: Not surprising really. We couldn't be as
stupid as we are when we're sober. If the Athenians took my
advice they'd always get drunk when going on diplomatic
missions. As it is, you see, we go to Sparta sober, and so
we're always looking for catches. We don't hear what they
do say, and we hunt for implications in what they don't say
– and we bring back quite incompatible reports of what
went on. And yet we only have to have a few, and everything's all right. Even if one of them starts singing 'Telamon' when he should be singing 'Cleitagora',[77] all we do is
slap him on the back and swear that 'Telamon' was just
what was wanted!

[*They go out. The* LAYABOUTS *return.*]

DOORKEEPER: Here come these no-goods again. Bugger off,
all of you!

FIRST LAYABOUT: We'd better. They're coming out. [*They
run off.*]

[*Enter* ATHENIANS *and* SPARTANS, *one of whom carries
bagpipes.*]

SPARTAN: Here, my dear fellow, tak the pipes, and I'll dance a
reel and sing a song in honour of the Athenians and of
oursel's forby.

ATHENIAN: Yes, do. There's nothing I enjoy so much as a good old Spartan dance.

[*The* PIPER *takes the pipes and strikes up. The* SPARTAN *dances a solo as he sings.*78]

Raise the song o' Sparta's fame,
And tae valiant Athens' name
Kindle an undying flame,
   Holy Memory.

How they focht in days of yore79
Off the Artemisium shore –
They were few, the Medes were more –
   Theirs the victory!

While we Spartans quit oor hame –
Boarlike from oor mouths ran faem –
Brave our King, and high our aim –
   'Hellas shall be free!'

Nocht cuid frighten us that day,
Nocht cuid mak us run away,
And we won renown for aye
   At Thermopylae.

Artemis the Virgin Queen,
Huntress in the wuids sae green,
Come and bless this happy scene,
   Come, we call on thee!

Pour thy grace upon oor peace;
Make the artful foxes cease;
Let guidwill and love increase
   And prosperity!

[*The Propylaea opens wide, and* LYSISTRATA *appears,
flanked by all the Athenian and Spartan women.*]

LYSISTRATA: Well, gentlemen, it's all happily settled. Spartans, here are your wives back. And here are yours. Now
form up everyone, two by two, and let us have a dance of
thanksgiving.

> And may the gods vouchsafe to give us sense
> Ne'er to repeat our former dire offence!

CHORUS:[80]

> Come, let us on the Graces call,
> Apollo next who healeth all,
> On Artemis and Hera too,
> On Bacchus and his Maenad crew,
> And most on Zeus above:

> Let all the gods come witness now
> The making of our solemn vow
> To stay our hands from mutual war
> And keep the peace for evermore
> Made by the power of Love.

> O great Apollo, hail!
> O let it be that we
> May win the victory!
> O great Apollo, hail!
> O great Apollo, hail!
> Evoi! Evoi! Evoi!

[*The* CHORUS *dance joyfully out. The* ATHENIANS *and*
SPARTANS *and their wives remain.*]

LYSISTRATA [*recitative*]:

> To hail the peace for which we've pined so long,
> There's time, I fancy, for another song!

SPARTAN: [81]

[*as a spectacular dance is performed by a soloist and everyone
else dances in the background*]

    Muse, now be Sparta praisin',
    Muse, Phoebus' name be raisin',
    And in her temple brazen[82]
      Let Pallas hear:
    Come, sons of Tyndareus's,
    Castor and Polydeuces,
    Favourites of a' the Muses,
      Famed far and near.

    Dance, dance tae Sparta's might!
    Swing, swing yer sheepskins light!
    Let's praise oor noble city,
      Home o' songs and dances pretty –
    Home of the sacred chorus,
    Home of our sires before us,
    Stout shield and mantle o'er us,
      Sparta the brave!

    Girls, shake your pretty tresses,
    Whirl roond yer Doric dresses,
    See your display expresses
      Joy and relief:
    Joy at the end o' slaughter –
    See, Leda's beauteous daughter,
    Purer than mountain water,
      Helen's the chief.

    Dance, dance for Helen fair!
    Smooth, smooth yer flowing hair!

Tak off wi' both yer feet and
Stamp on every ither beat and
Pray that Athena never
Her link tae Sparta sever,
May she protect for ever
Sparta the brave!
[*All kneel facing the shrine of Victory.*]

ALL:

Athena, hail, thou Zeus-born Maid!
Who war and death in Greece hast stayed:
Hail, fount from whom all blessings fall;
All hail, all hail, Protectress of us all!
[*General dance.*]

Notes

NOTES

THE ACHARNIANS

1. Cleon had apparently induced some of the allies to bribe him, in the hope of getting their tribute reduced. The 'Knights', i.e. the young aristocrats who furnished the Athenian cavalry, forced him to hand the money over to the Treasury.

2. Theognis was a tragic poet whose 'frigidity' had earned him the nickname 'Snow'. We shall meet him again later.

3. A piper from Thebes, mentioned in *Peace* and *The Birds* as a scrounger.

4. In the Greek this is called 'the Orthian'; it was a martial tune by the famous Lesbian composer Terpander.

5. When an Assembly was due to begin, all exits from the Market Square not leading to the Pnyx were blocked, and the Scythian policemen marched from end to end of the square holding between them a rope with red paint, so that any who did not quickly leave for the Pnyx were branded for the day.

6. Each of the ten 'tribes' supplied fifty members to the City Council, and each tribal delegation formed a committee which managed the business of Council and Assembly for one-tenth of the year. The members of this committee were called the *prytaneis*; this term is here rendered as 'the Executive Committee'.

7. The Greek has a pun on *prio*, 'buy', and *prion*, 'a saw'. Attempts at rendering this directly have not been very successful; I have had to resort to quite a different pun.

8. Before the Assembly was formally opened, a sucking-pig was carried round the place of meeting as a rite of purification. Its path marked the boundary of the 'consecrated enclosure', within which everyone attending the Assembly had to remain while it was in session.

9. That is, some time between June 437 and June 436 (several years before the war had begun!).

10. As a matter of fact the Persians did indeed bake oxen whole on special occasions; but the average Athenian would not have been aware of this. (In the original the ambassador makes the thing ridiculous by saying that the ox was baked in a *kribanos*, which was the name for the pot in which bread was baked.)

11. One of Cleon's hangers-on, better known later (after his exploit at the Battle of Delium in 424) as 'the shield-dropper'.

12. The Greek name for the bird, *phenax*, is invented for the sake of the pun on *phenakizein* 'to cheat' in the next line.

13. This title was really given to various major Persian officials.

14. Dikaiopolis first compares Pseudartabas' eye to the eye painted on each side of the bows of a warship; then to an oar-hole, which would be partly filled by a leather pad fitted round the oar to stop any water coming in. Presumably there was a similar leather casing around Pseudartabas' eye.

15. I.e. 'Ionian', as all Greeks were called in the Middle East.

16. A continual target of the comic poets for his effeminacy. He was, of course, beardless.

17. In the Greek he is called 'son of Sibyrtius', a famous athletic trainer, a person as unlike Cleisthenes as could be imagined.

18. Adapted from a line of an unknown play of Euripides ('O thou that plottest in thy passionate heart'), apparently addressed to Medea.

19. Nothing is known of Strato, except that he was another Cleisthenes. The two are coupled again in *The Knights*.

20. Early in the war this non-Greek ruler had become an ally of Athens, and his son was made an Athenian citizen. In 429–8 Sitalces launched an expedition against Macedonia and the Greek states on the Thracian coast, but achieved nothing except a great deal of devastation.

21. A satellite of Cleon's, mentioned again disparagingly in *The Clouds* and *The Wasps*.

22. See note 2.

23. That is, the Apaturia, at which children were admitted to their clan societies ('phratries'); it was held only at Athens, so Sitalces' son was exceptionally privileged in being made a citizen (which entailed being a phratry member) without going there. It would appear that sausages were to the Apaturia what turkey is to Christmas (or Thanksgiving).

24. An absurdly high rate for soldiers; it was what the ambassadors to Persia had been paid.

25. A 'sign from Zeus' such as a rainstorm or, especially, thunder meant that the Assembly had to be immediately dissolved. Dikaiopolis is distinctly lucky in finding that the Executive Committee agree with his exceedingly generous interpretation of this rule.

26. Added point is given in the Greek by the fact that *spondai* means both 'treaty' and 'libation of wine'.

27. See Introductory Note.

28. The reference to rocks is intentional. The expression in the original is

'look towards Ballene' with a pun on *ballein* 'to pelt' and probably also on the name of the village Pallene.

29. Phales (the name is connected with *phallus*) was a minor deity of whom we know very little, but whose attributes may be sufficiently gathered from what follows.

30. The Chorus is here used out of character to convey an unusually clumsy aside from the author. In the Greek he says that he will cut the luckless Cleon up into pieces 'to make shoes for the Knights'; this is appropriate treatment for a tanner, and the Knights were Cleon's most determined enemies (see note 1), but it may also be that Aristophanes had already had the idea of *The Knights*, produced the following year, in which Cleon appears as an arrogant and toadying slave, and I have suggested this in the translation.

31. Here we meet for the first time Euripides' *Telephus*, which is used to splendid effect throughout the next part of the play. In the tragedy the hero, seeking justice from the Greek commanders, says that he will speak his mind 'even if Agamemnon threatens to behead me with an axe'.

32. *Telephus* again. This time it is the scene in which Telephus secures himself a hearing by seizing and threatening to kill the infant son of Agamemnon.

33. Hieronymus was a poet, whose long hair was a byword. The 'invisibility hat' in the next line resembled his hair in that it was a magic helmet which made the wearer totally invisible.

34. Famous for his cunning, and for the punishment he suffered in Hades.

35. Cephisophon was the leading actor in many of Euripides' plays. According to stupid gossip he had a considerable share in writing them, and according to possibly less stupid gossip he had cuckolded Euripides.

36. It was a stock joke about Euripides that his tragedies were full of beggars and cripples. There was no doubt much exaggeration in this; his only surviving play with such a character is *Helen*, which scarcely pretends to be a tragedy.

37. In Euripides' play *Oeneus*, the hero, formerly King of Calydon, has been deposed and disgraced by his nephews, and reduced to the utmost squalor. The play concerns his restoration to the throne by his grandson, the great Diomedes.

38. Phoenix was falsely accused of attempted rape by his stepmother, and blinded and banished by his father. Peleus afterwards took pity on him and made him tutor to his son Achilles. (The story is Homeric, but it seems to have been Euripides who first made Phoenix blind.)

39. Philoctetes was marooned on Lemnos by the Greek chiefs on their way to Troy, and had to live for ten years on what he could kill with his bow and arrows.

40. In trying to ride Pegasus to heaven, Bellerophon was thrown and lamed, and it was in this state that he appeared in the play named after him.

41. Thyestes was banished by his brother Atreus, King of Mycenae, after seducing Atreus' wife. It was probably after his banishment that he appeared in rags in Euripides' play.

42. Ino, having been given up for dead by her husband, suddenly reappeared after he had remarried. Preferring her to his new wife, he brought her back into his house under pretence of being a servant – whence presumably the rags.

43. This and the couplet in Dikaiopolis' next speech are taken direct from Euripides' *Telephus*.

44. A reference to the evergreen legend about Euripides, that his mother sold vegetables in the market.

45. Again a quotation from *Telephus* (or possibly *Oeneus*).

46. The opening of the speech is modelled on that of the great speech of Telephus in Euripides' play:

> 'O hold it not against me, lords of Greece,
>   If, though a beggar, I make bold to speak
>   Among the great and noble.'

47. See Introductory Note.

48. Poseidon (who was god of earthquakes, among other things) was worshipped on Taenarum, in Spartan territory.

49. The famous mistress of Pericles, Athens' leading statesman at the outbreak of war.

50. Here we leave fantasy for history. Pericles' decree excluded all Megarians from the Athenian market and from all harbours throughout the Athenian empire, and was a major cause of the war.

51. An insignificant island dependency of Athens.

52. Which they played to set a rhythm and tempo for the oarsmen.

53. A final tag from Euripides' play (context not known). Here, of course, 'Telephus' has to be interpreted to mean 'Sparta'.

54. On embassies. The people named are not otherwise known. Chaonia was a remote district in the north-west of Greece. There is not the slightest evidence that Lamachus ever made use of an embassy to dodge active service.

55. Aristophanes often uses the name 'Coesyra' simply to suggest a

woman of great wealth. Her 'son' sounds as if the reference is to some
particular individual, but we do not know who it is.

56. The ambassadors would quote the famous ode to Athens by Pindar:

> 'O rich and shining, with violets crowned,
> In song and story aye renowned,
> Hail, Athens, Hellas' bulwark strong!'

57. At the beginning of the war the Athenians had expelled the
pro-Spartan inhabitants of Aegina, their neighbour and old enemy
but since the 450s their subject, and given the land to Athenian
settlers. It appears that Aristophanes or his father was one of these,
though it is hard to believe that the poet was living in Aegina in
425.

58. Unknown.

59. This Thucydides – not the historian, but the man who had formerly
been the leader of the political opposition to Pericles – returned from
exile about 433; the trial here referred to was later than this. It is
mentioned again in *The Wasps*, where we hear that Thucydides was
unable to speak in his defence. Meanwhile an opportunity is not lost
to taunt his chief accuser with his alleged foreign extraction.

60. In the original, 'or any other pheasant-man', with a pun on *phasis*,
'denunciation', and *phasianos*, 'pheasant'.

61. The long-drawn-out joke, which begins here, on the double meaning of the word *choiros* is hard to render. I have been forced to invent a
dialect word for the purpose (no connection with the genuine Scots
word 'cantie', which means something like 'good').

62. Part of the initiation rite at the Eleusinian Mysteries was the sacrifice
of sucking-pigs. The Megarian forgets that his daughters are too
young to remember the times when the Mysteries were open to
Megarians.

63. A Megarian hero, and (to complicate the joke still further) one of
the great legendary homosexual lovers of Greece. His death was
commemorated at Megara by a boys' kissing contest.

64. In the Greek, 'Tragasae', with a pun on *trogein*, 'to guzzle'.

65. He is in need of the very commodities which Megara in normal
times exported in large quantities.

66. This chorus may be sung to 'John Peel'.

67. See note 11.

68. Afterwards Cleon's successor as the leading radical politician; exiled
in 417 or 416 and assassinated in 411.

69. Probably *not* the comic poet, but a much younger namesake who
was a lyric poet.

70. Mentioned again in *The Poet and the Women* and *Plutus*. He was a painter, and permanently on the edge of starvation.
71. Despite his masochism, a member of high society and a notorious practical joker. We hear more of him in *The Knights* and *The Wasps*.
72. Heracles' faithful Theban squire, worshipped jointly with him at Thebes.
73. Parodied from the way Thetis is addressed in Aeschylus' *The Judgement on the Armour* as 'O eldest of the Daughters of the Sea'.
74. This comes from Euripides' *Alcestis*, where, however, the ending is 'from my faithful wife'.
75. On Theban lips this means Amphion and Zethus, sons of Zeus, who built the walls of Thebes.
76. See Introductory Note.
77. An extremely fat man. The real prize was a skinful of wine.
78. The leading medical man at Athens, and a state employee.
79. This is a reference to one of the many drinking-songs about Harmodius and Aristogeiton, who assassinated Hipparchus in 514 (see note 41 to *Lysistrata*). This one began 'Beloved Harmodius, thou livest yet'. The song was associated with parties, hence with dancing-girls; and Harmodius himself is supposed not to have been averse to wine or women.
80. Not otherwise known; he had evidently been Aristophanes' *choregus* in 427 or 426.
81. Almost certainly Aristophanes, who felt that the author had a right to be invited to the celebration whether or not he had personally produced the play.
82. See note 69.
83. With several editors, I omit the eight lines that follow in the manuscripts at this point. As, however, this is a subjective decision, I append a translation of them (in blank verse, since they are mock-tragic):

> Then up he roused the Gorgon on his targe,
> And dropped his boastard-plume upon the rocks,
> Lamenting thus: 'O glorious Eye of heaven,
> This is the last that I shall ever see thee:
> I am no more.' Then fell he in a ditch,
> And, rising, stayed his fleeing troops and charged
> The fleeing rustlers with his trusty spear.

84. See note 78.
85. The King-Archon (an annual official, nominal successor to the ancient kings of Athens, but with virtually no power) presided over the drinking contest on Pitcher Day. But he also presided over the

dramatic contest at the Lenaea, and Aristophanes is thinking at least as much of the judges and prizes in that contest as he is of Dikaiopolis' wine-skin.

THE CLOUDS

1. Interest became due at the end of the month.
2. Literally, 'I should have had my eye knocked out with a stone', with an untranslatable pun on *ekkoptein*, 'to knock out', and *koppatias*, 'a horse branded with the letter koppa (Q)'.
3. For 'Coesyra' see note 55 to *The Acharnians*. The name Megacles is likewise suggestive of riches and high birth; it was the name of Pericles' great-grandfather.
4. In the original 'she weaved too closely', i.e. she was extravagant.
5. A hemispherical cover; the coal was placed underneath it.
6. One of Socrates' earliest and most fanatical followers. His pallor, here and elsewhere in Aristophanes, is due to his alleged aversion to fresh air.
7. The first Greek scientist, who lived at Miletus in Asia Minor in the early sixth century, and whose name had become a byword for scientific knowledge.
8. See Introductory Note to *The Acharnians*.
9. In certain territories conquered by Athens the land was confiscated and distributed in allotments to Athenian citizens; such a settlement was called a cleruchy. This had been done at Mytilene in 427.
10. Pericles led the expedition to Euboea which suppressed an anti-Athenian revolt there in 446.
11. In Sophocles' *Athamas* the hero, who had vowed to sacrifice his children, was almost sacrificed himself after they had escaped; he was actually led to the altar, wreathed as a victim, but was rescued by Heracles.
12. The mystic rites of Demeter and Persephone, celebrated at Eleusis and famous throughout Greece and beyond. Initiates of these Mysteries form the Chorus of *The Frogs*.
13. The writers of this form of lyric verse were proverbial for never talking sense. One of them, Cinesias (not the character in *Lysistrata*), actually gets up in the clouds in *The Birds* with his wares, but not for long.
14. Apparently this is Hieronymus (see note 33 to *The Acharnians*).
15. Unknown apart from the references in this play.
16. See note 11 to *The Acharnians*.
17. See note 16 to *The Acharnians*.

18. A scientist, philosopher and writer from the island of Ceos, who had acquired a considerable reputation even outside intellectual circles.

19. In the Greek the etymological point is based on the similarity of the words *brontē* (thunder) and *pordē* (a fart). I have had to adapt.

20. See note 21 to *The Acharnians*.

21. The Greek has 'at the Diasia', a major late-winter festival.

22. This trio may be sung to 'My eyes are fully open to my awful situation', from Gilbert and Sullivan's *Ruddigore*.

23. He is thinking of the cave of the oracle of Trophonius in Boeotia, where clients brought honey-cakes for the resident snakes.

24. 427 B.C., four years before the original production of *The Clouds*.

25. *The Banqueters* was produced for Aristophanes by Callistratus.

26. Electra, in Aeschylus' *Libation Bearers*, found a lock of hair on her father Agamemnon's tomb, and recognized it as that of her brother Orestes, who had been abroad for many years.

27. This dance was frequently used in comedy, but was regarded as indecent in any other context.

28. A remarkable assertion in view of the final scene of the play!

29. See note 68 to *The Acharnians*. Hyperbolus' mother is attacked as a usurer in *The Poet and the Women*.

30. *Maricas* was produced in 421 – which shows that the revised version of *The Clouds* dates from later than that. Eupolis, Phrynichus and Hermippus were contemporary comic poets.

31. In *The Knights* Cleon had been compared to a man fishing for eels, who can only catch them by stirring up the mud.

32. Cleon was in the tannery business. He had been caricatured in *The Knights* as a slave from Paphlagonia ('Blusterland').

33. The moon was eclipsed late in 425 (actually some months before the election referred to).

34. Artemis.

35. The Athenian calendar was lunar, with months of twenty-nine or thirty days and a complete intercalary month every two or three years. Somehow or other, at this time, something had gone wrong and the month was not beginning, as it should, on the day of appearance of the new moon. In heaven, evidently, the calendar is regulated solely by the moon.

36. In the original the joke is not about feet but about fingers, since the word *daktylos* (dactyl) also means 'finger'.

37. Socrates recommends that the word *alektryon*, used for chickens of both sexes, should be replaced by *alektryaina* for the female and *alektor* for the male.

38. The word *kardopos* (a kneading-trough), in spite of its masculine-

sounding ending, was grammatically feminine. Socrates says it would be more logical to call it *kardopē*.

39. Philoxenus is mentioned in *The Wasps* as a homosexual. Aristophanes does not actually use the name 'Alexander' but 'Ameinias' (see next note).

40. In the original the point is that the vocative form of 'Ameinias' (see previous note) is 'Ameinia', which sounds like a woman's name.

41. In the Greek 'Corinthians', with a pun on *koris* (a bug).

42. Literally 'a cockchafer' which Greek children used in the same way.

43. Strepsiades is confusing Socrates with Diagoras, a philosopher from the island of Melos, an atheist who mocked at all aspects of religion and in particular at the Eleusinian Mysteries, and was eventually outlawed (the decree of outlawry, with a reward of 6,000 drachmas to whoever kills Diagoras, is quoted by Aristophanes in *The Birds*). The implication, of course, is that Socrates too is an atheist.

44. Pericles had once entered a large sum under this heading in his accounts, when in fact he had given it as a bribe to procure a Spartan withdrawal from Attica.

45. Aristophanes probably intended to insert here a song for the Chorus.

46. The chaining of Cronos, ex-king of the gods, by his son Zeus, was the classic instance used by philosophers and others seeking to prove the 'immorality' of traditional myth.

47. See *The Acharnians* passim.

48. The Greek mentions one Pandeletus, who according to an ancient commentator was a politician, but of whom nothing further is known.

49. A lyre-player who flourished (in all senses) around 450. The comic poet Pherecrates describes him as having 'twelve notes on seven strings'.

50. The Greek refers to the Dipolieia, an ancient festival of Zeus, which had never, like other festivals, been brought up to date with athletic, musical and literary competitions. Grasshopper brooches in the hair had gone out of fashion in the early fifth century. Ceceides was a poet, but we know nothing else of him.

51. At the Panathenaea youths performed a ritual dance naked except for a standard heavy infantry shield.

52. Perhaps the Antimachus of *The Acharnians* (see note 80 to that play), perhaps not.

53. Warm springs were called 'Heraclean baths'.

54. Actually only to one other person (Peleus, as a matter of fact); for Homer, moreover, the word in question (*agorētēs*) meant 'eloquent speaker' and had nothing to do with the market-place.

55. Peleus (who afterwards became the father of Achilles) got into a Potiphar's-wife situation with the wife of Acastus. Acastus, believing her accusation of attempted seduction, left Peleus naked among wild beasts, where he would have perished had not Hephaestus, knowing that it was Acastus' wife that had attempted to seduce Peleus, brought him a knife to defend himself.
56. Which, though remote and inhospitable, was at least rainless.
57. This was the day before the new moon, so called, presumably, because there was no moon and the day might have been regarded as belonging to either the outgoing or the incoming month.
58. This exchange may be sung to 'Oh, my adored one!' from Gilbert and Sullivan's *The Sorcerer*.
59. Carcinus was a tragic poet. He had four sons, three of them dancers (they performed in *The Wasps*) and the fourth, Xenocles, also a tragic poet, mentioned several times by Aristophanes, always with contempt.
60. From Xenocles' tragedy *Tlepolemus*.
61. 'Falling off a donkey' meant getting into a mess for which one had only oneself to blame.
62. In the Greek 'of Crius', whose name means 'ram'.
63. This was traditional at drinking parties when singing, and Strepsiades wanted his son to make at least a gesture to the tradition.
64. The speech will have been from Euripides' *Aeolus*. Euripides' portrayal of this incest is attacked again in *The Frogs*. The point of 'on both sides' is that brother and sister marriages were permitted if they were children of different mothers.
65. The actual quotation (from *Alcestis*) is, 'You want to live; do you think your father doesn't?', spoken by a father who has been asked by his son to die in his place; Pheidippides has thus turned it inside out.
66. In the original production it seems that there was a cup (*dinos*) on a pillar outside the Thinkery, symbolizing the new god Awhirl (Dinos). Strepsiades says, 'Awhirl hasn't driven Zeus out; I only believed that because of this cup (*dinos*). How could I have been so stupid as to worship a piece of pottery?'

LYSISTRATA

1. Strictly, the drums would only be needed for the Bacchic rites; but the women were very liable to turn anything into a Bacchic celebration.
2. See *The Acharnians*, p. 89.

3. These two are only mentioned together because they gave their names to the two ships used for special State missions.

4. There is a pun in the original on *kelēs*, which can mean 'a rowing-boat' (in which the Salaminians would have crossed the strait to get to Athens) and also has an erotic sense.

5. To find out whether it was safe for her to leave home. Theagenes was a *nouveau riche* politician, who had already been got at in *The Wasps*, *Peace*, and *The Birds*.

6. In the original 'Anagyrus', which was also the name of a shrub that gave off a horrible smell.

7. Sacrificial victims were prodded to make sure they were fit to be offered.

8. To a Spartan, this means the Heavenly Twins, Castor and Polydeuces.

9. The Greek text names him as Eucrates; it seems he was suspected of intriguing with the enemy.

10. Still in Athenian hands.

11. For an Athenian, this meant Demeter and her daughter Persephone.

12. The highest mountain in Laconia.

13. After the capture of Troy, when he had intended to kill her for her infidelity.

14. A contemporary comic poet.

15. From *The Seven against Thebes* – except that in that play it was bull's blood that was used. That would have been too masculine for Lysistrata.

16. An attempt to disguise the fact that she was proposing to use wine instead of the regulation blood.

17. Athena, also called 'Pallas' and 'The Protectress' (*Polias* or *Promachos*).

18. This lady, one Rhodia, is mentioned here for no other reason than her reputation for immorality. Her husband was a minor politician, who afterwards took part in the prosecution of Socrates.

19. In 508 B.C. a Spartan force under King Cleomenes entered Athens at the request of the aristocratic party there, to impose a solution in the dispute over the constitution. Popular resistance forced him to retire into the Acropolis, where he was besieged for two days, after which he and his troops were allowed out on condition they left Attica immediately.

20. This chorus may be sung to 'The Grand Old Duke of York'.

21. It was a standing joke against Euripides that he was prejudiced against women.

22. The pun in the original is on the name of the island Lemnos, where there was a volcano, and *lēmē*, 'an inflammation in the eye'.
23. Samos was at this time the headquarters of the Athenian navy.
24. This chorus may be sung to the aria 'Oh goddess wise' from Gilbert and Sullivan's *Princess Ida*, which shows signs of having been inspired by *Lysistrata*.
25. Bupalus was a sculptor, who was violently assailed (though only in words) by the satirist Hipponax for making caricatures of him.
26. The water for bridal baths was always drawn from the 'Nine Springs', which is also where the Women's water comes from.
27. An Asiatic god, like Dionysus worshipped mainly by women.
28. At the women's festival in honour of the young and beautiful boy loved by Aphrodite and killed in his prime.
29. In the Greek *Cholozyges*, a name compounded of *cholos* (anger) and Demostratus' nickname Buzyges. I have supplied Demostratus with an imaginary deme.
30. There was a serious shortage of timber suitable for this purpose, as almost all of it had to be imported at considerable cost.
31. This, as well as 'the Giver of Light' and 'the Bull Goddess', are names of Artemis; but Pandrosus was also a minor Attic goddess in her own right, with a shrine in the Erechtheum, the oldest of the temples on the Acropolis.
32. A prominent politician of oligarchic leanings. A few months later he was to play an important part in the setting up of a short-lived oligarchic regime at Athens. When it fell he took refuge with the Spartans at Decelea. There are other references to him in *Peace* and *The Birds*.
33. That is, the war which had ended with the Peace of Nicias in 421.
34. The treaty made in 421, a copy of which was engraved on a pillar set up on the Acropolis. Three years later the Athenian Assembly voted to inscribe below the treaty the words: 'The Spartans have not abided by their oaths', which was equivalent to a denunciation of the treaty.
35. Hector's parting words to his wife in the *Iliad*.
36. Priests of the Asiatic goddess Cybele, who wore full armour for her ritual.
37. A honey-cake was placed in the hand of a dead man for him to distract the attention of the hound Cerberus with when he arrived at the gates of Hades.
38. The ferryman Charon, whom we meet in *The Frogs*, charged one

obol for conveying spirits across the infernal lake. It appears that
Lysistrata does not have an obol handy, and the Magistrate has to
make do with two halves.

39. See note 16 to *The Acharnians*. Cleisthenes, being neither man nor
woman, was obviously ideal as a go-between in negotiations between
the sexes.

40. The main source of income for many of the older citizens.

41. When Hippias, son of Peisistratus, had been autocrat of Athens, in
514, Harmodius and his lover Aristogeiton had attempted to assassi-
nate him at the Panathenaic festival. They succeeded only in killing
his brother Hipparchus, and were both themselves put to death, but
they were ever after known as the 'tyrannicides'. A famous song
about them began:

> 'I'll bear my sword in a myrtle bough
> As did Harmodius and his love,
> Who dared the tyrant to remove
> And Athens city did endow
> With Equal Rights, our treasure now.'

42. In the festival of Artemis held every four years at Brauron, near
Marathon, where Artemis seems to have replaced an ancient local
bear-goddess.

43. Containing ritual objects for the Panathenaic festival. This was the
greatest honour that could be bestowed on an Athenian girl, and
parents took pride both in getting their daughters selected for it, and
in dressing and adorning them for the occasion.

44. The tribute from the subject states of the Athenian empire, which
had been created as a result of Athens' part in the defeat of Persia.

45. In the Greek *leukopodes* ('whitefeet'), with a pun on *lukopodes*
('wolf-feet'), the name given to those who had risen in rebellion
against Hippias (see note 41) about 511. Apparently the Chorus are
wearing white sandals, and I have made use of this to introduce a pun
on 'partisan'.

46. Artemisia, who fought on the Persian side at Salamis in 480.

47. A fresco in the Painted Portico at Athens, depicting the battle
between Theseus and the Amazon army.

48. In the fable (by Aesop) the beetle's young had been stolen by an
eagle, and the beetle took revenge by destroying the eagle's eggs.

49. The Greek mentions one Orsilochus, a well-known brothel
proprietor.

50. The goddess of childbirth.

51. It was not lawful on the Acropolis, since that was all holy ground.

52. The helmet from the colossal statue of Athena the Protectress (not that in real life it was detachable).

53. Children were named at a feast held when they were ten days old. I suspect that the rule was that until then neither mother nor child was permitted to leave the house in which the birth had taken place.

54. Supposed to dwell in the Erechtheum and symbolize the protection of the City by Athena. The Fourth Woman must have been the only person who ever saw it, since it did not exist (as everybody knew).

55. Owls nested in great numbers on the Acropolis, and the bird became the emblem of Athens.

56. The oracle refers to the story of Tereus and Procne, who were transformed into a hoopoe and a swallow respectively, after which he went on chasing her.

57. The general largely responsible for the great Athenian conquests on the Greek mainland in the 450s.

58. The Athenian admiral who virtually drove the Spartans from the sea between 430 and 428.

59. The famous misanthrope. His devotion to women is invented for the purposes of the story; according to the comic poet Phrynichus he shunned women as much as or more than men.

60. Heracles was traditionally a voracious eater, and when he appeared in comedy he was often kept waiting for his dinner. This is mentioned in *The Wasps* as a comic cliché which Aristophanes loftily shuns.

61. The following song may be sung to 'The Blue Bells of Scotland'.

62. Another leading entrepreneur in the call-girl business.

63. The Spartans sent cipher messages by writing them on strips of parchment wound round a rod, so that they could only be read by the intended recipient, who alone possessed an identical rod.

64. Pellene was a city of the northern Peloponnese, which the Spartans were at this time trying to induce to contribute to the armada to be sent against Athens. It was also the name of a well-known woman of pleasure.

65. And had to keep our bodies to windward of them, to prevent their being blown out.

66. See note 16 to *The Acharnians*.

67. In the Greek 'Hermae'. Shortly before the Sicilian expedition sailed, all the statues of Hermes in the Athenian streets were mutilated by the removal of their heads and phalluses. This resulted in a witch-hunt of 'Popish Plot' proportions, which dragged on for many years.

68. This refers to the mutilation of the Hermae (see previous note).

69. I have taken this chorus, with slight modifications, from that which greets the entrance of the heroine in Act Two of *Princess Ida*.

70. The beginning of this speech is taken from Euripides' *Melanippe the Wise*, and the whole of it is close to the diction and metre of tragedy.
71. To sprinkle on the altars.
72. In 464 Sparta was almost totally destroyed by an earthquake, and the serfs (the 'Helots') took advantage of this to rebel. Sparta appealed to Athens for assistance, and it was sent. However, Sparta was not 'saved' by Cimon's force; she suspected the Athenians of sympathizing with the rebels, and soon informed them that she would have no further need of their services. Lysistrata skates over these inappropriate facts.
73. See notes 41 and 45. Hippias was dethroned by a Spartan force aided by dissident Athenian nobles in 510.
74. Pylos had been a useful base for stirring up Helot risings.
75. Who were notoriously lustful.
76. See note 43.
77. At the after-dinner singing session, when each singer, as his turn came, had to choose a song which had some connection, however fanciful, with that sung by his predecessor.
78. This song may be sung to 'Scots wha hae'.
79. While the Spartans and their allies were making their heroic attempt to block the Persian advance at Thermopylae in 480, the united Greek navy, consisting mostly of Athenian ships, engaged the enemy fleet off Artemisium in Euboea, and, with the help of a storm, inflicted heavy losses on them.
80. This chorus may be sung to 'Oh joy, oh rapture unforeseen' and 'For he is an Englishman', from the finale of Gilbert and Sullivan's *H.M.S. Pinafore*.
81. The Spartan's song may be sung to 'Scotland the Brave', and the final chorus to 'Hail Poetry' from Act One of *The Pirates of Penzance*.
82. At Sparta, where Athena was worshipped as 'Goddess of the Brazen House' (*Chalkioikos*).

SELECT BIBLIOGRAPHY

1. Editions of Aristophanes

Complete plays: F. W. Hall and W. M. Geldart, Clarendon Press, Oxford, 1906–7.
   B. B. Rogers, George Bell & Sons, London, 1902–15 (with translation and commentary). Text and translation reissued by Loeb Classical Library, London and Cambridge, Mass., 1924.
   V. Coulon, Collection Budé, Paris, 1923–30 (with French translation by H. Van Daele).
The Acharnians: E. W. Handley, Clarendon Press, Oxford, forthcoming.
The Clouds: K. J. Dover, Clarendon Press, Oxford, 1968.
Lysistrata: U. von Wilamowitz-Moellendorff, Weidmannsche Buchhandlung, Berlin, 1927.

2. Aristophanes and his work

K. J. Dover, *Aristophanic Comedy*, B. T. Batsford, London, 1972.
V. Ehrenberg, *The People of Aristophanes*, Basil Blackwell, Oxford, 3rd ed., 1962.
T. Gelzer, *Aristophanes der Komiker*, Alfred Druckenmüller, Stuttgart, 1971.
G. G. A. Murray, *Aristophanes*, Clarendon Press, Oxford, 1933.
C. H. Whitman, *Aristophanes and the Comic Hero*, Harvard University Press, Cambridge, Mass., 1964.

3. Greek drama and its production

P. D. Arnott, *Greek Scenic Conventions in the Fifth Century B.C.*, Clarendon Press, Oxford, 1962.
C. W. Dearden, *The Stage of Aristophanes*, Athlone Press, London, 1976.
A. W. Pickard-Canbridge, *The Theatre of Dionysus in Athens*, Clarendon Press, Oxford, 1946.

Select Bibliography

A. W. Pickard-Cambridge, *The Dramatic Festivals of Athens*, Clarendon Press, Oxford, 2nd ed. revised by J. Gould and D. M. Lewis, 1968.

T. B. L. Webster, *Greek Theatre Production*, Methuen, London, 2nd ed., 1970.